THE
RUBY CODE

THE RUBY CODE

JESSICA KHOURY

SCHOLASTIC PRESS
NEW YORK

All rights reserved. Published by
Scholastic Press, an imprint of
Scholastic Inc., *Publishers since 1920.*
SCHOLASTIC, SCHOLASTIC PRESS, and
associated logos are trademarks and/or
registered trademarks of Scholastic Inc.

Library of Congress Catalog-in-
Publication Data available

ISBN 978-1-338-85928-7

10 9 8 7 6 5 4   24 25 26 27 28

First edition, June 2023
Printed in the USA 61
Book design by Christopher Stengel

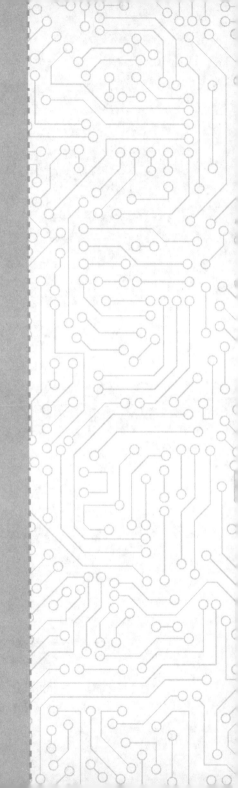

For the gamer kids

1. ASH

Every good quest begins with a setback.

That's what I tell myself, anyway, as I shimmy out of my bedroom window.

Rain pings on the fire escape, on the tops of the metal dumpsters below, on the hoods of passing drones. The sound is almost musical. Maybe some people would find it soothing. To me, it sounds like a countdown. Like any minute, thunder could crash and I could topple off this rickety fifth-floor fire escape and fall down, down, down . . .

"Stop it, Ash," I mutter. "You can do this."

Heights aren't my thing.

But the apartment door is out of the question. My mom's boyfriend is parked on the couch, and if he sees me trying to sneak out, it will lead to a *whole* bunch of questions I don't particularly care to answer.

Like: *Where are you going at ten p.m.? What's with the huge wad of cash in your allowance account? Didn't I say I was going to start charging you for the food you eat out of my fridge, boy? Give me that phone!*

One press of a button, and Luke could drain all my precious savings in an instant.

He's done it before.

So the fire escape it is.

I go quickly, climbing down before I can chicken out. Relief hits me like a cool breeze once my sneakers finally find the pavement of the alley below. I hurry out of the dark and onto the main road.

The city at night is a blur of shadow and color and movement. Neon signs sprout along the skyscrapers like glowing fungi. Ribbons of light trail behind passing drones and autocabs. Overhead and all around me, flickering holograms light the air, distorted slightly by threads of rain.

Head bent against the drizzle, I weave my way down the busy sidewalk. My camo-coat, with its blend of plastic and pixelcloth, shimmers with shifting color and shadow, making me blend into the crowd. Most people don't even notice me slip past them.

How do you survive these streets as a lone thirteen-year-old?

The same way I survive living in Luke's apartment: by being as invisible as possible.

Just ahead of me, a glowing hologram panda leans out of a shop window, words appearing in a speech bubble over its head. *Try the new Fifth Dimension visors! Augment your reality today! Play Scavenge, the ultimate game of—*

"No, thanks," I murmur, walking through the hologram. The panda shimmers and re-forms behind me. True, I've wanted an augmented reality visor since I was five—I mean, who wouldn't want to turn the real world into a living video game?

But I don't want a slightly improved version of this world.

Tonight, I'm going to another world entirely.

My veins buzz with electric purpose, pushing me to walk faster, leaning into the press of bodies. I imagine I'm an avatar being controlled by some gamer in the sky. *Play* Sidewalk Runner! Navigate the kid to his destination without getting robbed by crypto-muggers, run over by jetbikes, or flagged by suspicious cop drones, and you win! It's harder than it looks at first, though. This game only comes with *one* life.

The flow of the crowd stops suddenly as a streetlight changes. Autocabs roar through the intersection ahead. Someone jostles me, knocking me sideways. I nearly topple into traffic, teetering on the curb for a heart-stopping moment.

Worse, my phone tumbles from my hand, skittering across the street.

NO!

Without thinking, I dive after it. Behind me, a woman screams, and someone shouts at me to stop.

I pop up again—right in the path of a speeding autocab. The blue glow of its headlights blinds me temporarily. I snatch up my phone just as it bears down, then throw myself backward.

The autocab speeds by with a growl, the spray from its tires drenching me. The backdraft makes my hair whip.

"That was stupid," says a little girl on the sidewalk behind me, not even looking up from her phone.

"Yeah." I haul myself back onto the sidewalk, standing on wobbly legs. Autocabs turn people into human pancakes every day in New York. I can't believe I was dumb enough to nearly become one of them. My heart is racing, my breath coming in jagged gasps.

But I got my phone back, and with it, my funds for tonight.

The quest continues, unless . . .

I anxiously pull up my account. Half the time when you get pushed in a crowd, it's so some crypto-mugger can hack your credentials and digitally drain everything you own.

Eight hundred and forty-three dollars. It's all still there. I exhale in relief.

For the past year, I've taken every weird job on GigSnap I could find. I can't tell you how many disgusting things I scrubbed off people's floors, or how many times I got bitten by dogs no one else would walk. I've beaten countless levels of *Dark Seas* for gamers more interested in mining loot than playing the game.

Eight hundred and forty-three dollars. A fortune to most other thirteen-year-olds I know. But that's the cost of escape. Well, an hour of it anyway.

I hold my phone *very* tightly for the rest of my journey. It's a relief when I leave behind the busier streets and turn onto an all-but-deserted side road.

The virtual reality arcade appears as a blur of lights at first, slowly materializing as I approach. The name, Immerse, floats as a brilliant blue hologram over the sidewalk, slowly rotating in place. Its windows shine with holographic ads, each one promising fantastic journeys to different destinations: unwind on a tropical island, run with dinosaurs in the Jurassic era, pilot a starship galaxies away, experience superhuman strength and flight as a god of your own domain.

That last one is the game I'm planning to try. Is there anything more freeing than being able to fly? I've never actually been in one of the full-body immersion tanks, but from what I've heard, the experience is life-changing. It's supposed to feel as real as this street and the rain pinging off my hood. Way, way better than my clunky old-school VR helmet back home.

I slow in front of the window, reading the words racing in neon pink over the ads.

Reality is better here, it promises. *Let us take you away.*

Already I can feel the tension draining from my tight muscles. I lift my hand to the door.

Then I hear the scream.

Yes, I know I should ignore it. I *know* this part of the Bronx is infamous for its murders, muggings, kidnappings, and general shadiness. I *know* it's smarter to keep your head down and not get involved with these kinds of things. I mean, even if I didn't know that, the graffiti plastered on every wall within twenty blocks screams it at me in two dozen different languages. The one by the arcade literally says *Stick around and DIE.*

I pull open the door. The air inside is cool and fresh, unlike the oily wet-asphalt smell of the street. The interior is pristine, and a woman waits behind a counter in a crisp blue dress. She looks like an airline attendant.

"Coming in, young man?" she asks, smiling.

"I, uh . . ." How many times have I walked past this arcade, dreaming of going in? I've skipped school trips and bound shoes together with tape, just to save up for this one single hour of blissful, total escape.

"Young man?" The woman tilts her head.

Glancing back, I can dimly make out scuffling shadows in the alley. Another cry of pain sounds, weaker this time.

"Sir?" The woman's voice is a little sharper this time.

"Forget it," I mumble, letting the door shut. "Another time, maybe."

Ash, you idiot!

What am I doing?

Why, oh, *why* can't I just mind my own business?

I pull out my phone and start tapping quickly, hunched in the rain. After waiting for a break in traffic, I hurry across the street and press myself against the wall by the alley. There's a sleek white jetbike propped there, fixed with an anti-theft lock but otherwise forgotten. With its electromagnetic wheels powered off, it looks a little like a regular old-fashioned bike, just missing its tires.

Unlike a regular old-fashioned bike, it's fitted with a pair of jet engines on the back.

I'm hoping its owner is one of the guys in the alley.

It takes me all of two tries to enter the right code into the lock, which falls away with a whisper.

"C'mon, c'mon," I mutter to my phone. "What's taking so long?"

A cartoon llama winks on the screen below a chat bubble. *Hold tight, AshTyler9368! We are processing your request now!*

Neon raindrops patter my transparent coat, droplets catching the pink and blue light from the arcade across the street. I cast it a longing glance.

Stupid, stupid, *stupid!* Why couldn't I have just kept walking? I could be neck-deep in an immersion pod right now, flying happily around some virtual sky, the way I've dreamed of for years.

The alley beside me is dark, choked with the stench of wet concrete, garbage, and trapped exhaust fumes. In that darkness, the muffled sounds of laughter, scuffling, and cries of pain are barely audible over the hum of the rain and static buzz of neon.

I'm not even sure how many guys are back there. Three, maybe, plus the guy they're beating on.

An autocab drones by, its electric motor barely making a sound. Its headlights flash over the graffitied bricks around me but barely touch the shadows in the alley.

Another pained shout echoes out of the dark, followed by harsh laughter.

If this digital llama doesn't get his digital butt in gear, this rescue mission could turn into a cleanup mission.

The notification finally comes through with a *ding*. The cartoon llama does a happy twirl.

Great news, AshTyler9368! Your requested pickup is inbound! ETA 20 seconds! Thank you for using LlamaPost!

Finally!

Right on time, I hear a sound over the rain: the familiar buzz of a delivery drone. It flies in from the north, gracefully navigating the tangle of wires, street lamps, and neon signs that clogs the streets of the Bronx. Its eerie red eye glares while long, articulated legs bundle waspishly beneath its belly. When it reaches me, it beeps in greeting, then hovers on twelve spinning rotors while lowering hook-ended cables.

Grabbing hold of these, I latch them onto the jetbike, working fast, trying to stay out of the shafts of light beaming down from the arcade. The hooks grip the bike's frame and tighten like robotic fingers. Once they're all in place, I enter a command on my phone, the screen slick from the rain.

Package secured comes the automated reply. *Ready to ship, friend?*

I select *Yes*, then stand back as the drone's rotors throw themselves into overdrive in their attempt to lift the heavy bike. Biting my lip, I cross my fingers that this dumb operation doesn't go completely, magnificently to pieces. If it does, *I'll* end up in pieces. Like, literal pieces. I've heard about the kind of stuff that goes down in this neighborhood.

Finally, the drone heaves its cargo into the air.

Then, just as the bike leaves the pavement, I reach up and flick the ignition.

BrrrrrrRRRRRAUGHHHHHH!

The mini jet engines on the back roar to life, twin streams of thrust causing the bike to buck against the drone's clutches. Red lights blast on around their rims, giving it the illusion of spitting fire. The bike does manic loops in the air.

Shouts and curses erupt in the alley as the punks realize what's happening.

Ha!

My little ruse worked. I'd cackle if I weren't terrified out of my mind—and still ruing the cost of the drone. Those things are *not* cheap. That adorable llama might as well have mugged me in this alley.

I pull back quickly, pressing a button on the inner lining of my raincoat. A sensor on the back of the hood takes a silent scan of the wall behind me, then the translucent material glazes over, re-creating the image on the front of the coat. I stay very, very still, hood low, a chameleon blending in.

It's the oldest rule in gaming.

When facing bosses of a higher level than you, your only option is *stealth mode*.

Well, that or *game over*. In this case, probably with my face smashed into wet concrete.

Three men come sprinting out of the darkness, bigger and meaner than I'd feared. They're all wearing black tactical gear, like undercover soldiers or something.

Definitely higher level than me. I've never been so glad for my camo-coat.

"What the—someone's lifting my bike!" the biggest one yells. His face and neck swirl with living tats, inks that shift constantly to reflect his mood. And right now, that mood seems to be *murdery.* The cobra head on his jugular opens its mouth and hisses in silent fury.

While his buddies jump in vain, trying to grab the bike, Tats looks around. His eyes skip right over me.

I'm pretty sure my camo-coat just saved my life.

"What do we do?" cries one of the others, a dude with ice-blond hair in a Mohawk.

Well, buddy, for a start, don't make your bike lock code *1234.*

Honestly, it's like they *wanted* it to get stolen.

The LlamaPost drone is pulling away. The jetbike bucks and sputters against the cables, engines churning the air with a sound like a chain saw cutting through a metal fence.

"Follow it!" roars the leader.

"What about the job?" whines Mohawk. "We were ordered to—"

"Forget the stupid job! We'll finish it later! Go, go, *go!*"

They take off at a sprint, darting into traffic and setting off alarms in the autocabs speeding by. The drone buzzes over the road. There's no way they'll catch up to it before it reaches the Hudson.

Still, I don't breathe again until the sound of blaring horns, curses, and snarling thrusters finally fades into the night.

Then I run down the alley as the power cell in my camo-coat drains the last of its juice. The material turns translucent again.

"Hello?" I click a switch in the heel of my boots, and small red lights turn on in the toes, illuminating the alley. The beams bounce off piles of garbage and the lumps of broken-down autocabs; the place looks like a dragon's lair, and I've just stumbled into the nest of eggs.

"Are you back here?" I *know* I heard shouts of pain earlier. Is it horrible to hope I didn't just blow almost eight hundred bucks on a rescue mission only to find out there's nobody *to* rescue?

Then a groan sounds somewhere in the junk around me. I kick over a pile of wet, soggy cardboard and finally find him—a middle-aged man with a dazed look, greasy beard, and blood running from his forehead. Judging by the state of his clothes and general hygiene, I'm guessing he's homeless. He throws up his hands when my boot lights strike his face.

"Sorry, sorry." I click off the lights and creep closer until I can see his face illuminated in the pale glow of my phone. "I just want to help. Do you need a medic drone or something?"

He shakes his head. "No hospital," he says hoarsely.

Well, he doesn't seem to be in mortal agony. And besides, by the look of him, he couldn't afford the emergency airlift any more than I could. Medic drones operate on a strict pay-to-play policy, and I just blew every penny to ship some neo-punk bully's jetbike to Jersey.

I sigh, waving him over. "C'mon, there's a shelter six blocks east of here. I'll take you."

He cocks his head, blood dripping from his swelling ear. Those punks did a number on him. "You coulda just called a cop drone."

"You know what those things do to . . ." I gesture vaguely at him.

"People like me?" He scratches his beard. "Point taken. But . . . kid, why stick your neck out like that? You *looking* to get a beating? How old are you? Ten?"

"Thirteen. And let's just say I knew someone in your position once."

"Yeah?" He laughs, sounding more than a little unhinged. "How'd they end up?"

I don't answer.

It hadn't been Dad's fault. His mind was sick and he couldn't afford to get well. I remember the last time I saw him; I was eight and he'd only been on the streets for a year. Still, he was so out of his head he hadn't even recognized me. He'd died a week later, on a greasy bench overlooking the Hudson.

Maybe this guy is someone's dad. Maybe if someone had stopped long enough to help *my* dad on that bench, he'd still . . .

I hold out a hand to the man. The homeless guy waves it away and tries to stumble to his feet by himself. "What's a skinny punk like you gonna do for me, eh? I can walk on my own . . ."

But he can't. He's either too injured or too ill to find his own feet, so I slip an arm around him and we start trudging down the alley. He smells like old cheese fries and cardboard.

"You got some kind of savior complex?" he asks.

"Yep," I say through my teeth. "That's me. I love hero crap."

At the street, I hail an autocab. Several pass us by, either occupied or too expensive for my wallet, which their sensors can remotely scan. Finally, a beat-up, rusty old model slows to a stop, the door popping open and a robotic voice asking me for an address. I tell it the name of the shelter, then help the man inside.

"Good luck, I guess," I say, still smarting from the loss of my savings. I'm only human, after all. Maybe I'll drain my account out of some extremely misguided sense of charity, but I don't have to be *cheerful* about it.

"Wait," he says, fumbling in his pocket. "You're an idiot, you know. That big heart of yours'll just lead you into a life of pain. You gotta toughen up, boy. Learn when to keep walking."

I roll my eyes. "You're *welcome*."

"Yeah, yeah, thanks or whatever. I don't know. Here. Have this. I can't take it where I'm going anyway. And like you say, I owe you."

He puts a small metal box in my hand. "You remind me of someone," he says, his voice suddenly clear, the fog in his eyes burned away by some inner light. He catches my wrist, ignoring the impatient beep of the autocab wanting him to shut the door. "I think you'd be good for each other. Just don't be stupid about it. And . . . don't tell anyone you have it, okay? That's crucially important. *Don't. Tell. Anyone.*"

"Riiiiiight." Maybe I should be sending him to a psychiatric hospital instead.

He shudders and settles into the cab, letting the door close. I hear him order the cab to take him to some address in the opposite direction of the shelter I recommended. It glides back into the flow of traffic.

Well, fine. The guy's on his own now, and whether he wants to go to the shelter or Coney-fraggin'-Island, that's his business.

As for me, I'm now soaked to the bone, irritated, and flat broke.

Feeling drained of more than just my savings, I wander through the street and stand in front of the arcade. My forehead presses to the glass, my flop of blue-streaked hair dripping water onto the toes of my boots. The window is glazed, so I can only see vague silhouettes inside, white pods in neat rows waiting to carry their occupants out of this polluted, dying city to someplace wonderful, magical, and new.

"It would have been a stupid waste of money anyway," I mutter.

Opening my hand, I look down at the little box Homeless Guy gave me. Glancing at a trash bin by the arcade door, I almost just toss it. Who knows what's inside? Could be drugs, a lock of some dead person's hair, a tooth. No, thank you!

What was it he'd said?

"I think you'll be good for each other."

In the end, I'm just too curious to resist.

I open the box.

2. ASH

Well.

Talk about an anticlimax.

Instead of something horrifying or illegal, I find a single golden coin lying on a small cushion of dark blue silk. Not a scrap of dirt or oil on it.

Weird.

I hold the coin up to the neon glow of the arcade sign. In the shifting light it gleams blue, purple, pink. Four nicks on the edges tell me at once that it's not currency, but a tiny electronic drive. It's the sort that was popular a few years ago, when people wanted a throwback to retro compact discs.

It's a video game.

VR-optimized too, judging by the tiny symbol stamped on one side, beneath the title.

The Glass Realm.

"Wait a minute," I murmur. "I've heard of this."

It's an old fantasy RPG, or role-playing game, released maybe three or four years ago. I remember seeing posters and ads for it, but it seemed to drop away pretty quickly, drowned in the tide of thousands of virtual reality worlds released every year.

Why the guy was carrying this around like a precious family heirloom, I've no idea. It's not worth much; I could sell it for maybe the price of a burger.

Sighing, I replace the game coin in the box and stow it in my pocket.

As I begin the long walk back to my apartment, my phone chirps with a text from my best friend, Hakeem.

So? How was it? Worth breaking the old piggy bank?

Wiping raindrops from the screen, I type back, *Something else came up. Another time, maybe.*

Really? Those pods are all you've been talking about for months.

I groan inwardly. *Did you win your match?*

Nah, lost 6–1. They dragged us to the trash, dude. It was ugly.

Ouch. Hakeem's into minor-level e-sports, mostly battle royale–type stuff. Not my brand of VR, but I join him every now and then when he needs backup.

My mom says you can come over if you want. She's making baklava.

Tempting, but— I press a hand against the lump in my pocket, the homeless guy's weird warning suddenly flashing in my brain.

"*Don't tell anyone.*"

Just as quickly, I shake off the thought. Because that's completely stupid, right? It wasn't like he gave me the president's diary or a stack of photos from Area 51. What could possibly be illegal or dangerous about some old video game?

I got a new RPG, I finish, then hit send.

DUDE. You and your elf games. C'mon. Baklava in all its honey nutty doughy goodness!

It's true there's nothing you could possibly put in your mouth that's remotely as delicious as Hakeem's mom's baklava.

But still . . . there's a coin-shaped hole burning in my pocket.

I'll come by tomorrow. Swear.

Hakeem replies with a holomoji, a sobbing cartoon dog that leaps off the screen to hover in the air. Rolling my eyes, I flick it and it dissipates into nothing.

By the time I reach home thirty minutes later, I'm shivering. I enter the passcode to unlock the door and slip inside, shedding my coat and boots in a soggy puddle on the front rug. My mom's jacket and shoes are missing. She's still on her artists' retreat upstate, off painting waterfalls or deer or whatever. Lately it seems like she's always going off to paint things—flying all over the world, visiting galleries and museums.

The apartment is huge, four times the size of the old place my mom and I lived in up until last year. The furnishings are all high-end leather and marble. It doesn't feel like home. Mom said to just give it time.

About fifteen seconds through the door, I remember Luke is on the couch. Stupid, stupid, stupid! If I hadn't been so distracted by the whole thing with the homeless guy, I'd have remembered to go back in through my window.

I swallow hard, trying to sneak past Luke.

It's no use.

"Where have you been, boy?" he calls out, without turning around. "I know you snuck out like a little rat."

It's always *boy* or *kid* with him. Never my name.

Not that I want to hear him use it.

"Can't you mind your own business?" I mumble.

Luke sits up.

I freeze, realizing too late that I just made a *big* mistake.

He turns to give me a narrow stare. He's a tall guy, with a long, round jaw and hair that's too perfect to be natural. "What did you just say?"

Suddenly, he's standing right in front of me, six feet of crisp business suit and overpowering cologne.

"Uh . . ."

"*Uh,*" he mocks. "You walk into *my* house, dripping all over *my* rugs, eating *my* food and showering in *my* water, and you have the nerve to say it's *none of my business*?"

I look down at my damp socks. I know better than to keep talking when Luke's in this mood.

"Nothing to say?" Luke sneers. His work clothes are barely creased from his cushy office job rigging stock markets or whatever it is he does. I usually zone out when he brags about it.

Without another word, he turns and walks down the hall to my room.

"W-wait!" I lurch forward. "What are you doing?"

He pauses in my doorway. "Minding my own business."

I run down the hall, skidding into my room just as he yanks the blankets off my bed.

"Mine," he says, grabbing the bed frame, mattress and all, and heaving it onto its side with a loud clang.

I flatten myself against the wall. My finger scratches my wrist, where my camo-coat button would be if I still had it on. Not that it would hide me from him in here. Even my camo-coat has its limits. Sometimes stealth mode just isn't an option.

Sometimes the boss just wins.

Callister, my mom's fluffy little spaniel, runs in and barks at Luke. Quickly, I grab him and hold him tight so he can't get in the way of Luke's shoes.

Luke drags the bed out of the room. Then he returns and dumps out every drawer in my dresser and drags it out too. Then the rug, the mirror on the wall, the desk that has my school tablet and gaming stuff. He jerks it, letting everything crash to the floor. His movements are sharp and violent, the crashes loud enough to make the windows rattle.

"Mine, mine, and mine," he says calmly. "My money paid for them, so they're *my* business."

"My mom—"

"Won't get back from her retreat until Monday night," he says. "Maybe you'll have learned your lesson by then. Or maybe you won't, and I'll dump you and your mother back in the trash heap where I found you." He steps closer to me. I can't possibly get any smaller, but I try anyway. He puts his hand on the wall right by my face and leans in close. "I can take it *all* back, if you want. All the clothes I've bought her. The stupid painting lessons she loves so much. Her precious, ridiculous dog."

He scowls at Callister, who snarls in my arms, wiggling to get free. I hold his snout shut, fearing that if he did manage to bite Luke, it would be the last thing the little dog ever did.

I stay silent.

"I can take it all and more, kid. You'll be *less* than you were when I found you. Back to digging in garbage and begging for handouts. Living on borrowed cash, borrowed time. Is that what you want?"

I shake my head.

By the time he finally leaves, my room is a wreck. All my furniture is piled in the living room. Clothes, electronics, shoes, and other stuff are strewn everywhere. I stare for a long while, waiting for my heart to stop racing. Callister leaps down and burrows into my rumpled blankets, then emerges with one of his toy ropes.

By the time my mom returns, Luke will have made me drag all the furniture back in and clean up. She'll never even know this happened. And I won't tell her.

Because he's right.

He can take everything away from us, all the stuff that makes Mom happy. She doesn't even know scary Luke exists. She only gets doting Luke, puppy-eyes Luke, who buys her anything she wants and makes her laugh like no one has since my dad. Luke is her knight in shining armor. He saved us from poverty and gave her back her painting.

I remember what she was like before she met him. Always struggling to make ends meet, working three jobs, her artistic talent abandoned while she tried to feed me and keep us housed.

Her reality changed for the better when she met Luke.

And me?

Well, at least I can escape reality altogether. For a while, anyway.

I make a kind of bed out of my clothes, piling them up in the corner. Then I crack open the floorboard under the window and take out my secret stack of VR equipment: headset and motion-tracking gloves and anklets. I learned the hard way it's better to hide my more fragile stuff from Luke, after he smashed my backup VR set in another fit of rage.

Taking out the game coin, I pop it into a slot on the side of the headset and turn the unit on.

Once I'm geared up, I lean against the wall, Callister snoozing beside me.

The *Glass Realm* opening sequence plays: clouds parting over a vast, lush landscape of mountains, valleys, rivers, oceans. Not a hint of air pollution, not a skyscraper to mar the horizon. I can almost taste the purity of that sky.

Already I'm liking the feel of this world. Maybe that homeless guy wasn't as spaced as I'd thought.

"I think you'll be good for each other."

Or had he been talking about a person? Something about how I reminded him of someone . . . ?

On second thought, yeah, he was *galactically* spaced.

The Glass Realm's logo fades into a cutscene showing various realms, mobs, and NPCs, a kind of trailer for the game itself, set to sweeping orchestral music. Even on my old equipment, the immersion experience is all-encompassing. Everywhere I look, there's no sign of my ransacked bedroom, the walls of Luke's apartment, the rain drumming on the fire escape outside the window. Best of all, the *Realm* is a single-player game—a rarity in this age of multiplayer worlds, battle royales, and e-sports, the stuff Hakeem and most other kids seem to prefer.

There will be no real people here but me.

Perfect.

Welcome to the Glass Realm, the world of the ever-curious, a cool voice whispers in my ear. *Are you ready to begin your quest, brave adventurer?*

"Yeah," I murmur. "Just get me out of here."

3. RUBY

Eyes open, Ruby. Rise and shine.

I blink, my vision blurry. Slowly, wooden rafters sharpen into focus. Fragrant herbs hang from them—lavender, thyme, rosemary. I stare for what seems an eternity, engrossed in the shapes of the leaves, the gentle sway of the bundles, the intricacy of the flowers.

Then the Voice returns, prodding me gently.

Sit up, now. Get out of bed.

I sit up. My hands are folded in my lap. I'm in a narrow bed in a small room in a wooden house, wearing a plain brown dress and soft leather shoes. It all feels . . . strange and familiar at the same time. New and old. Surprising and expected.

I carefully stand, bare feet finding smooth wooden floorboards. A pair of plain leather slippers waits, perfectly sized for me. I slip them on.

This is your home, Ruby. And this is you.

I look into a round mirror hung over a pitcher and basin. See a face staring back at me through red-gold eyes. I touch the reflection, then my face. I run my fingers through my long white hair, then, guided by the Voice, twist that hair into a tidy bun.

"Who are you?" I ask aloud, looking around. There doesn't seem to be anyone here but me. But the Voice speaks from just over my shoulder. In the very corner of my vision, I almost see . . . *something*. A shadow hovering on my back. Once I'm aware of it, it's like I can feel its weight on my shoulders, a slight *pressure* against the nape of my neck.

Focus on the path, it says.

And just like that, it doesn't matter anymore who the Voice is or why there is a shadow behind me. All that matters is the path, just like the Voice said. I should do what it wants me to. It's just . . . easier that way.

It feels right to listen to it. I can't really imagine doing otherwise.

The Voice guides me down a narrow stair. I go as it commands, passing crude wooden furnishings, rugs of bear and wolf skin, a wall of hoops strung with yarn. A room downstairs reveals a simple kitchen, a wood-burning stove, stacks of firewood, plain chairs, and a table. An array of fruit, vegetables, herbs. I walk around, touching everything, absorbing textures, curves, colors.

It is time to go to work, Ruby. Out the door, there you are. Good.

I open a door and step into sunlight.

A cobblestone path leads away from my door, down a grassy hill toward a small town. A carpet of farmlands surrounds it on three sides while to the north rises a dark forest, mist oozing from its shadows. Smoke rises from a cheerful cluster of buildings in the town, and the clear ring of a hammer striking an anvil mingles with birdsong and the bleating of sheep. Daisies nod by the corner of the house.

This is Timberton, says my guiding Voice. *In the eastern region of the Glass Realm. You are due at Tomtock's Hinterland Sword and Supply Shop in five minutes.*

Out of the house I go, down the cobbled path, toward the town. I pick three daisies and pull their petals off one by one as I walk. At the bottom of the hill, a little girl runs with a shaggy brown dog.

Porsha and Morto.

I recognize them, know them. I catch my breath in anticipation the moment before Morto sniffs out a hare and bounds away, Porsha chasing him. They run right past me.

"Hi, Ruby!" Porsha shouts, waving.

I wave back, smiling. "Watch for wolves in the northern wood!"

Porsha rolls her eyes. "I always do! Besides, Morto protects me!"

I continue on, passing more people. A blacksmith, a baker, an ostler, a huntress. Each of them calls a greeting to me, which I return warmly. Otherwise, they seem very set on their own paths and tasks. Perhaps they too have little Voices in their heads, directing their every motion. I wonder if—

Focus on the path, Ruby, says the Voice, and the pressure on my neck increases slightly.

Yes. Of course. The path. Instantly, the questions in my mind seem silly and pointless, and they evaporate. Instead, I focus on the route to my shop.

There are eleven buildings in Timberton, most of them houses. Stone foundations support wooden walls and brightly painted doors of red, yellow, blue. Chickens flutter and squawk among the people and hurry out of my way as I walk.

It's a beautiful town. Peaceful. A good place to belong. I go slowly, enjoying the giggles of the children running in the apple orchard. A feeling of contentment bubbles inside me, along with the odd, happy sense that I've been walking this path forever, and that I'll gladly continue walking it forever.

My shop waits at the far end of town, small and tidy. It has four windows with blue shutters, a red door, and a wooden sign with the name— TOMTOCK'S HINTERLAND SWORD AND SUPPLY SHOP, with three symbols carved below it: sword, flask, shoe. When I put my hand in my pocket I find a key, which opens the front door.

Inside, banners of sunlight unfurl across neat shelves and a swept wooden floor. There are items of every type there. Cheeses (price: 1 aurin) and potions (25 aurins each), daggers and shoes (100 aurins and 425 aurins), spinning wheels and morning stars (630 aurins and 1,200 aurins).

I take my place behind the small counter, noting the clockwork till, the more expensive items hidden on the shelves below, and the window to my left that looks out to the road. A few gold aurins are scattered on the counter.

I run my hand over the rich golden wood of the counter, feeling a sense of pride.

Now you wait, Ruby, says the Voice.

Yes. I wait. That's what I do every day, isn't it? I wait in this shop for . . .

"For what?" I murmur. Have I asked that question before? Why can't I remember?

Polish the sword, Ruby, says the Voice, nudging my attention to the counter.

I look down and see a rusty sword (14 aurins) and a polishing rag. I pick them up and set to work.

------◇------

Eyes open, Ruby. Rise and shine.

I blink, my vision settling on the bundled herbs above my bed.

It's morning again.

Sit up now. Get out of bed.

I swing my legs out of the bed and go downstairs. Nothing in the room has changed, not a single mote of dust.

This is your home, Ruby. And this is you.

I look around thoughtfully. "Could do with a touch of class, don't you think? Maybe a fountain? A tiled lobby? Spiral staircase?"

The Voice doesn't reply. I suppose it doesn't appreciate jokes.

It is time to go to work. Out the door, there you are. Good.

By the time the Voice finishes its sentence, I'm halfway down the hill, plucking apart my three daisies. I exchange greetings with Porsha again, warning her once more of the wolves in the wood. She rolls her eyes and tells me Morto protects her.

She scampers off, and I stop.

Wait. How do I know about the wolves in the wood? Have I seen them before?

Focus on the path, the Voice says.

"I am," I murmur. "But what about—"

Focus on the path. The Voice is firmer the second time. The shadow on my back presses against me.

Just like that, I forget what I was thinking. Why am I stopped in the road? I need to get to my shop.

"Good morning, child!" calls Variel the milkmaid. "Anything new in your father's shop today?"

"We just got some lace from Lantisea," I reply. "Come by and see!"

She smiles. "I'll stop in this afternoon."

I start to walk on, but then slow and look back at her. "No, you won't."

Variel just continues to smile.

"You always say you'll come by this afternoon," I say. "But you never do. And how is it that we *just* got lace from Lantisea *every* day? That doesn't make sense."

Focus on the path, urges the Voice. *Focus on the path, Ruby.*

"Why do you never come to my shop?" I ask Variel, resisting the Voice. Its shadowy form seems to grow larger and heavier.

The milkmaid doesn't reply. Instead, she picks up her pails of milk and walks on without so much as a glance my way, her dark braids swinging. She catches the eye of the blacksmith Rauf, who pauses in his hammering to watch her go by.

"Didn't you hear me?" I ask her. "Variel?"

Focus on the path, Ruby. Focus on the path. Focus on the—

The path. Right. What was I saying? Why am I facing the wrong direction? My shop is the other way.

I complete my route, arriving at the door a few moments later.

In my shop, I find everything in its place, as expected. Taking my seat on the stool, I blink at the polish rag and rusty sword before me. All that polishing yesterday, and it's just as rusty as it was to begin with.

Now you wait, Ruby.

"Yes," I reply, picking up the sword and rag. "I know."

- - - - -◇- - - - -

Eyes open, Ruby. Rise and shine.

I roll out of bed. What morning is this? The ninth? The tenth? Hundredth? Why have I never asked that question before? I try to think back . . .

Sit up now, says the Voice. *Get out of bed.*

Right. Up I go.

Open the door. Pick the daisies. Pull their petals.

It's time to go to—

"I'm going!"

Down the hill. Past the milkmaid.

"Hello, child. Anything new in your father's shop today?"

My father. Suddenly, it occurs to me that I can't picture my father's face. For a long moment, I stare at nothing and try to remember him. Tomtock is his name, right? It's the name of his shop. Where is he? Why did he leave?

Focus on the path, Ruby, the Voice says.

26

The effort of trying to remember becomes too much. My father—or the hole in my memory where he should be—melts from my thoughts.

"We just got some lace from Lantisea," I tell Variel. "Come by and see!"

She smiles. "I'll stop in this afternoon."

I stop. Turn around. "Will you?"

She stands between her buckets, smiling vacuously at the sky. I look up, see nothing but blue. Look down at her blank eyes.

A sudden, inexplicable splinter of anger strikes me like lightning splitting a tree.

I kick over one of the buckets. Milk spreads across the road, irritating a few nearby chickens. They cluck and hurry away, beady eyes glinting.

Variel picks up the bucket anyway, carries it empty, casting her usual flirtatious looks at Rauf. Never once acknowledging me.

"I'm sorry!" I shout. "I don't know why I did that. Variel!"

She ignores me and my apology.

Why can't I remember my father?

Focus on the path, Ruby. Focus—

"I KNOW."

Yanking the key from my pocket, I open the shop.

I pick up the rusty sword.

I begin polishing.

- - - - - -◦- - - - -

Eyes open, Ruby. Rise and shine.

- - - - - -◦- - - - -

Eyes open, Ruby. Rise and shine.

- - - - - -◦- - - - -

Eyes open, Ruby. Rise and shine.

- - - - - -◦- - - - -

This is what I do: I wake. I open my shop. I polish a rusty sword that never gets any cleaner. I go home and to sleep.

In the morning, I start all over again.

Outside my shopwindow, townsfolk wander past, on the same predictable schedule:

Lord Toffton hurries by, yelling about a wolf attack in the mountains.

Lilia, the huntress, exchanges a tense greeting with her nemesis, the blacksmith Rauf (they're both in love with the milkmaid Variel).

Porsha, the village child, walks by next, followed by her faithful dog, Morto.

Routine is my life; my life is routine. I polish that sword as if I truly believe it will one day be clean.

And I wait. I wait. I wait.

I wonder what I'm waiting *for*.

No. No wondering. When I wonder, the Voice nudges me gently back onto my path. And it's not a bad path, really. Boring, yes, but my town is beautiful. My neighbors are peaceful and welcoming. I love my little shop, its clean surfaces and neat rows of inventory and the way the sunlight slants just so through the windows.

But still, sometimes I wonder if . . .

"What if I throw it out the window?" I ask aloud one morning.

I pause, startled by the thought. It's been days, maybe months since I kicked over Variel's bucket. That day is fuzzy in my memory, so faint I sometimes think I imagined it.

I could just do it. Toss the sword away. Interrupt the routine for good.

Yes. But . . . no. No, I can't do that. Couldn't possibly.

I'm not supposed to toss things out windows. That's not my job. What I *am* supposed to do is polish this sword all day, go to bed at dusk, wake up at dawn, and do it all over again.

Focus on the path, I remind myself.

I'm supposed to polish the sword fourteen times a day while waiting for . . . What? The answer is still elusive. Easier not to think about it. Easier not to think at all. Easier to just *be*. There's a peace in that. A contentment. Questions only bring me struggle, against the Voice, against myself. It's tiring to ask questions, to swim against the Voice's stronger current.

But . . . what if I *did* throw the sword?

What if I threw it in the well behind the blacksmith's shop, where I couldn't get it back? What would happen? What would I do all day then?

Polish the sword, Ruby.

The Voice gets louder.

Polish the sword.

Polish the sword.

Polish the—

"Oh, all right!" Relenting, I resume my task.

I'm still polishing when the shop door bursts open.

I'm so astonished that I drop the sword. It clatters on the countertop, and I shoot to my feet.

In all my days, I've never known that door to open by anyone's hand but my own. But there in front of me, large as life, stands someone *new*. Not a townsperson.

A stranger.

An adventurer, the Voice tells me, and I know this is the one I've been waiting for.

Well, they could be a slavering gobspider and I'd still be glad to see them, just because it's something different. Something not in the routine.

This adventurer is a boy, short and pale, with shaggy black hair. A streak of blue threads through it. He's dressed in battered armor, his sword even rustier than the one I've been polishing. His feet are bare on the wooden floor. He has a triangular face, with a small pointed chin, bright green eyes, and a little scar under his left eye.

"I want to sell some—" he starts, but in his rush to the counter, he knocks over a set of clay urns (2 aurins each), which go rolling noisily across the floor. They clatter in the corner, shatter into pieces, and knock over a broom, which tilts toward the newcomer. He squeaks and pulls his sword, batting it aside.

Then he looks at me.

I sweep a hand over the counter. "Good afternoon, adventurer. I'm keeping shop while my father is off battling the troll hordes." Wait. What troll hordes? My father is fighting *trolls*? The Voice feeds the words to me, a continuous whisper in my ear, ignoring my questions as usual. "It's a hot day out there. Care to cool off with a Stagfen Ale?"

Smile, says the Voice, and I do.

"How much will you give me for these?" the adventurer asks. From the pouch on his belt, he pulls a bundle of gamper grass, three blanche melons, a vial of gobspider milk, and a riverwolf pelt.

I blink at the mess and wonder how in the name of the Realm all that junk fit into his little satchel.

"One aurin for each, and three for the gobspider milk." I can resell that for ten. "What's your name, traveler?"

"My name?" His head tilts. "Why would you want to know . . . It's Ashton—uh, Ashlyre, I mean. What's yours?"

I stare at him.

He answered my question.

He answered my question.

Nobody ever answers my questions! And for once, the Voice doesn't shush me. I wait for the inevitable *"focus on the path"* or some other command, but it doesn't come.

I'm so stunned that for a moment I almost forget the boy asked *me* a question.

"Ruby," I say quickly. "My name's Ruby."

"Okay, Ruby. Give me twelve vitality potions, one super-vitality potion, and a Brayvern apple."

"Wouldn't you rather have a pair of boots?"

"What?"

I point at his bare feet. He looks down as if surprised to see his toes wiggling there.

"I must have lost them in the troll king's cave," he groans. "See, *this* is why I need haptic shoes, so I would at least know when . . . Oh, forget it. It's not like *you* would understand. Just give me your cheapest boots."

I frown, offended at the insult to my intelligence. "*'Please.'*"

"What?"

"Did you lose your manners along with your shoes?"

He blinks, then bursts out with "*Seriously?* I've been mauled to death three times today, fell off a cliff, drowned twice, got my butt kicked by a fragging *zombie chicken*, and now the game wants to get *sassy* with me?"

Hmm. Adventurers are, I conclude, a rude bunch. Also melodramatic. Obviously no one who'd actually experienced all those things would be standing in my shop, in one piece, with only missing shoes to show for it.

But he answered my questions. And for that, I might forgive worse things than bad manners.

Primly, I take a pair of rusty sabbatons and place them on the counter with a *clank*. "Ten aurins."

He hands over the coins, each one shining gold.

I beam another smile, then thrust a hand at him. "Thanks for doing business, Ashlyre!"

"Uh-huh . . ." He looks confused as he shakes my hand. "Right. Well. See ya."

He leaves as quickly as he arrived, the door banging shut behind him. I look over at the broken urns, thinking I should clean up.

Except . . .

I blink, stupefied.

The urns are sitting in their original spot, whole and unbroken. The broom is propped against the wall. Everything is as it was, as if the adventurer had never been. As if, for a moment, time stopped when he entered the shop and now the clocks tick again.

As if nothing had ever happened.

Or . . . no. No, it's the other way around, isn't it? Time was frozen, but when Ashlyre arrived it began to move, a melting glacier. For a brief and wonderful few minutes, my world *changed*. Even the Voice was quiet for once.

Then the adventurer left, and everything froze over again.

I blink, something tugging at the back corner of my mind. A whisper, a thread of wind beneath a door.

"Voice?" I whisper. "Are you there? What just happened?"

The shadow behind me stirs. *Pick up the sword, Ruby.*

"But why—"

Pick up the sword.

Pick up the sword.

I resist as long as I can, pressing my hands over my ears, shutting my eyes, unable to silence the commands.

Pick up the sword.

Pick up the sword.

"All right!" I shout. "You win. You win."

I pick up the stupid sword and at once the Voice relaxes. The current eases. As I polish the blade, it polishes the sharp edges of my memory. It tries to erase the adventurer from my mind the way it erases all my questions. It wants to patch me up as it did those urns.

As if nothing had ever happened.

But that . . . that I resist.

I remember.

4. ASH

I can hear the troll king breathing in the dark, his heavy sighs punctuated with wet, shuddering snorts. Only a thin wall of rock separates us. My enchanted wayfinding amulet, dangling around my neck, casts pale blue light over the stone and my rusty iron armor—only to be swallowed by the darkness in the tunnel ahead. My toes tense in my new sabbatons.

A line of green saliva glistens on the ground leading to the troll king's cavern, both a warning and an invitation. With a shiver I grip the hilt of my sword and review my plan of attack.

I got this.

I *totally* got this.

Third time's the charm, right?

With a mighty yell, I throw myself into the darkness, sprinting out of the tunnel and into a large cavern. Stalactites hang down like broken, dripping teeth, and below them, on a dais of bones, sleeps a monster as big as a house. The moment I cross the threshold of his lair, Bamoorg wakes, all nineteen hairy, toothy, snot-soaked feet of him. No wonder he's the most feared creature in this region of the Glass Realm.

"YOU!" he roars. "Human worm, how dare you trespass here!"

He swipes, claws slicing the air, and I dodge with a sideways roll.

"You are *nothing*!" he roars. "A failure! You will die in this place!"

He grabs one of the fallen stalactites and wields it like a club, knocking me hard across the chest and throwing me through the air. I collide into the wall and crumple into a shallow, murky pool of water. With terrifying speed, Bamoorg leaps high, the stalactite clutched in his hand like a spear aimed for my heart.

As he soars through the air, he bellows, "You! Will! *Lose!*"

Gasping, I flick my hand and yell, *"Pause!"*

Bamoorg freezes in midair. His jaw is wide open, teeth shining and sharp black eyes merciless. A glob of saliva twinkles where it's just fallen from his lower lip, close enough that I could reach out and poke it. Gross.

Sighing with relief, I open the satchel on my belt and take out a small vial of golden liquid. It shimmers like sunlight, and when I pop the cork, bright, fizzy sparks erupt and melt into the air.

"To your looming defeat, sir," I say, lifting the vial in a toast to the troll suspended above me.

I swallow the golden potion, eyes sliding to the lower left corner of my field of vision, where my health bar appears. It's blinking, alerting me of dangerously low vitality, but as I drink, the bar slowly refills to the quarter mark.

"Hang on," I tell my salivating friend in the air. I toss aside the empty vial, and it vanishes. "I'll be with you in a sec."

I delve into my satchel again—only to come up empty. Heart missing a beat, I rummage deeper while my eyes follow the alphabetized list of items that pops up in front of my nose.

Thirst-Quenching Ring (damaged)

Trueflight-Enhanced Arrows (18)

Tumbleweed (3)

Vitamin of Strength

Wampus Whisker (4)

With a groan, I pull my hand out of the satchel and the list vanishes. "Are you *kidding me*? I forgot to load up on vitality potions?"

I think back to the shop in the Hinterlands, and the white-haired NPC shopkeep who talked me into buying shoes instead of potions. And, distracted by her weird obsession with manners, I did just that.

I glance mournfully at my quarter-filled health bar, then search desperately through my satchel once more. There's gotta be something. *Anything.* I check my ascension points again, in the lower corner of my heads-up display, but I haven't landed enough hits to fill the little golden bar. Until it's full, I can't use any god-tier attacks.

Maybe if I'm quick enough, I could roll aside and stab the monster in his ugly poison-sac throat. It's a long shot, but I've already died two times in this stupid cave. I have to try *something*.

There's a speed-enhancing berry in my satchel. I eat it, and at once my body begins to glow with the purplish aura of time magic.

I may actually have a shot at this.

"Okay, ugly . . ." My hands clench around my sword. "It's just you and me. Let's end this."

With a flick of my hand, time resumes.

Bamoorg descends through the air toward me, his stalactite-spear flashing. Boosted by the berry's power, I roll aside, prepared to drive my blade through—

Ssshhhnnnnik!

The sound of a stalactite piercing flesh.

I look down to see a pale, glistening rod of stone protruding from my belly. The sharp end went right through my abdomen, impaling the wall behind me.

Oh, come *on*!

Bamoorg roars in victory, lifting me on the stalactite like a cocktail weenie on a toothpick. "You have lost, pitiful adventurer! You are weak. You are *nothing*!"

Then he chucks me into his mouth, stalactite and all, and grinds me in half with his teeth.

My vision slowly turns red.

You Are Dead, a pop-up grimly informs me.

Then everything goes black.

I yank off my VR headset, then blink hard as the neon streetlights pouring through the window momentarily blind me. Coming out of virtual reality is always disorienting, no matter how many times I do it. It's a moment more before the words *You Are Dead* fade from my vision. Every time I blink, they're inscribed on the underside of my eyelids.

"Stupid, ugly, hairy son of a *fart*," I mutter, unstrapping my haptic gloves and anklets and tossing them into a pile.

I've been playing *Glass Realm* for nearly twenty-four hours straight, with only a short break to sleep and eat. My school tablet alarm's gone off twelve times, I see, glimpsing it sticking out of my backpack in the corner. *Study for Monday's biology exam, Ashton*, it urges me.

Pulling a face, I turn over and pick up my phone. I've got a whole day between now and then. I'll just cram Sunday night.

There's a message waiting from my mom.

Hey, kiddo, missing you! Everything okay at home?

I pause, swallowing hard as my thumbs hover over the screen.

Then I quickly type out, *Fine, miss you too*, and hit send.

I skim through my usual websites, checking for updates on my favorite online mangas, flicking away a few hologifs from Hakeem, scrolling through Chattr.

But then a local crime alert buzzes, a holographic alarm flashing over my phone with an attached news story. It's the sort of thing I'd usually dismiss without even reading it, but I *know* the guy in the picture.

Homeless Man Found Shot Aboard Skytrain. Suspects at Large. Police Caution Public Within the Area to Stay Alert.

It's him.

The guy from the alley.

The picture is blurry, taken from some old ID, judging by the trim of his beard. I scroll through the story.

The victim has been identified as Owen Locke.

I sit back, head thumping against the wall. An inexplicable sense of loss settles in my gut, like he was an uncle or something, not some random guy I knew for, like, five minutes. Then again, I did spend my life savings helping him get away from those sadistic punks.

The article says he was shot Friday night. Which means he was killed only hours after I met him, maybe less.

A shiver runs through me.

Maybe I was the last person he talked to. The last person who treated him with anything like kindness.

Who shot him? And why?

He hadn't seemed scared when I last saw him. But he had seemed . . . resigned. *I can't take it where I'm going anyway*, he'd said as he handed me the game coin.

Had he possibly known . . . ?

No. No, that's crazy. If he'd been worried for his life, surely he'd have gone to the police or somewhere safe.

Anyway, it's not like there's much I can do about it. There aren't even funeral details, so I can't pay respects. And if I did, that might be kind of hard to explain to his family. *I'm the kid who could've saved him, if I'd just taken him to the shelter myself instead of shoving him into an autocab.*

A flashing light on my wrist catches my attention. There's a paracord braided around it, holding a small metal disc. It blinks repeatedly—three flashes, pause, three flashes, pause. A secret message only one other person could have sent.

It means Hakeem's coming up.

Seconds later, I hear a tapping at my window. Callister leaps out from somewhere and starts yipping at the casement, his butt wiggling with excitement.

I squint at my best friend through the glass. Hakeem is perched on the fire escape like some kind of Middle Eastern Peter Pan, grinning and waving a paper bag.

I slide open the window and he slithers inside, a sweaty tangle of gangly limbs, gym clothes, and black hair. On his wrist is a matching paracord bracelet, also flashing, until he taps it off.

The smell of the city wafts in with him—hot metal, baking concrete, pizza, autocab fumes. Lines of delivery drones buzz past in endless queues, like wasps flitting to and from a hive.

"Hey, Keem."

"Hey, Ash. Hey, Fuzzbutt!" He picks up Callister and gives him a squeeze, then looks closer at my face. "*Hey.* You okay? You look like you're about to hurl."

"It's nothing." I don't feel like explaining I'm gutted because a homeless guy I barely knew is dead. It sounds pathetic, even to me.

"Yo, you put it up!" He points proudly at the poster of our school soccer team, where he poses front and center, clutching the ball. "Go Sharks! You know, Coach said he hoped you'd come to the tryouts next month."

"Keep it down, poster boy," I tell him. "Luke will kill us both if he finds out you're here."

"He'd have to get his butt off his expensive couch long enough to try, so I'm not too worried." With a snort, Hakeem shoves the bag at me. "Here, from Mom. She made me bring it, since you wouldn't come over. Or respond to any of my texts. Remember last year, when you told her once she's like your second mom? Yeah, that was a huge mistake. She took it *way* too literally, dude."

Inside the bag is a container of Dr. Jawabre's out-of-this-world baklava.

"For this," I say, cramming it into my mouth, "she can literally adopt me."

"Luke the Puke took all your furniture again, huh?" Hakeem looks around my trashed room. I did try to fold the clothes, but Callister just tore through them. "That dude has one twisted brain."

"Don't worry about it," I mumble.

Hakeem's been my best friend since we were toddlers. I've started wondering when he's going to realize how uncool I am and decide to dump me. After all, he's on the soccer team, he's practically famous in his e-sports league, he's got the world's most amazing family, and unlike me, he's got plenty of other friends he could be hanging out with. Everyone likes Hakeem. But here he is, sprawled on my floor, licking baklava off his fingers and scratching my dog's ears like he seriously doesn't have anywhere cooler to be.

I feel a rush of gratitude that he's still sticking by me.

That evaporates when he proceeds to use those sticky fingers to pick up my VR headset. "Playing that new game?"

"The Glass Realm." I snatch the headset away, rubbing off a glob of honey.

"I think my sister was into that for a while," he says. "Not my thing. Good graphics, though."

I spin my chair slowly, grabbing another piece of baklava. "Did Nadia ever meet a weird NPC girl there? White hair, red-gold eyes, runs a shop in the Hinterlands?"

"How would I know? And why do you care?"

"I don't know. She's strange. Different. Not sure how yet. I think she might be some special side quest."

He sighs and pushes to his feet. "All right, all right, hint taken. I'll leave so you can get back to your elf game."

"There aren't actually any—"

"You should think about those tryouts," he says. "We could really use a striker."

"Yeah . . ." I look down.

"Is this about Chase?"

I shrug.

Hakeem scowls. "Look, he's a total trashface, and what he did to you was uncool, but—"

"He broke my leg, Keem," I mumble. "On purpose. You know that."

"Because he knew you were better than him! If you try out, Chase won't make the team."

"If I try out, what's to stop him from breaking my leg again?"

"Me, that's what." He frowns, picking at the window. "It's like you're disappearing, man. You spend so much time in fake worlds, it's like you're fading out of *this* one. You quit soccer. You quit that

school writing club you loved so much. You quit everything except the bare minimum. I never see you anymore. My mom was asking why you don't come around like you used to. She thought maybe we got into a fight." He raises his hand, pointing at the paracord braided around his wrist. "Whatever happened to best bros forever, man?"

I touch the matching friendship bracelet on my own wrist, where it's been since first grade. Sappy? Well, yeah. But deep down, I kind of like the reminder that I'm still his best friend after all these years. "I'm not a zombie, Keem, if that's what you're saying."

Virtual reality addictions are no joke. In the old days, lots of people were addicted to computers, gaming, and social media. But VR addictions take it to a new level. People are found dead every day in their beds or couches, with their VR helmets still on, their games still running. They die of starvation, thirst, heart attacks. It's a big problem, and *zombies*—people with severe addictions—are as common as alcoholics or drug addicts these days. Many of them can't function in the real world anymore. They don't go to school or work or go outside. They couldn't even if they wanted to. The way Hakeem's mom explained it to us—in an effort to scare us from ever letting ourselves go that route, I guess—people with severe VR addictions have flipped the real and virtual worlds in their minds. To them, reality is the simulation, and VR is reality.

"I didn't say that," Hakeem insists. "I just . . . I don't know. Forget it."

What can I tell him? That in those *fake* worlds, I feel more real? That there, I can actually solve my problems, even if it takes me a hundred tries?

That's the thing about virtual reality. There are no consequences, not really. But in real life?

In real life, if you don't beat the boss in the first try, you just . . . lose.

I look at him. He looks at me. Then he sighs and shakes his head. "Whatever, dude. If you change your mind, let me know. Keem out!"

He slips out the window and is gone.

"Right," says the adventurer as he strides through the door of my shop. "I need vitality potions. And if you mention my manners again, I'll fill your shop with homicidal zombie chickens. That's a promise. Those mother-cluckers do *not* play."

I look up, polishing rag paused on the blade of my sword.

"Greetings, adventurer. It's a hot day out there. Would you care to cool off with a stagfen ale?"

"It's dark out." He points at the darkened window.

Ashlyre looks battered. Clearly he's been in a nasty fight, because there are dents, scratches, and tears in his armor to prove it.

"I can repair that for you," I offer, prompted by the Voice. We've been playing nicely for the last few days. No more thoughts about chucking swords through windows.

"Yeah? You do kind of owe me one, letting me leave here without a full stock of vitality potions." He begins peeling off pieces, tossing them onto my counter with noisy clangs. Cuirass, gauntlets, pauldrons, greaves. When he's done, he stands barefoot in a thin linen tunic and leather leggings, his hair fading from black to blue as it flops over his forehead.

"What kind of monster did this?" I hold up the left pauldron, which has a gouge running through it.

"Bamoorg," he groans. "The troll king."

Troll king. My father is off fighting the troll hordes. Why don't I have any memory of my father?

Irrelevant, says the Voice.

Irrelevant? How is my father—

Return to the script, Ruby.

What script?

I grimace at the dried snot on the cuirass. "Friendly fellow, this Bamoorg?"

"Yeah, a real bundle of charm."

I use my polishing rag to rub away the dents, stains, and scratches, and even the tears close up when the cloth passes over them. Seeing how quickly the repairs will go, I make myself slow down, to pretend it's harder than it looks. I don't want Ashlyre to leave. I want him to keep talking, to tell me of the strange and wonderful things he's seen and done.

Anything to keep time running, to stave off the monotonous dream of my existence. And when Ashlyre is here, I've noticed it gets easier to resist the Voice, to deviate from its repeating pattern. It still offers me words to speak, but I find I can ignore them.

"You should have a seat," I say. "This will take time. How about that ale?"

"I'm only thirteen." He tilts his head. "I guess that doesn't matter here. But still . . . nah. Gotta save my gold for vitality potions."

I try to think how old *I* am. But the further back in time I reach, the foggier my memories become. All I seem to know is my little wooden house, Timberton, and this shop. Is that all there is of me?

"Tell me about the troll king," I say.

His eyebrows shoot up. "You want to hear about it? Okay. Um, so I was just wandering in the northern forest, you know, exploring, and . . ."

I polish slowly—really, a snail could make quicker work of the job—listening to his every word. He's fascinating: the way he gestures as he talks, his ever-changing expressions, his punctuations of laughter and animated reenactment of the battle's more exciting bits. I watch him more than I listen to his actual words, trying to figure him out. Where is he from? Where did he learn to fight? Why is he so different from Toffton and Rauf and Porsha and all the others?

Why does he seem *more real*? Is it merely because he sees me, and they don't?

His tale doesn't last nearly as long as I hoped it would.

"Where will you go next?" I ask.

"A cavern to the west. There's supposed to be a legendary boar—" He pauses, cocking his head. "You hear that?"

I do. Distant thunder, I think, but as the sound gets louder, I realize it's feet. A lot of very *heavy* feet, closing in fast on Timberton.

"Quick!" cries Ashlyre. "My armor!"

I bring it over and help him clasp it on, cinching the cuirass and cauldrons. He sheaths his sword and stands there like a shining knight, his helmet snapping shut so that only his green eyes are visible.

"You're ready," I whisper, feeling a strange twinge.

Envy?

He opens the shop door and steps into the night. Seeing no reason to stay put, I follow, grabbing my rusty sword.

Return to the shop, Ruby, the Voice commands.

I ignore it.

Return to the shop, Ruby.

"Oh, go jump in a hole," I mutter.

I have far more interesting things to see right now than the inside of that dusty shop.

Rushing down the main road is a horde of enormous hairy gobspiders, each one bigger than a horse. Their pincers drip with foam, and the joints of their legs bristle with bladelike barbs.

"The Night Swarm," breathes Ashlyre. "But they're, like, ten levels higher than me." He smacks his hand to his forehead. "Ugh, this is because I triggered that quest back in the Gloom Cavern, isn't it? I knew I shouldn't have cut down that web! Now they're out for vengeance."

"They see us!" I say, nodding at the leader. It clacks its pincers, its eight eyes all seeming to fix on us.

"Great," moans Ashlyre. "Well, see you when I respawn, I guess."

"When you what?"

He draws his own blade; it flashes in the moonlight.

The Swarm bears down on us ruthlessly, its members beginning to chitter and screech. They leap high in the air, their eyes turning red with bloodlust, and lash out with whips made of white webbing.

"Get back inside!" Ashlyre says. "They'll shred you, and I don't know if you'll respawn!"

"What is that word you keep using?" I shout.

Without answering, he leaps in front of me just in time to sweep his sword at the first of the gobspiders.

The others circle us, cutting off all escape. Ashlyre fights valiantly, but clearly he will soon be overwhelmed.

I react without thinking.

My hand tightens on the hilt of my rusty sword. I whirl it around, impaling a screeching gobspider in its glowing fourth eye. Instead of dropping, the spider bursts into dust. Where it had been standing, there's now a spool of gobspider silk, some coins, and a sword—starsteel, magic forged, worth 1,745 aurin.

Wait—what?

Where did all *that* come from? Where's the creature's corpse? Is all that junk just stuff the thing . . . swallowed? It makes no sense. I stare at the pile, bewildered, but it's like trying to add three plus purple.

Something feels very, *very* off.

But its buddies don't give me much time to ponder.

Spinning, I cut down another with a slice at its legs. The one behind it lunges through the dust cloud. I kick hard, snapping its carapace, then follow up with a plunge of my blade.

It's all so . . . *easy*.

"Hey!" Ashlyre calls, grinning over the teeming horde. "You're *good!*"

I barely hear him. A red haze fills my vision as if the world is on fire. The sword becomes a part of me. My body becomes a mere tool. It's as if I separate from it entirely and manipulate my limbs from above.

I see Ruby the shopkeep spin and whirl and flip, her eyes alight and teeth bared in a vicious grin. She stabs and strikes, wreathed in the dust of her victims. With a leap, she plants a foot against the wall of the shop and backflips through the air, over Ashlyre's head, to run her sword through three gobspiders at once. The movement tears her brown skirt from hem to knee. She lets out a whoop of glee and hurls herself at the next monster.

That girl is *me*?

In one moment, I'm aware of the location of every one of the spiders, how they are moving, their velocity, their intention. I kill them as easily as if I were brushing dirt off my shoulder.

As I whirl and stab and parry, my vision flashes, and I see another road in another place—red dirt in a desert. Scraggly grass and sharp rocks beneath a sizzlingly hot blue sky.

Gasping, I blink the vision away, trying to focus on the fight.

But the image intrudes again. The battle around me transforms. Instead of giant spiders, I'm suddenly surrounded by humans wearing long-sleeved shirts and trousers the color of sand. Their uniforms are dusty, their heads encased in round, hard helmets. They carry not swords and spears like most Glass Realm folk, but long metal tubes.

Guns, I think. *They're called guns.*

I hover above them, with arms of metal and whirring blades and a humming, thrumming metal heart. I guard them from on high, directing their movements through their helmets' earpieces, buzzing above like a wasp of cold, indifferent doom. What am I doing here? What are these soldiers after?

Do I want to know the answer?

Then I blink and find myself back in Timberton, where I've somehow acquired another sword and am whirling both with deadly precision. Gobspiders fall shrieking before me, bursting into dust. Where they die, items appear on the ground—swords, armor, vials, and a lot of coins.

I force myself to pause, swords gripped high above my head, as the last gobspider cowers before me, legs raised in submission. Taking its chance, it turns and scuttles into the dark, chittering.

I lower the swords slowly.

The rest of the Swarm is gone, two by Ashlyre's hand, twenty-three by mine. On the road where they'd been, I stand still, swords held at my sides, my own body unscathed.

So you have left the shop, the Voice suddenly sighs in my ear. As always, when it speaks, I sense its shadowy form behind me, just out of sight. *Very well, then. You have earned this.*

"Voice?" I whisper, still shaken by the image of the desert road. "Earned what? What just *happened*?"

The Voice doesn't reply. Instead, a scroll appears in the air before me, shining as if dipped in molten gold. Dropping one of my swords, I reach up and take the scroll.

Okay. Something really weird is going on here.

I may not have seen much of the world beyond Timberton's bounds, but I'm pretty sure dead things, even supernaturally large spiders, shouldn't just *disappear*. Or turn into piles of treasure, for that matter. And scrolls shouldn't just *appear* in midair.

And how did I kill them all so easily? I'm not a trained fighter . . . am I? I'm just the shopkeeper's daughter! I clean swords and sell them. I don't *wield* them, like some kind of warrior. Then there's the vision I saw—which makes even less sense. Whatever place it was, it didn't look anything like the world I know.

And yet . . . it felt familiar.

It's all wrong, wrong, wrong. I press a hand to my head, waiting for the Voice to explain, to tell me what's going on. But it's silent. Instead, my head is filled with screaming questions.

What is happening?

Why does nothing make sense anymore?

And, worst of all: *What am I?*

6. RUBY

"Ruby!" Ashlyre steps in front of me, his eyes as round as moons. "You— you *wasted* them. Without getting a scratch. That was *brilliant!*"

Brilliant? I don't know about that, but the fight *was* invigorating. It's like a part of me had been sleeping all this time, only to come fully awake once there was a battle to be won. Even still, my eyes scan the world around me, looking for more enemies, ready to spring back into action.

I *enjoyed* fighting. The thrill pumps through me, sizzles in my finger-tips. It's a weird feeling, this sense of power. Like I could do anything. Beat anyone.

But where did those movements come from? Why did it all feel so . . . familiar? It's like I transformed into an entirely different person, and it's not someone I'm sure I like. Super-skilled and deadly, yes. But behind all the excitement, a shadow of unease lurks. Like a second part of me— the shopkeeper's daughter—isn't sure she *should* like all this slicing and dicing. "Is it over?"

Ashlyre nods. "Yeah, I'd say you ended it pretty definitively. What *are* you?"

"I . . . don't think I'm just a shopkeep."

"Uh, yeah, that seems obvious." He laughs. "You're *incredible*! That triple flip you did through the air? Like, *how even*? You're totally OP!"

"OP?"

"Overpowered. Never mind, it's a—a real-world thing."

Real world?

He picks up the extra sword I dropped and hands it to me. "Keep it. You won it fair and square."

I hesitate, recalling how much I'd relished the fight. "I don't know if I should."

His eyebrows lift. "Oh? Okay, well, if you won't, I will." He drops it into that unfathomable, bottomless satchel. How *does* it all fit in there? Some kind of enchantment, maybe?

I look at him through the white curtain of my hair, wondering at his nonchalance. All that killing, all that death, and he's *whistling*. He almost got his head snapped off several times back there, but it's like he just brushes it off. Maybe he has battles like this all the time?

It's like he doesn't even *fear* death.

And for someone who fights as badly as he does, that seems . . . concerning.

"Sweet!" he says, focused on something I cannot see. His hand makes gestures in the air, as if he's searching an invisible scroll suspended before him. "Leveled up! That's a ridiculous amount of XP. I have to take you questing more often now that I know you're an ally."

"Ally?"

"Someone who can follow me around, help me fight, carry my loot."

I frown, drawing myself up to my full height—which is still a good foot shorter than his. "Excuse me, adventurer, but I am *not* a pack animal."

"Okay, okay!" He waves his hands. "Just the following and fighting, then."

"Will it always be like this?" I ask. "The fighting, I mean?"

"Mostly, but let's at least prepare a little before our next big encounter. I mean, you're great and all, but I'd like to get in a few hits. Once you jumped in, you pulled all the aggro. Leave some for us mortals, eh?" He laughs again. "I am *so* glad I dropped by your shop."

He moves around, picking up weapons and armor and storing them in his satchel, still talking about the fight as if it were some kind of show just for his entertainment.

I notice then that tear in my skirt has closed up as completely as if it had never happened, just like those urns patching themselves up in the shop. More magic at work? What is going on here?

"Voice?" I whisper. "What's happening? Did *you* do this?"

The Voice doesn't answer.

I run my hand over the fabric, angry that it's able to just *undo* the past like that. As if it's trying to make me forget what it felt like, fighting for my life. *Being* alive in the first place.

As I glare at the untorn skirt, the fabric . . . *changes*. Just for a moment, only faintly. Through it, I see numbers shimmering inside the fabric—1s and 0s.

What?

Wonderingly, I *press* my hand to the skirt, watch my fingers pass through the fabric and comb through the numbered web inside it. Where I touch it, the numbers shiver and rearrange, like a school of small fish.

When I withdraw my hand, they vanish.

And the skirt is torn once more, right to the knee.

"Ruby?" Ashlyre is several paces away, watching me in puzzlement. "Are you okay?"

Magic. That must be the answer. Right? I look up the road toward the rickety, narrow cabin where an old woman named Ezrina lives. According to the gossip between the housewives one street over, she's a witch who performs questionable magic.

Am *I* a witch?

Or was I cursed by one? If so, why? And how? Is there a way to break it?

I don't know what happened here. I don't know what I am. I feel the answers are there, somewhere very close, but my mind can't quite grasp hold of them. They whisper in my ear but vanish when I turn my head.

I *saw* things tonight I've never seen before. Or . . . have I seen them, and just forgot? The vision I had, of the desert, the men in those tawny uniforms and hard helmets—the word *soldiers* pops into my mind suddenly. It all felt so weirdly familiar.

What if they were not a vision at all, but a memory?

I don't know which would be more unsettling.

Shivering aftershocks of the vision still run through me. I can feel the whir of those metal hands, the ticking of that mechanical heart, the cold, ruthless calculations running in my head, reducing people to numbers, to targets. *That* is what's making me truly uneasy. The feeling that inside the grinning, laughing warrior I became, something *colder* is hiding. Something even deadlier.

"Ruby, I said, *are you okay*?"

"Absolutely," I say, forcing a grin. "I am fine, Ashlyre."

Whatever that was, it's over. Ashlyre doesn't seem bothered by the fight, so why should I be? Those spiders would have killed my adventurer if I hadn't stopped them. And who would I wait for then, all day in my little shop, while I polish the sword I just used to kill two dozen creatures?

"What's that?" Ashlyre asks.

"What's what?" Oh. I look down at my hand. "It's a scroll. I . . . found it."

Or rather, *earned* it, according to the Voice. Whatever that means.

"What does it say?" Ashlyre hurries to my side, peering over my shoulder. "Go on, open it!"

The scroll is sealed by crimson wax, stamped with a ruby-red seal. Breaking it, I unfurl the parchment. It rustles under my fingers. Faded, handwritten script curls across the page.

If it's truth you seek, the past you'd find,

Then listen, child, to me:

The road you'll travel you've traveled before

But once left willingly.

Seek your fate, walk in light,

To reach . . . uh . . . farthest . . . something . . .

Ah, shoot, I'm no poet. Here's the quest: If you want—I mean really *want—the truth about the desert road, then seek the next door. King under mountain, mountain under crown. But I'll warn you. The path won't be easy. What you learn along the way and what is revealed in you may change your mind. Once you know the truth, there's no going back. If you start down this path, you must follow it to its end.*

—The Wizard

At the bottom of the scroll are two words: *Accept* and *Deny*.

"Weird," says Ashlyre. "What's the desert road? And who's the Wizard? I mean, there are loads of wizards here, but which one is *the* one?"

I'd nearly forgotten he was there, reading over my shoulder.

He takes the scroll from me and reads it again, aloud. I stare at the rip in my skirt.

"Well," Ashlyre says. "I guess it can't hurt to accept the quest."

He taps the paper, but nothing happens. I'm not sure what he expects, but apparently this isn't it, because his brow furrows in confusion.

"I don't get it. It won't let me accept. Maybe I'm not a high enough level for this one? It *did* drop from the Night Swarm, I guess. But why offer it to me?"

The answer beats in my heart. It claws its way up my throat and, with heavy reluctance, loosens my tongue.

"Because it's not for you," I whisper.

He looks up. "Huh? Of course it's for me. I mean, who else? This is a single-player—"

"Give it to me."

Ashlyre stares for a long moment, his eyes wide.

Then, wordlessly, he gives me the scroll.

I bite my lip, reading it once more. *The truth about the desert road . . .* I know exactly what it means. That somehow, by fighting the gobspiders, I unlocked some secret. A vision, a memory, a prophecy, I don't yet know. But *I* was the one who saw that road, not Ashlyre. That desert road over which I soared like a wasp of death.

Once you start down this path, you must follow it to its end.

Do I even like what the battle awoke in me? I mean, there was a kind of freedom in it, the joy of being alive and fighting to *stay* alive. But then there was the feeling of losing control of myself, of being a spectator as my body wielded destruction like a third limb. The taste of it still burns in my mouth, metallic and cold. I never want to experience *that* part again.

"Hello, adventurer," says a velvet voice. "Care to cool off with a glass of fresh milk?"

I turn to see Variel the milkmaid smiling coyly at Ashlyre, having emerged from whatever hidey-hole she crawled into during the fight. So she *can* talk! Just not to me.

"Keep walking, farmgirl," I growl. "If he's going to cool off with anything, it'll be a glass of my stagfen ale. And can't you see we're busy here?"

Ashlyre clears his throat. "Um. If anyone cares, I'm not actually thirsty."

"Too bad, adventurer. Maybe next time." Variel winks at Ashlyre and then keeps walking, her buckets sloshing in her hands. She never even mentions the spiders.

"Hey!" I shout after her. "Aren't you going to thank me for saving you and your precious cows?"

She doesn't even turn her head.

It's not just Variel. All of Timberton is going back to normal. Porsha and Morto emerge from their hiding place. Lord Toffton resumes his hand-wringing around the town. Everyone is going right back into their routines as if nothing at all had happened. Just like the broken urns in my shop, they repair themselves, unbroken. Unchanged.

As I look back at the scroll, my finger hovers over the *Deny* button.

There *is* a choice.

I could be like the other people in Timberton. Go back to waking up in my little house, opening my quiet shop, sitting alone in a beam of sunlight, polishing that rusty sword. Submitting to the Voice. Forever. If monsters attack the town again, I could hide inside my shop and pretend nothing is happening, just like Variel. She seems happy enough.

At least when I follow my little path, I don't turn into a wild killing machine. I don't have visions of other places. I could go back, and I could be safe. Life was no adventure as the shopkeeper's daughter, but I was content most of the time. I love my shop, and I love Timberton. And if I'm not here, who will warn Porsha about the wolves?

I could let the Voice polish the memories out of me the way I polish the nicks out of a sword. I could be whole again, without the questions screaming in my mind. What if the answers are terrible? What if the truth is worse than the monotony of my life in Timberton?

But if I follow this path, this *quest*, maybe I'll understand what happened.

And from that, maybe I'll understand the Voice in my head, the restlessness in my bones, the difference I know exists between me and the other people of Timberton. The thing that makes me more like Ashlyre.

More *real*.

Maybe that's not what Ruby the Shopkeeper's Daughter wants. Maybe she would be content with that quiet, safe life.

But I don't think that I am Ruby the Shopkeeper's Daughter.

I think I might be someone else entirely. And I want to know who that is.

With a trembling finger, I press the word *Accept*.

With a sound like twinkling chimes, the scroll disintegrates into glittering golden dust that rains through my fingers and melts into the air. In a moment, it is gone entirely. Another enchantment? Or . . . something more? Something I don't yet understand? Because one thing *is* clear. There is much, *much* that I don't yet understand.

As if disappointed, the Voice in my head sighs. *Quest accepted, then.* Strangely, the Voice sounds different this time, as if it's another speaker entirely. *This is where I leave you. I hope you're ready, my ever-curious Ruby. Because now there's no going back.*

7. RUBY

Timberton is a speck in the distance, barely even discernible as a town. I take one last, long look from atop the rocky hill the adventurer and I just finished climbing.

"We'll make camp up in those rocks," Ashlyre says, gesturing with his sword.

Bleached white, the boulders cast long shadows over the pale golden grass. The setting sun flares on the horizon beyond, where the land turns wild. Forests tangle over rocky rivers, and a desert spreads to the south.

"All of this was just a day's walk from my house, and I never knew it," I say softly.

Ashlyre sheathes his sword. "Uh-huh. C'mon, if we're caught out at night we'll get swarmed by worse things than gobspiders."

Worse things?

I hurry to keep up with him.

At the boulders, Ash lets out a shout. I hurry over, sword in hand, ready for anything.

But instead of slavering spiders or hulking trolls, I find him bending over an old wooden chest tucked between two boulders. He kicks it, and the lid pops open.

"Sweet," says Ash. "Golden antelope steak!"

He pulls a hunk of meat from the chest and shoves it into his satchel, as well as some coins and potions he finds under it.

"Uh . . ." I blink. "You're going to *eat* that?"

"Golden antelope steak," he says, shrugging. "It makes me immune to poison for the next twenty-four hours. Of course I'm going to eat it."

"But—you don't know how long that meat's been sitting in there. It could be months old and rotten. You could *die!*"

He gives me a strange look. "Um . . . that's not . . . how this works."

"Why is there a chest up here with raw steak in it anyway?" I ask. "Who would just leave a steak in a box in the middle of nowhere?"

Ash stares as if stupefied by my perfectly rational questions. Honestly, I can't help wondering how he's survived this long on his own.

I kick the chest, but it doesn't pop open for me the way it did for him. "It must be a trap. I bet the steak is poisoned. Pretty stupid trap, though, for pretty stupid people. Because *who* eats a steak they find in a box in the wilderness? Stupid people, that's who."

Finally, Ash laughs. "Oh, I get it. You're supposed to be funny."

"Funny! I'm trying to save your life!"

"Yeah, yeah." Ash takes out a cord of firewood from his satchel and tosses it on the ground.

"How do you *do* that?" I ask.

He looks up. "Do what?"

I gesture at the wood, then his satchel. "Fit all of that in there! Is it magic?"

Ashlyre frowns. "You mean . . . my inventory?"

"Inventory. Is that a kind of spell?"

"Uh . . . no." He gives me an odd look, then mutters something under his breath and points at the wood. It catches fire immediately.

"Okay, *that* was magic!" I say.

He shrugs as he spears the questionable steak on his sword and props it over the flames. "I know some spells. But to be honest, I put most of my skill points into stealth. By the time I'm done, I'll practically be invisible. Till then, though, I'm going to need another invisibility cloak. Lost mine in the last fight with Bamoorg."

He sits beside the fire and pulls two bundles of wool from his satchel, and a skein of gobspider silk. I watch in fascination and utter bewilderment as he moves his hands over the items. With a puff of smoke and a flash of light, the objects vanish, replaced by a silvery cloak.

"Voilà!" he says. "Invisibility cloak."

Eyes wide, I watch as he puts the cloak on. Everything below his head vanishes.

"You're a wizard," I conclude.

"I told you, I'm more of a stealth guy. Well, stealth and archery. And some paladin skills, but only for the armor buffs. I prefer to fight from a distance." He chuckles. "Not that you understand any of that. I can't believe I'm talking to you like you're real."

"What? I'm real. Why wouldn't I be real?" I sit down opposite him. The fire crackles between us. But he's right about the other part—I don't understand half of what he says.

"Sure, sure," he mutters.

"I'm *real*," I insist hotly. "And I'm a wizard too. See? I made this!" I point at the hole in my skirt.

Ashlyre's eyebrows lift slightly. "Um . . ."

I grab a handful of grass and hold it up like a pathetic bouquet. "Watch."

Concentrating hard, I stare at the grass, pushing, *pushing* . . . There! I glimpse the murky soup of numbers—1s and 0s—teeming behind the grass. What the stuff is, I have no idea. Maybe magic itself? Just like I did with my skirt, I *press* my thoughts against the numbers, willing them to do what I want.

And just like that, the grass bursts into flame.

I quickly drop the smoking bundle into the fire, but not before Ashlyre sees what I did.

He laughs a little, then claps his hands slowly. "Okay, yeah, so you're equipped with magic. To be fair, though, a lot of characters here are."

So I'm a *character*, am I? Rude way to refer to someone who just saved his mangy neck. Grumbling to myself, I draw my knees up to my chin and glare at the flames.

So he wasn't impressed with my magic. Fine. Maybe it's not all that impressive, but it was a surprise to me that it even existed. I didn't know I could do those things. Who taught them to me? The father I can't remember?

Ashlyre takes some items from his satchel. Two swords, a bow, a bunch of arrows, and a pile of potion bottles. He begins pouring potions onto the weapons, nodding in satisfaction when they hiss and steam and begin to glow faintly. It all looks very mysterious and wizardly.

"What are you doing now?" I ask.

"Enchanting my gear. Their magic stats run out at sunset."

Magic stats. Armor buffs. Paladin skills. It's like he's speaking a whole other language. It irritates me, not understanding. Is this the stuff they teach in adventurer school? Is that even a place?

"Do you hear the Voice too?" I ask.

He pauses, giving me a long stare. "Uh . . . You, uh, hear voices?"

"Not voices. *The* Voice. Singular. Do you hear it? Does it tell you what to do, where to go?"

"You . . . you mean the tutorial? I finished that ages ago. Well, I skipped most of it, to be honest." He frowns, his voice dropping to a whisper as if he's speaking only to himself. "But how would *you* know about the tutorial?"

Tutorial? Is that the Voice's name? And why haven't I heard the Voice since we left Timberton? It doesn't answer even when I ask for it. Granted, it *did* say it would "leave me" after I accepted the quest, but I hadn't really expected it to.

Ashlyre puts down the potion bottle and studies me. "What's your backstory, Ruby?"

"My backstory?"

He waves a vague hand in the air. "You know. Your history. Tragic past. All that."

"I . . . don't have any of that. I'm just Ruby the Shopkeeper's Daughter."

"Your childhood. What was it like? Where did you learn to fight? Everyone here has backstory, even the urchins in the streets." Again he drops his voice, speaking to himself. "Trust me, I've skipped through enough dialogue trees to know."

"Um . . ." I try to think back. Childhood. I was a child. I had to have been, right? But I don't remember anything about *being* a child. As far back as my mind will go, there's only my little house, the path through Timberton, the supply shop.

Unsettled, I stretch my hands toward the flames but feel no heat. Shouldn't flames be hot? I try to remember other fires I've seen before but can't recall a single one.

What is *wrong* with me?

"So she's a shopkeeper who can fight like a warrior, but she has zero backstory." Ashlyre shakes his head. "That's just bad writing if you ask me. Unless it's an amnesia situation? Maybe you forgot your backstory."

"Yes," I say. "That must be it. This quest, it should reveal everything."

Like who my father is, and why I have magic powers, and why I can fight like a warrior.

"Makes sense. Except for the part where it's *your* quest, not mine. Argh!" He lunges for his sword. "Almost burned my steak."

I frown. "Why shouldn't it be?"

"Burned?" He gives me a confused look.

"Why shouldn't it be *my* quest? Because I'm a shopkeeper's daughter, and not some fancy adventurer wizard-boy with terrible manners?" I grimace as he takes a bite of the charred meat. "If you drop dead from that, it's your own fault."

"Mmmm, delicious." He grins, then swallows the rest whole. "Look, Ruby, *everything* here is for me. That chest with the steak? It was put there for me. The gobspiders? They were in your town seeking vengeance against *me* because I chopped down some of their sacred webs or whatever. This whole world is an enormous playground, all for *me*."

With a snort, I smooth out my skirts, feeling the tear in the fabric. "The only enormous thing I see around here is your ego, adventurer."

"Ha ha ha," he says humorlessly. "So you're a snarky one, huh? Okay. Cool. You're more fun than the other characters I've met. I hope you don't get killed off in some dungeon raid."

"Um . . . thank you?" I raise an eyebrow at him. "Though with *your* fighting skills, you might want to worry more about yourself."

He laughs. "Yeah, you're probably right. I'd have been spider chow back there if it weren't for you."

"What's *your* backstory?"

Ashlyre looks away thoughtfully, and a few moments later replies, "I grew up in a far-off city, in the slums. My mom was a hard worker, and my dad . . . he got sick, in his mind, you know. Then he, well, he died. A few years later, my mom met a . . . wealthy lord, and he seemed nice at first. But turns out he was actually super evil, so I ran away."

My eyes go wide. "And your mom?"

"I'm going back one day to rescue her," he says quietly. "That's why I have to go on these adventures. To get stronger."

I watch him for a moment. He looks down at the grass, his hands curled into fists.

Then I slide around the fire and sit beside him, slinging my arm across his shoulders. "Then I'll help you on your quest, since you're helping me on mine. We'll find my truth, and your strength. No matter what kind of monsters stand in our way. What did you call us? Allies? Well. Isn't that what allies do—help each other?"

Ashlyre meets my eyes, looking a bit startled. For a long moment, he seems not to know what to say.

Then, with an odd, soft laugh, he says, "Yeah, Ruby the not-just-shopkeeper. That's what allies do."

"So we have a deal, then?" I put out my hand.

"Yeah." Ashlyre shakes my hand. "We have a deal."

8. ASH

"Trouble ahead," I murmur.

Ruby and I lie in tall grass, peering up at a flock of shadows circling above.

"Razorscales," I say. "Fifteen levels above me. I wouldn't mess with them if they were fifteen levels *lower*." I shiver, remembering the last flock I found. They'd torn my avatar into pieces, then devoured half my gear.

RIP, epic ruby-encrusted chestplate.

"Why are you so obsessed with ranking everything? Is that some kind of adventurer hobby?" Ruby peers up, her eyes intent, as one of the creatures dives on a wild sheep that's wandering around in the grass. It grabs the creature and bites off its head. The sheep drops two bundles of wool. "Big scaly bullies. Those poor sheep don't deserve that."

"Better them than us. Hey, whoa! What are you doing?"

She's got her hand on the hilt of her rusty sword, tugging it loose from the sheath I gave her for it. "I may not know my backstory, adventurer, but I *do* know I hate bullies. It takes a special kind of coward to pick on someone smaller and weaker."

"Uh, if you haven't noticed, those are level forty-seven razorscales,

Ruby. *We* are smaller and weaker. Like, much, *much* smaller and weaker."

She looks up at the razorscales again. "Do you always hide when things get a little tough?"

I'm glad my blush doesn't translate into my avatar's face. "There's tough and then there's stupid. According to the lore I've read, those big, scaly bullies are invulnerable."

"Every enemy has a weakness."

I snort. "You wouldn't say that if you met Bamoorg."

"Ah yes, the troll king who kicked your butt three times. Are you sure you don't want to pay him a visit? I'd love to introduce him to old Rusty." She twirls her sword, grinning fiendishly. "Fourth time's the charm, right?"

"We are *not* going up against that guy! Stop bringing it up." What I don't tell her is that I'm worried even she couldn't beat Bamoorg. And if she dies, I have no idea if she'll respawn or not. As far as allies go, she might be the coolest one I've ever met. Sometimes it's almost like she's a real person. Her dialogue is creepily good.

"Just saying. Maybe the reason you failed all those times before was because you didn't ask for help."

"Look, forget Bamoorg. And forget those razorscales! I'm the player here, and I say we sneak around. C'mon."

I start crawling away, keeping low, but when I look back, Ruby is standing up, in plain sight of the razorscales. She has her rusty sword in hand and a manic grin on her face.

"Ruby!" I hiss. "You have to obey me! I command you to stay put!"

She glances at me, anger flashing in her eyes. I'm taken aback. For a moment, I forget she's an NPC. There's just something so . . . *human* in that expression.

"I don't have to obey anyone," she snarls. "Not you, not the Voice, not anyone."

"The voice? What voice? Are you talking about the tutorial again?" I still haven't figured out why an NPC would know about that.

She doesn't hear my question, though, because she's already sprinting over the grass, howling like a deranged baboon.

The razorscales dive with murder in their eyes, claws shining like shards of broken glass. There must be six or seven of them—the biggest flock I've seen yet.

"Ruby!" I yell, panicking. "Stop! If you get killed, you might not—"

Ssssshhhhhhhing!

The rusty sword speeds through the sky like an arrow, slung from Ruby's hand.

With a scream, a razorscale plummets to the ground, impaled through the neck. It disintegrates the moment it lands, leaving a pile of loot—three scales, a claw, five arrows, and a vitality potion. The others converge on Ruby, but she moves like a beam of lightning, collecting her sword from the ground and slicing the throat of the nearest razorscale.

"You want a fight, you overgrown lizards?" she bellows. "Pick on *me*, then! I'm not such easy prey. And *you*!" She shoos away the sheep. "Get out of here, you big lumps! Can't you see I'm trying to save your woolly butts?"

The sheep run off, bleating in terror, as Ruby distracts the razorscales.

I huddle in the grass, eyes wide as she wreaks destruction on the creatures. She scoops up the five arrows and drives two of them into the eyes of another razorscale, before flipping neatly out of the path of yet another's jaws. Her sword severs its neck, then spins in a silver blur to stab the chest of a fourth. The last two close in together, hunting in formation, and Ruby drops into a low crouch, her sword raised horizontally across her face. For a moment, she and the razorscales are locked in a standoff.

Ruby attacks first.

She charges at one, slides under its belly, and rakes her sword down the length of its soft underside. Guts spill out. As the creature falls in a cloud of dust, Ruby shoots high into the air, pirouetting as she slings her three remaining arrows. Each one buries itself in the last razorscale's hide, and as it recoils in pain, she falls on it in a whirlwind of steel.

When the bodies disintegrate, she's left standing atop a pile of loot, calmly looking around like she's disappointed the fight was so easy.

"Well," I say, standing up, my stomach still in knots. "Okay, then."

"Told you every enemy has a weakness," she says. "Turns out, razorscales' is their throat." Ruby digs through the loot, then holds up two bundles of wool. She beams at me. "Now you can make me an invisibility cloak with your magic!"

"Um. Yeah. Sure." I add the wool and a bunch of the loot into my inventory while staring at Ruby. "We, uh, should probably get you a better weapon. That sword is about to crack. And think of what you could do with a *real* piece of steel."

She looks down at the rusty blade, which has splinters running through the steel, a sure sign the weapon is about to burst into useless pixels. Before now, I would have said a sword like that couldn't ding a razorscale.

But then, I'm starting to realize that even a soup spoon might be deadly in Ruby's hands.

Those were not the first mobs she's killed on our journey. But they *were* the highest level, even stronger than the gobspiders. And she acts like it was nothing.

Shaking my head, I turn to look northward. "We're almost there."

"The mountain under the crown?"

"Maybe. Those are the only mountains in the game so it has to be there, right?"

"Game? What game?"

I turn back to her, not sure I heard her correctly. "What did you say?"

"What game?" She stares at me blank faced, like any other NPC.

But there is *nothing* normal about that question.

"Is this some kind of fourth wall thing?" I ask. "A joke by the developers?"

She looks around. "I see no wall. And what's funny about it?"

"It's just that NPCs don't usually . . . act the way you do." They also don't get *quests*. Or ask about the tutorial. Or give you grief for eating a steak you found in a random chest.

"NPC?" she echoes. "What's that?"

I shake my head. This is getting a little too weird. "Let's just finish your quest. Maybe it'll . . . explain things."

Such as why a programmed character is asking questions like *"What game?"*

It's got to be a joke hidden by the developers. I've seen them before—tongue-in-cheek NPC dialogue like "Sometimes this world doesn't feel real" or "Do you ever feel like you're being played with?"

Except if this *is* a joke, it's running kind of long. I mean, building a whole quest around it?

I have to know *why*.

I guess that's why this game's subtitle is *The World of the*

Ever-Curious. It does like to hide secrets under every rock. The more you explore, the more questions you ask, the more rewards you get. It's a world *designed* to make you curious. And nothing I've seen so far has made me more curious than Ruby the Shopkeeper's Daughter.

I pause the game again to check the time. It's late. Or early, I guess. In fact, it's almost morning. Pulling off my helmet, I shut my eyes for a moment, feeling how tired they are. Then I check in with my IRL body. My stomach growls with hunger, and I realize with a start that I haven't had anything to eat since lunch. *Yesterday.* All I have in here is a case of Zero Gee energy drinks, half of which I've already downed. But finding food means leaving my room, and leaving my room means risking running into Luke. He'll be getting ready for the gym soon.

I can wait till he's gone. Anyway, I want to see if I'm right, and if the *mountain under the crown* is ahead of us. It's taken us hours to get this far, since I haven't unlocked fast travel yet. And because Ruby wanted to explore every digital blade of grass and flip over every digital rock to see what might scurry out from under it.

It's almost as if she's as *ever-curious* as I am.

Blinking rapidly to flush my dry eyes, I pull my VR helmet back on—only to scream.

Ruby is RIGHT THERE.

Like, in my face. *Poking* at it.

Did I accidentally unpause the game?

No. There are birds still frozen in flight above, and the perpetual wind isn't blowing the grass around. Everything in the Realm is still fixed in place, from the environment to the creatures to my own armor-clad avatar.

Everything . . . except Ruby.

71 ------ọ

The pause menu floats by her, but she seems oblivious to it.

"Hello?" she mutters, prodding my avatar. "Ashlyre? You there?"

Hastily I unpause the game, and the grass begins to rustle again. The birds continue their flight pattern. My avatar relaxes.

Eyes widening, Ruby steps back.

"What did you just do?" I whisper. "I—I paused the game."

"The game," she murmurs. "You keep mentioning this game. Where did you go just now? It was like weird magic froze everything. You froze up. *I* froze up."

"But . . . you didn't stay frozen," I point out.

That should have been impossible.

"No," she says. "Whatever it was, I broke free of it. Why didn't you?"

"I . . ." I must be hallucinating. Duh. I've been playing this game for nearly thirty hours straight, with only a few hours of rest. That's just unhealthy. My brain's probably fried. "I should go get some sleep. Yeah. Sleep."

I motion to pause the game again but hesitate. Ruby watches me with intense curiosity, her gaze flickering from my face to my hands, like she's trying to memorize every move I make.

It's creepy, is what it is.

Shaking my head, I pause the game again. The world around me freezes.

Stomach churning, I glance at Ruby.

She smiles. Waves.

Definitely *not* paused.

Okay! *SUPER* creepy!

Instead of just letting my VR sit idle like I usually do, I power it down completely. Then I tear it off and remove the power cell. Now it's completely dead.

Maybe we both need a rest.

I heap my clothes into a pile and flop onto them, pulling my blanket over myself. After commanding the lights to turn off, I scrunch down, expecting to drop off within seconds. I'm so tired.

But fifteen minutes later, I'm still tossing and turning, and it has nothing to do with how uncomfortable a bed made out of T-shirts and jeans is.

"Night lights on," I say. The strips around the top of the wall illuminate, flooding the room with soft blue light. Sitting up, I reach for my VR kit. The power cell slides in with a crisp click, and the gloves are still warm.

I can't stop thinking about Ruby. There's something strange going on there, and I won't be able to sleep until I know what it is. There are *rules* in VR. In all games. That's kind of the point of them. Games are the one place where you *know* how things work. When you duck into tall grass, mobs can't see you. When you get an NPC ally, they obey your commands.

When you pause the game, it should *stay* paused.

I hunker down in my clothes pile, pulling on the VR set. I power it up, but before I open *The Glass Realm*, a thought strikes me.

With a few haptic gestures, I open the settings and turn off the internet.

The Glass Realm is meant to be a single-player game, but it does have a multiplayer feature. I guess there's always a chance I activated it. Maybe Ruby is some internet rando messing with me.

That done, I open the game.

My avatar pops back into the field where I'd logged off. Ruby is there, standing in exactly the same position, still smiling and watching me curiously.

Okay. So, not a real person. She's definitely a part of the game itself.

"Well?" she asks. "Are you going to sleep or not? Strange place for a nap, though, if you ask me. I'll keep watch for more razorscales till you wake up."

"Uh . . ." I blink, unprepared for her barrage of questions.

She has no idea I logged off or shut down the game. In her world, no time has passed at all since our last conversation. For some reason, that makes me feel a little relieved. She didn't somehow stay active when the VR kit was powered off.

I manipulate the game, jumping out of my avatar and into third-person POV. Then I circle the camera, studying Ruby as she studies *me*. Or, well, my avatar.

"There's something different about you," we both say at the exact same time.

In the real world, I freeze.

In the Realm, Ruby freezes.

Okay. This just keeps getting weirder.

"What are you doing with your hands?" she demands. "You've been doing it since we met. Is it a magic spell thing?"

I look down, hardly even realizing what I'm doing. My hands and fingers move in a kind of sign language called haptic. In the real world, my hands control everything in the game—my UI, movement, communication. Sensors in my gloves read each tiny gesture. I double-tap my right thumb to my middle finger, zipping back into my avatar and looking through its eyes at her.

She looks back, both of us wary as two alley cats.

Here's the thing. I've played hundreds of games like *The Glass Realm*. In terms of a fantasy RPG, it's really not anything special, though the graphics are good and the combat fun. But I'd yet to find any feature of the world that's truly unique.

Until I met her.

I walk in a circle around Ruby, looking for anything I might have missed. IRL, my right hand is slightly curled, tilting as if pushing an invisible controller that directs my movement. True, full-body immersion is only possible in a gel tank like the ones at the VR salons, but even so, I'm barely aware of my physical self, my haptic motions so instinctual that I don't even have to think about them.

Her white hair and red irises are already unusual—I haven't met any Glass Realm races with coloring like that, but then, games often have characters who stand out for one reason or another. Her clothes are identical to the ones I've seen on the NPC girls in other villages. Visually, she *looks* like a part of this world. Her graphics fit the vaguely anime aesthetics of the Realm, with crystal-clear details like eyelashes and skin pores, but overly large eyes and too-perfect features to be realistic.

But the way she speaks is all wrong.

NPCs have scripts they have to follow. Rote responses, recycled phrases—everyone knows that. But she acts more like one of the bots you meet in a chat room, AIs programmed to act human. You can carry on whole conversations with them and never know they're computers.

Of course, *real* AIs are outlawed now, ever since the Great Vuum-Vuum Disaster of 2032, when a whole network of AI-powered vacuums fritzed out and started sucking down everyone's pets. Apparently they'd developed a rudimentary sense of "jealousy." I've seen recordings of those dark days.

Let me tell ya, it was not pretty.

"Ruby," I say slowly, "what do you know about . . . yourself?"

She frowns. "I'm Ruby. I tend shop at Tomtock's Hinterland Sword and Supply shop while my father is away . . ." Her voice trails off, a look of intense struggle on her face. "I *am*. Aren't I? Who *is* my father? Why can't I remember his face? Or my mother's? What *is* my backstory?" She thumps her fist against her forehead. "It's like there are walls all around my memory! I can't get out. I can't remember. I can't—"

"Ruby!" I grab her arm before she can hit herself again.

She looks up at me. There are *tears* in her eyes.

"I don't know what's wrong with me," she whispers. "I don't know what I am. Please, Ashlyre. Will you help me?"

When you're fighting a horde of zombie wolves, let me tell you: Axes are your new best friends.

I hold one in each hand, admitting to myself that the adventurer was right. That rusty sword *was* holding me back. These silver-bladed battle-axes are much more efficient, especially when facing multiple enemies. Or *mobs*, as Ashlyre calls them.

It's night, and we're deep inside Mistmoon Forest, standing back-to-back. I've already dispatched a dozen undead wolves, but twice that many circle us now, their eyes glowing blue in the mists.

Ashlyre grips his broadsword with both hands, the blade dripping with blue wolf guts.

"Here," he says, "try this."

From his magic pack, he takes out a hornbow and a bundle of arrows.

"They're explosive," he warns.

Sticking the axes in my belt loops, I string an arrow in the bow and aim it at the pack. I glance up for a moment, at the tall, dark blue mountains rising above the trees. Anger boils in me. I'm *so close* to finding the next clue on my quest, and these slavering, zombified dogs are only slowing me down.

I let the arrow fly.

A huge explosion of fire, shards of wood, and chunks of zombified wolf flesh shakes the forest. I stumble backward, throwing my hand in front of my eyes. Not because the blast is blinding, but because for a second, I can't see the forest or wolves at all.

Instead, I see a jungle, hot and humid, and a metal building hidden under the trees. Instead of a bow, I'm holding some kind of steel tube. And instead of an arrow, I'm launching a metallic missile. It strikes the building and blows it apart.

What?

The vision vanishes as soon as it came, but it's far from the first time it's happened. The desert road was only the first of a string of visions like it. Sometimes it's a desert, sometimes a jungle, sometimes a frozen forest. And there's always violence. People fighting, screaming, running.

And me in the center of it all.

"RUBY!"

Hearing Ashlyre's shout, I pull myself back to the battle at hand. Dropping the bow, I snatch my axes up and whirl into action, driving off the wolves that were about to chomp off his head. They fall back, snarling, and I work methodically. Axe here, axe there, swing and twirl, jump and kick. It's almost *boring*. The thrill of fighting is wearing off. It's like the closer we get to solving my quest, the more the world tries to stop me. We've battled monsters, lava fields, tar pits, freak ice storms, not to mention the curse that witch in the desert put on Ashlyre, making him tiny as a newt. I had to carry him in my pocket until we found the magic potion to reverse the spell. It cost me three days, but I couldn't risk my only guide getting swallowed by a random cat.

I zone out, trying to remember the details of that building in the jungle. It didn't look like anything in the Realm. It looked . . . more real.

But what does that even mean? *This* is real, this forest and this battle and these zombie wolves with their bodies half decayed and leaking guts. How can something be more real than real?

It makes no sense!

Suddenly, Ashlyre screams.

I whirl around. I was so lost in my own thoughts I let myself get separated from him. And Ashlyre is . . . Well, let's put it this way: He's not *great* at fighting. I mean, he's not bad. But he keeps going on about his level and how it stops him from being able to fight most things.

Just something else that makes no sense.

Now he's in big trouble. A sea of wolves separates us. He swings his sword, but there are too many enemies.

"NO!" I yell, trying to fight my way back to his side. But I can't reach him in time.

He collapses with a strangled shout, and I gasp in horror as the wolves fall on him, tearing, ripping . . .

Ashlyre vanishes.

Just like all the mobs I've killed, he disintegrates into nothing, shimmering out of existence.

"NOOOOO!" I scream.

I go into a frenzy, hacking brutally at everything in my path. Teeth clamp on my arm. I chop off the head behind them. Wolves dive at me from every side. My axes meet them in midair. The forest is a cacophony of snarls, howls, and death cries.

Then, suddenly, I'm alone, axes held wide, the forest silent.

The wolves are gone.

Ashlyre is *gone*.

I fall to my knees, dropping the weapons, and clutch my chest. What is this *feeling*? This pain inside me I can't escape?

"No, no, no, no, no, *no*!" I pound the ground as if it could spit him back out, feeling tears run down my face. He was supposed to help me. He promised to help me! He knows this world better than I do. He was going to take me to the mountain under the crown, where there will be answers. Answers I *need*.

"ASHLYRE!" I wail.

"Yeah?"

I nearly fall over at the sound of the quiet voice.

Whipping around, my axes in my hands again, I stare.

Ashlyre stands there, casually buckling on a battered leather chest-plate. "Those dumb wolves broke my good armor," he grumbles. "I might as well go into battle wearing paper as this thing. Ruby? Why are you—"

I throw myself on him, checking him from head to toe, feeling his neck. I *saw* a wolf bite down on his throat! I *saw* him die!

"You're alive," I whisper. "You came back."

"Of course I did." He shrugs. "And I see you took care of those wolves while I respawned. They didn't drop any good armor, did they? Ruby? Why are you looking at me like that?"

I step back, shaking my head, gaping at him. *Respawned? Of course I did?*

"You've died before?" I whisper. "And come back?"

He frowns. "Yeah . . . It's a game. I didn't die for real, Ruby. I always come back."

A game.

Again with the *game* talk.

He didn't die for real.

I look around the forest. The mist seeps through the trees, but the sky overhead is turning pink. The dusty stars fade, and in moments, it's morning.

Real. The word echoes through me, hollow as the wind.

"How?" I ask.

"How what?"

"How did you *die and then come back*?"

His eyes widen at the snarl in my voice, and he takes a step back. "Whoa, easy! I guess you could say my soul, uh, got recycled into a new body. That happens whenever I die."

"Your *soul*? Is that a magic thing?"

"No!" He pushes his hair back, looking exasperated. "Not everything is magic, Ruby. A soul is . . . it's what makes you real. Or I guess I should say it's what makes *me* real. It's the part of you—uh, *me*—that can't be seen or touched. It's . . . I dunno, emotions and feelings and stuff. Argh!" He tosses his hands in the air. "Why am I explaining this to you? You keep making me forget you're not . . . uh . . ."

"Not what?"

With a wince, he just shakes his head, unwilling to say whatever it is he's thinking.

"Back in Timberton," I say, "you told me not to fight those gobspiders or I might not respawn. That's the word, right? Respawn. That's what you call *coming back*."

"Well, yeah, but—"

"Why wouldn't I respawn like you, Ashlyre? What about *my* soul?"

He grimaces, stammering, "Uh, well, uh, I'm not sure. It's different for—"

"Different!" I snap, making him jump. "You've been *different* since the day we met! Why? Because you have this *soul*?"

"Well, yeah! Anyway, you think *I'm* different? Ruby, when I was gone you kept fighting! How did you *do* that? The game was *stopped* but you just . . . kept fighting!"

"I thought you were dead." For some reason, I feel foolish. And that makes me angry. I point an axe at him. "I thought I was avenging you."

"No, I mean, I get *why* you kept fighting. It's the *how*. You're not supposed to be able to do that."

"You keep saying that. Ruby shouldn't be *able* to fight a razorscale. Ruby shouldn't be *able* to disobey the all-mighty adventurer's commands." I'm seething now, and I don't know why. Partly because of how dumb I feel, thinking he was dead when he was just fine.

"Because you're an NPC!" he blurts out. "You're just a—a script. A character somebody else wrote! But you don't act like one! And it's weird, to be honest. It's kind of freaking me out!"

My hands tighten on my axe handles. Just a script? A character?

"You're not *real*, Ruby," he adds.

"I'm real," I whisper.

"You're not! You're just a . . . You don't have a soul."

Not real?

Fury surges through me. With a roar, I throw my axes to either side. They go spinning, one thudding into a tree trunk, the other biting into the ground.

"Not real?" I say. "*No soul?* Then tell me, Ashlyre the adventurer, who knows *so* much, what is real?"

Then, like I did with my skirt days ago, and the time I lit the bundle of grass on fire, I *push* on the world around me. I see *through* the trees, through the ground, even the air itself. Behind it all is that never-ending storm of 1s and 0s. They blink and dance, always changing positions, but somehow, I can see the pattern they spell out.

I push on the numbers, forcing my will on them. Making the world change to the way *I* want it to be. Only this time, the magic is far, far bigger than when I've touched it before. I have no idea what the limits to my magic are, but the more I push, the easier it gets.

As if there are no limits at all.

One by one, the trees flicker out of existence. The mossy ground turns brown and dusty. The sun grows brighter, scorching the earth.

The land around us for thirty paces becomes dry desert.

Ashlyre stares.

I stare.

I had no idea my magic was *this* strong.

"What is that?" I ask him, pointing at the metal contraption to my left. "Is it real?"

"It—it's a car," he says. "Some kind of military SUV, I think. But how did you—"

"And that?" I point to a spidery-looking thing hovering in the air.

"That's a drone."

"And this?" I hold up a metal box, another relic from one of my visions.

He blinks. "Where did you get a computer? That shouldn't be here. None of this should be here. These things don't belong in the Realm."

These things don't belong in the Realm.

I relax my grip on the world and the desert vanishes. The trees are back, and the moss, all as it had been before I changed things.

If those things didn't belong in the Realm, do *I*?

Ashlyre looks at me as if he's wondering the same thing. "How did you do that?"

"Um . . . magic?"

He shakes his head, his eyes never leaving my face. "Ruby, that's not like any magic I've seen in this game."

I look around at the landscape, then down at my hands. "It's not?"

My anger seems to melt away, leaving only weary confusion. I'm so *tired* of not understanding. I'm so tired of questions with no answers.

"You're . . . not an NPC, are you?" he says softly. "You really don't know what you are?"

I shake my head. "I think . . . I think I used to be somebody else. I have memories of other places. Not of the Realm, but of places like the one I just showed you."

"Maybe you're from a different game," he murmurs, studying me thoughtfully. "A mod. Yeah! That would make sense. Someone coded you into this world, but maybe you belong to a different one. I can find out. Back in the real world—"

"The real world." I step closer to him, my chest aching with the need for answers. "The place you're from? Is that where you go when your body freezes here? Is that like some kind of . . . other dimension, where people have *souls*?"

"Yeah, sort of." He waves that off; he's still thinking hard, talking more to himself than me. "Doesn't make sense how you just did that trick, though, if you're a mod. You shouldn't be able to change the game's landscape, right? I need to do some research. Someone must know who you are."

"Ashlyre—"

"Call me Ash," he says.

"Fine. *Ash*, you're saying you don't belong to the Realm?"

"No. I'm from . . . Earth. Uh. The real world. Reality."

"And this place? The Glass Realm?"

"Oh. Um. This is . . . this is a game, Ruby, for people in my world to play. If you come down to it, it's a computer program. Just . . . code."

"Code?"

"Yeah, you know. Ones and zeros. The stuff this world is made from."

Ones and zeros! I suck in a breath, and for a moment, I can glimpse them shimmering all around Ash, a smoky, glowing aura of flashing numerals.

It's not magic at all.

It's something called *code*.

And *I* can control it.

I shake my head. "When you froze up the other day . . ."

"I left the game," he says.

"You went back to your world."

"Yeah."

I nod. My head is spinning, and I have a thousand more questions, but I feel this is the truth. Like maybe, for the first time, I'm getting a *real* answer, even if I don't fully understand it yet. This idea of two worlds makes sense, even though it shouldn't. But what does it all mean? Who am I? How did I get here? Am I part of Ash's world or this one?

"I can get answers," he says. "I think I can, anyway. I'll go back to my world and do some reading, then tell you everything I find."

I nod reluctantly. I don't like relying on him to tell me everything. I want to find the answers myself.

I *have* to finish this quest.

10. ASH

"Dude, you've *got* to check this out!"

"And hello to you too," yawns Hakeem, opening his apartment door so I can slip inside. He's wearing long pajama bottoms with candy canes all over them. "You realize it's seven in the morning? On a *Sunday*, the holiest of days for those of us who still worship the God of Sleep?"

"Does your sister still have her copy of *The Glass Realm*?"

"Huh?"

"*Glass Realm*, Keem! Keep up!"

He groans. "It's still on the computer, I think."

I charge past him and into his bedroom, slinging down my duffel bag with my VR kit inside. One corner is devoted to Hakeem's refurbished Ion Turbowar ultra-gaming tower, with two monitors and a sweet VR e-sports setup. He moans and falls face-first onto his bed while I power up his PC. His walls are plastered with FC Barcelona posters. His stinky shin guards are on the desk, and I swipe them up and set them on the terrarium on the floor.

"Good morning, Tank," I say to the turtle inside.

"Why are you here?" mumbles Hakeem. "And how do I make you go away?"

"I thought we were friends." I waggle my wrist with the friendship bracelet at him.

"Friends let friends sleep in on the weekend."

"Well, I'm really only friends with you for your mom's baklava, so." I tap his password in and begin sifting through his game files. "Don't tell me you deleted it? You *have* to see this NPC I found. I think she's some kind of mod but, like, *freakily* human."

"You're here to show me some elf world NPC? *Seriously?*"

Dr. Jawabre appears in the doorway, dressed for her morning kickboxing class. "Good morning, Ash."

"Hey, Dr. J!"

She leans on the wall for a minute, watching me burrow into Hakeem's files. "You know," she sighs, "I miss when all parents had to worry about was drugs, alcohol, girls—"

"Mom," Hakeem groans.

She shrugs. "Just saying. At least we understood all that stuff. But this?" She waves a hand at the monitors, towers, VR equipment lying around. "It's another language entirely. All I can do is smile and nod and hope this vaguely uneasy feeling goes away on its own."

"Make *Ash* go away," Hakeem begs. "He's *perky*, Mom. It's seven in the morning on Sunday and he's *perky*."

"Want breakfast, Ash?" Dr. Jawabre asks. "I've got fresh manakeesh."

"Sure!" I chirp.

She frowns and looks at me closer. "How many Zero Gees have you had this morning, kiddo?"

I give her a jittery, slightly embarrassed grin. Can she really tell I've been chugging energy drinks? I guess they do make me look a little . . . unhinged. I had five, but I don't dare tell her that. My heart feels *sweaty*. "I, uh, haven't exactly slept in two days."

"*Ash*. Your mother—"

"She's out of town. She'll get back tomorrow. Painting thing. I gotta put my room back together before then. That baklava you made was really good, by the way. Do you have any more? Wait, no, I'm kinda in the middle of something now. Do you wanna see—"

"Whoa, slow down!" Dr. Jawabre waves a hand. "*Too many* Zero Gees, I see."

I hiccup.

Hakeem gives a sob and pulls his pillow over his head.

I locate the game folder and open it, toggling on the spectator mode so while one of us is in VR, the other can watch what's happening on the computer. My foot taps restlessly on the hard mat beneath the desk while the opening sequence plays.

"Uh, you said this was *Nadia's* game?" I roll the desk chair aside so he can see his older sister's *Glass Realm* avatar—a beefed-up, bulked-out, hulking marauder class, gripping an axe that has three skulls dangling from the angle. He's wearing nothing but a pink tutu and bunny ears. Not exactly what I would have expected from prim, straight-laced, first-year-law-student Nadia.

Hakeem peeps from under his pillow. "Don't be fooled by her pageant queen exterior. Her brain is a dark, terrifying labyrinth."

Grinning, I put on Hakeem's VR helmet and peer out at a familiar valley through Nadia's marauder. Instead of putting on haptic gloves, I navigate with an old-school controller.

"Right, so all we gotta do is . . ." I fast travel to Timberton, the tiny village where Tomtock's Hinterland Sword and Supply Shop is located. "You watching?" I stick a finger under my earpiece so I can hear Hakeem's reluctant grunt. "She should be in here."

I open the door of the shop—only to stop mid-stride.

The shopkeep sitting behind the counter, methodically polishing a rusty sword, is *not* Ruby.

Her face is plain, her eyes blue and her hair brown. I've seen her a dozen times over in the Glass Realm before. As I'd half expected, she's just another recycled NPC.

I go to the counter anyway, placing the marauder's meaty hands atop it. "Ruby?" My voice comes out deep and gravelly.

"Good afternoon, adventurer," says the NPC. "It's a hot day out there. Care to cool off with a stagfen ale?"

"What's your name?" I ask.

"I'm Laures," she replies, beaming cheerfully. "Can I interest you in silk from the Brayan Steppe?"

I look all around the shop. Everything else looks the same, not an urn or potion or bundle of dried gamper grass out of place.

"Do you know a girl named Ruby?" I ask.

The NPC tilts her head, still smiling vacuously, and says nothing. Meaning the question didn't register with her at all and was treated as junk dialogue.

Feeling strangely light-headed, I leave the shop and jog around the town. Lord Toffton runs up to me, begging for aid against a wolf attack, but I reject his quest and move on, searching the blacksmith shop, the houses, the barn.

Ruby isn't in any of them.

I yank off the headset, leaving the marauder jogging in place on the computer screen. "She's not there. I *knew it*."

Hakeem has rolled onto his back, his hands locked under his head. "This is getting weird, Ash."

"Exactly! She's not in Nadia's copy of the game, so she *has* to be some kind of mod. She's unique to my version."

"I *mean* you're here at seven in the morning yelling about some make-believe girl, your eyes are red, and you're kind of freaking me out."

Dr. Jawabre returns with a plate of pita bread smothered in spices, and a white pill on the side. "I want you to swallow that. I won't let you run off and suffer a heart attack. No more Zero Gees today, Ash."

She gives me a stern look. As a physician, Dr. J highly disapproves of energy drinks. Otherwise, she's pretty cool. You know. For a mom.

I obediently chuck down the pill, then rip into the manakeesh. The spices are powerful enough to knock you over—or startle you awake when you've pulled two all-nighters in a row. Better than any high-energy drink.

"Right, you two. I'm off." She blows a kiss to each of us, shoulders her gym bag, and heads out.

Hakeem sits up. "Did you think any more about tryouts next month? Coach wanted me to ask you. He really hopes you'll—"

"I haven't had time, Keem." I open the internet browser and start running searches. *Ruby NPC Glass Realm. Shopkeep in Timberton Glass Realm. Glass Realm OP NPC white hair.*

Nothing's bringing up Ruby. Not even the forums mention her. Something feels off about the whole thing. I wish I'd asked that homeless guy more questions.

Then I remember he's dead. Murdered on the Skytrain, just hours after I talked to him.

I shiver, suddenly remembering his last words to me. *Don't tell anyone.* About what? About Ruby? Why would a game mod be so top secret? He had to have meant something else. Maybe he stole the game and just pawned it off on me so *he* wouldn't get caught. I could be dealing with stolen goods! Maybe the people who killed him . . .

No, no, that's ridiculous.

Nobody ever shot anyone over a game coin you could find in a vending machine.

"Aaaa-sh," sings Hakeem. "Are you even listening to me?"

"Someone has to know about her," I say. "I think my copy might have been pirated, or modded. Maybe someone else downloaded the same mod."

Hakeem rubs his hand over his face and flops back onto the bed.

I create a profile in the largest *Glass Realm* forum I can find, then post a question:

Anyone here ever run into an NPC named Ruby, white hair, red eyes, fights like a demon? Maybe in the shop in Timberton? Could be a mod or something. URGENT!!

"Ash."

I pause my search at Hakeem's odd tone. He's picking at his bed-spread, which is decorated with the avatars of his favorite *Strikeforce Royale* team. "You're not . . . going zombie, are you?"

I spin in the desk chair, face hot. "Oh, come on! I'm not going zombie."

He frowns. "That's exactly what a zombie would say."

"I know how to set limits." Angry, I turn back around.

"Is it about Luke?"

"Luke?" I grind my teeth. "What about Luke?"

"I know he's a jerk," he mumbles. "You shrug it off like its nothing, but I know he scares you sometimes. Especially when your mom's gone."

I stare at the screen, but the words all blur.

"I'm sorry," Hakeem adds. "I just thought maybe this VR obsession might be because of him. Because maybe you're trying to . . . I don't know. Forget it. Just don't become a zombie, okay?"

I click out of the browser and turn around.

"There," I say. "See? I'm done for the day. What do you want to do?"

As he rolls out of bed, he doesn't quite lose the look of suspicion in his eyes. "I've got a preseason scrimmage at two. We're playing those rich kids from Northside."

"I'll come! I'll bring Nadia's old pom-poms." Leaping from the chair, I wiggle my butt and pump my hands in the air in an absolutely flawless impersonation of our middle school cheer squad.

Hakeem rolls his eyes. "Now you're just overcompensating."

"Excuse me, it's called school spirit!"

"I'm going to shower." He grabs a towel and heads down the hallway.

I clench my hands into fists, physically stopping myself from reaching for the VR headset to do just one more check for Ruby. Instead, while Hakeem showers, I pick up Tank and feed him turtle treats. Every few minutes, my eyes flick to the computer, wondering if anyone's responded to my forum post.

Okay, okay.

I'm not a zombie.

But I might be getting a teeny bit obsessed.

When I hear the shower turn on, I scramble to the desk and open the computer.

There's a response.

-----◇-----

BAMOORG2: *Dude, I've been looking for info on Ruby for MONTHS. You will not believe what I found out. Your profile says you're in Queens? No way, dude, I'm like 20 min away. Meet me today, @Cheeko's on 3rd.*

Not safe to talk here.

I glance down the hallway, toward the bathroom. Then I scribble a quick, vague apology note on Hakeem's whiteboard.

I grab my stuff and run.

11. ASH

Cheeko's is a holo-arcade that every kid in Queens knows—and avoids. It has a reputation for shady deals and police raids. The games are old and clunky, mostly fighting sims where you can slash hologram enemies with plastic katanas, or race a chipped, half-busted race car through holo-tracks. Unlike VR, which takes you *into* virtual worlds, holos bring the games into *our* world. But VR is way more popular, and the tech more advanced. I have no idea how the place keeps paying rent. Maybe the shady deals have something to do with it.

I slip inside the front door and blink hard, waiting for my vision to adjust to the dark interior. Blue strip lighting stretches ahead, leading me down a narrow hallway to a desk where a gaunt teenager sits. He's sprawled in his chair, face covered by a VR visor, completely oblivious to my existence. Jeez, even the employees in this place prefer virtual. Pulsing club music thumps through speakers, making the floor vibrate under my shoes. The place smells like old popcorn and mold.

Behind the teen, the hallway opens to a huge room divided into different gaming arenas. It's dark and murky, filled with mist that curls out of tired fog machines. Colorful lights flash all around, advertising everything from holo WWII sims to dance games where you face off with holo replicas of ancient celebrities. It wouldn't be *so* bad, I guess, if there were people here. But the place is completely deserted.

"Hello?" I call out.

I step through a glitching holoscreen of Elvis Presley doing the macarena. The hair on the back of my neck rises.

Why would BAMOORG2 want to meet here?

And why didn't I stop to ask myself that question *before* I came inside?

That feeling of wrongness comes back stronger than ever. Something is going on that makes my nerves short-circuit.

Surrounded by a labyrinth of darkness and flashing lights, my ears smothered in a blanket of pounding synthetic music, I look back at the exit.

Only, I can't see it.

I can't see *any* doors out. The lights and music and shadows have me completely disoriented.

My stomach tightens and my palms start to sweat. Is this what claustrophobia feels like? I have to get out of here. I don't care *what* BAMOORG2 may or may not know about Ruby. This all feels very, very wrong.

I pick a direction at random and begin walking, leaping over a rope cordon marking a battle arena. Activated by my presence, a dozen holographic robot-samurai materialize around me, slashing their blades over loud J-punk music.

Right. I'm out of here. If this person wants to meet up, we can do it somewhere more pleasant than this. Like a graveyard at midnight, or the sewers under the city.

When I finally bump against the damp, carpeted outer wall of the arcade, I give a sigh of relief. Now all I have to do is work my way along it until I find the exit.

"He's here," a voice says suddenly. "I saw him on the security cameras—a kid, maybe twelve or thirteen. Find the lights, block the exits, and *bring me that boy*."

I freeze.

The voice came from my left, deep and male.

Someone is here. And they're looking for me.

This is bad, bad, bad.

I've read plenty of stories of kids getting scammed by internet weirdos, sometimes disappearing. Geez, the first rule of the internet is *don't meet strangers from the internet*. I was just so caught up in the mystery surrounding Ruby that I left my brain in VR.

"Are we sure this kid even *has* what you're looking for, boss?" asks another voice, from somewhere to my left. I glance that way, just as a strobe of light bounces off the guy's face.

I clap a hand to my mouth, smothering a gasp.

It's Tats! The guy who was beating up Owen Locke before I boosted his jetbike.

I only get a glimpse before the darkness hides him again, but I know it's the same guy. His snake tattoos are writhing up the side of his face like living vines. Are his friends here? Best to assume they are, I guess.

But *why* are they here?

My stomach goes cold as it dawns on me.

They weren't just random punks having sick fun with an old homeless guy. They *targeted* Locke. I should have realized it earlier. Maybe they were even the same ones who killed him on the Skytrain.

And now they're after *me*.

I have to get out of here before Tats and whoever is with him find the lights.

I move faster, sliding along the wall, my eyes peeled open. In the strobes, I make out a figure in black tactical gear. It's Mohawk, Tat's buddy. There's another guy farther off who I don't recognize. He's muscled and bald and also dressed like some kind of military operative.

Slowly, horribly, I realize there are at least a dozen people in this room with me, all slinking through holograms, appearing only in brief flashes. Their movements are muffled by the thumping electronica.

Holy cats! *What* did that guy Owen get me into?

Suddenly, I bump into something large and solid—definitely not a hologram. A hand closes on my arm. I look up, terrified, into Mohawk's face.

"Hague!" he bellows. "I got him!"

Oh, no, you don't, big guy.

I twist, pressing a button inside my camo-coat. The sleeve disconnects and I dart away, leaving the guy standing in the dark, gripping an empty sleeve.

At that moment, the lights blast on.

My eyes burn at the sudden illumination, and for a moment, I stumble around blindly. The arcade looks dingy and sad in the bright beams of the fluorescent bulbs. Dingy, sad, and *teeming* with figures in black tactical gear. There are twice as many as I thought, and every single one of them looks at me.

"There he is!" one shouts. He's not as rough looking as the rest. Instead of the gear everyone else is wearing, he's in a sleek gray suit over a black turtleneck. I get the feeling this guy is *Hague*, the one Tats called the boss. He looks more like he should be giving political speeches on TV, with his perfectly combed hair and stripes of gray at the temples. But there's nothing diplomatic about the way he points at me—like he wants my head for a hacky sack. "Grab him!"

I spot the exit and sprint for it, sliding into the hallway. The teenager is still sprawled in his chair, lost in virtual reality. He doesn't even flinch as I run past.

Hearing heavy steps thundering behind me, I press for more speed, my lungs already burning. Busting outside, I pelt across the sidewalk, ducking into an alley as the door bangs open behind me and men spill out.

Ha! They may be bigger and meaner, but this is *my* neighborhood.

I jump a fence and turn down another alley. Then, eyes stinging with sweat, I climb a fire escape and run along a low rooftop before dropping into a church garden. There's a hidey-hole in the bushes where Hakeem and I used to hang out when we were little and my mom worked as a cleaner in the church. The bushes are all dry and dead now, the ground choked with garbage and the walls plastered in graffiti. But it's still as good a hiding spot as ever.

I curl up, my heart pounding, mind racing. It seems to take forever to catch my breath.

At least I know three new things now.

One, that forum post was a trap.

Two, that guy Hague and his men are intent on finding me . . . the same way they were looking for Owen Locke.

Three, it has something to do with the Glass Realm. Specifically, *Ruby*.

A sudden, terrible thought strikes me. I phone Hakeem. Like, *voice* call. Not a text; not a message on Chattr.

Hakeem knows the code. Voice call means top-level best-friend emergency. He answers on the second ring.

"Ash? What's wrong? Why did you run off—"

"ZERO GEE IS PROUD TO SPONSOR THIS CALL!" roars a third voice into the phone, way too deep and gravelly to be Hakeem's. It sounds like an amped-up wrestler screaming into my ear. *"The juice that defies gravity! Why crawl when you can FLY? Supercharge your veins with ZERO GEE and CRUSH THE LAWS OF PHYSICS! Zero Gee can cause heart problems, hallucinations, paranoia, diarrhea, toxic shock syndrome—"*

I sigh as the ad plays on. *This* is why no one makes voice calls anymore. It takes thirty seconds for the autotuned voice to rush through all of Zero Gee's many, many risks and side effects, before finally ending with an earsplitting *"ZERO GEE! PUNCH GRAVITY IN THE FAAAAACE!!!!"*

"Ugh, finally. Look, Keem, I think I'm in trouble." I talk fast. We only have one minute before the next ad will play. "I need to know if you have encryption activated on your computer." If those guys have even basic knowledge of computers, they could track my post back to Hakeem's address. That thought makes me want to throw up.

"Of course," he says. "You know I always do. Why?"

Right. I let out a relieved sigh. As an e-sports gamer, Keem *has* to keep encryption on, hiding his location from anyone who might want to get IRL revenge after a match didn't go their way. It happens.

Keem is safe. At least there's that. But now what?

"Ash, what's going on? I'm really freaking out over here."

"I . . . I'm not sure yet." I don't want to involve him in this, not until I know more about what I'm dealing with. "It's probably nothing. Uh . . . elf game stuff."

"You *voice called*."

"Yeah, sorry. I, uh, overreacted a little."

"Overreacted? You're acting full-blown insane! Is this about Luke?"

"No!" For once, it's got nothing to do with Luke. "I'm fine, Keem. Good luck at your game. I'll message you later, okay?"

"But you said you'd—"

"I can't be there. I'm sorry. Something came up."

"Elf game stuff?" His tone is flat. He knows I'm keeping secrets, and I can tell he's hurt. But that's better than him being *hurt*, hurt. Those guys in the arcade . . . they weren't messing around.

I saw guns in their jackets.

"I'm sorry, Keem, really. I—"

"ZERO GEE IS PROUD TO SPONSOR THIS CALL! The juice that defies—"

Hakeem hangs up. With a groan, I rap my phone against my forehead, trying to think. Then I realize I've taken the box out of my pocket, with the *Glass Realm* game coin inside.

I open the box and stare at the coin. "What *are* you?"

Maybe I'm looking for answers in the wrong place.

Or rather, the wrong *world*.

Hearing voices, I freeze, peering through a gap in the shrub. My heart helicopters in my chest.

A guy and girl walk into view, snooping through the garden. I relax in relief. They're not part of Tats's crew. They're just Scavengers, by the look of the augmented reality visors on their faces. The visors overlay the real world with an artificial one, turning it into a living video game. I've been begging Mom to let me have one. I always wondered what it would be like to live half in virtual reality all day long, but she said I spent too much time in fake worlds as it is. She's as bad as Hakeem's mom sometimes.

Scavenge is a kind of treasure-hunting game, where you find AR prizes that you cash out in real-world dollars. The girl squeals and grabs at the air, shouting about whatever prize she found, and then the two hurry out of the garden. Probably to cash in their loot. There's a Scavenger vending machine just one block down, if I remember right.

Once they're gone, I crawl out of the bushes and hurry through the overgrown garden to the back wall of the church. The place has been closed for years, but the small, ground-level window is right where I remember it, hidden behind a dead rosebush. Pushing aside thorny branches, I kick at the window until it swivels open. They never did fix that lock.

Sliding through, I land in a cloud of dust. I look around at the stacked pews, boxes of hymnals, and other clutter. Nobody's here, of course. Well, nobody except the bat colony I suddenly spot nesting over my head. Aaaaaand that's not just dust under my feet. Gross.

Upstairs, the air is clearer and there's considerably less bat poop. I sit down against the wall of the old sanctuary. Around me, beams of colored sunlight filter through the massive glass windows. Through them, I can make out the haze of neon, smog, and noise that makes up the city, but this place is like a time bubble, a throwback to an era before electricity.

My VR kit's power cell is fully charged. I pull on the helmet and pop in the game coin, then tug on the haptic gloves. I swipe my fingers through the air, selecting *The Glass Realm* from my digital library. As the game loads, I lean back and sigh.

If there are answers to what the heck is going on, maybe they're here.

I need to find Ruby.

We need to finish that quest.

"I'm back," the adventurer says.

I turn around, surprised. "Already? You just left."

We're standing on a footpath leading into the mountains, not far from where I killed all those razorscales. Ash had told me he'd return with answers about what I am, but that was *seconds* ago.

"Oh," he says, blinking. "Right. I forgot time doesn't pass here when I'm . . . there."

"How long were you gone?"

"Hours."

I think that over. "When you leave, this world freezes. Time stops."

"Yeah, I guess you could say that."

My lips twist in a scowl. I don't like the idea. It feels like . . . a cage.

And I may not know much about what I am, but at this moment, I realize I *hate* cages.

"Is there a way around that?" I ask him. "When you're not here, can you keep time flowing in the Realm?"

He cocks his head. "Yeah, sure. I could go AFK, let the game keep running, I guess."

"Do it. Next time you are away, go . . . AFK?"

"Away from keyboard." He shrugs. "It's an old-school term. And yeah, I guess I could do that."

I nod, though I realize I have no way of ensuring he keeps his word. If he can leave for *hours* and return like he'd never left, how could I know?

"Did you find any answers?" I ask.

He hesitates, then shakes his head. "Just more questions. Ruby, I think you're . . . special."

I raise an eyebrow.

"I mean, uh, not that I thought you were *not* special. Just *more* special than I realized. Special in a different way. Look, I think we need to finish your quest. That scroll said something about finding the truth, right? Well. Let's see what the game has to say."

Something happened to him out there, in this "real world" of his. He's talking faster, and his expression is different, like he's afraid.

"Ash," I say. "Is this how you really look?"

He seems surprised at the question and glances down at himself, brushing at his armor. "Well, sort of. I mean, maybe I'm a little shorter. And skinnier."

"This body you have here, it's a construct?"

"Yeah. An avatar."

"Avatar." I frown, looking down at my own hands. I *press* at them, the way I did on the world when I turned the forest into a desert. Immediately, my arms lengthen, fingers congealing, skin growing a coat of hair.

With a strangled shout, Ash stumbles back, gaping as I transform into a tall, sparkling white unicorn.

"How—how did you *do* that?!" he gasps. "It's like you're affecting the game's code itself."

I whinny, then prance in a circle, feeling out this new form. That was . . . easy. I'm getting better at reaching through the facade of the things around me and changing them to suit my wishes. Experimentally, I reach out again, like stretching invisible hands.

Pressing my consciousness against a rock by my hoof, I concentrate hard—until it pops, transforming into a red apple. Farther away, an old cart is broken down in the grass. I focus on it until it flickers, the 1s and 0s behind it shimmering into view. With a silent command, I rearrange the numbers, and the cart changes into a rosebush. Noting a flash of movement to my left, my mind flickers instinctively—and the rabbit that had been scampering by suddenly shifts into a hedgehog. It bounds on as if completely unaware.

Of course it's unaware.

It's not a *real* rabbit. I know that now. None of it is real. Not the grass or trees or birds or razorscales. And simply by *knowing* that, I find I have power over it all.

My mind spreads in every direction. As if the Glass Realm truly were made of glass, I peer *through* it. And everywhere I look, I see those numbers—01101001, on and on and on—and a part of me understands them. It's as if they were a language I forgot I was fluent in.

Next, my mind *presses* against Ash, curiously probing.

Sure enough, he's made of the same flowing digits as the rest of this place. Unlike the rocks and trees, however, he's made of a glowing knot of numbers so thick they look like one great source of light. His numbers— what did he call it? Code? Yes, that word feels right—his *code* is so complex and concentrated that it takes me a little longer to read it. But when I do, I find I can change it just like the rest.

"Whoa, whoa, whoa!" Ash yelps, dancing around as he suddenly sprouts wings. His skin turns to scales, his face elongating and his jaw sprouting fangs.

"You turned me into a razorscale?!" he shrieks. "Ruby! Stop!"

I do, releasing my influence on the world.

At once, everything returns to its previous state, including me. I'm a girl again, and this form, for some reason, feels more natural. More *me*. But why? Is this face *my* face, if Ash's face isn't really *his*? Is my body true, or an avatar like his? Is my real body somewhere else?

He pats his armor, hair, and face in relief. "Never do that again," he moans. "Please."

"You're right," I say. "We need to finish this quest."

"Cool!" His voice is a high squeak. "Cool, cool, cool. Let's go, then. And, uh, could you *not* make any volcanoes spontaneously erupt or canyons open under our feet along the way?"

I shrug. "You mean *you* can't do stuff like that?"

"Of course not!"

Interesting. He doesn't fit into this world the same way I do. It's like . . . he's a visitor here, who doesn't speak the language of the code. He knows things I don't, but I can do things he can't.

We set off up the mountain path, looking for the "king under mountain, mountain under crown." But there are dozens of mountains, each one looking like all the others. And it'll take us *ages* to search them all.

That will not do.

Maybe I can control this world in other ways. After all, none of it is *real*. The rules are all different now. Just *how* different, I plan to find out.

"Hold on to me," I tell Ash.

"What?"

I reach out and grip the hard rim of his chestplate's collar. "Hold on."

Shutting my eyes—I don't know why, it's just an instinct—I *press* again. This time, instead of changing the shape of things, I focus on Ash's code and my own. Weirdly, my *own* code is less clear to me. There are sections of it I can't seem to access, the numbers seemingly hidden behind twisting walls of yet more code. Maybe if I had time I could break through them, but for now, I wrap my mind around the pair of us, isolating our code from the rest of the game world's. It's like I reach down into wet sand and wrap my fingers around a pair of clams, then yank them up. Where that analogy comes from, I don't know. I have no memories of beaches or sand or clams, but somehow, I know what they are.

"Hold on," I say a third time.

Then I *fling* us through the air.

My eyes are still closed. I don't see the mountains zipping toward us or the ground falling away. Instead, I see mountains of code, streams of code, a vast landscape of code in all directions. Navigating that, I drop Ash and myself atop the nearest mountain peak. It would have taken ages to climb this high Ash's way. With mine, we arrive in milliseconds.

The mountaintop is all rock and snow, with the Glass Realm spreading like a quilt in front of us, all forests and fields, rivers and towns.

"Whoa," Ash says. "Did you just fast travel us?"

"Is that what it's called?"

He stares at me. "You're . . . incredible."

I smile. "See any crowns?"

We hunt all over the mountain, but nothing seems to indicate it's special in any way. There are no crowns carved into the rock or anything like that. I let Ash search with his eyes while I comb through the code. Nothing there either.

"Next mountain," I say, grabbing his chestplate again. He barely has time to yelp before I *fast travel* to the next peak.

We search the entire mountain range, but nothing turns up.

Frustrated, I kick a rock off the last peak, then nudge its code. It becomes a massive boulder rumbling down the cliffs, taking half the mountain with it.

Ash groans and holds on to me as the peak trembles. "You know," he says, "I'm usually not afraid of heights in VR. But you're starting to change that."

"It's a dead end!" I snarl. "This quest is broken!"

The rumbling stops, and Ash wipes a hand over his forehead. "Look, usually the trick is in the details. Like, maybe we misunderstood the words on the scroll. These kinds of games love to play with word puzzles."

I take out the scroll and shove it at him. "Well?"

He studies the words. "'King under mountain, mountain under crown.' That's weird, right? I mean, crowns go on kings' heads. Shouldn't it be king under crown?"

Shrugging, I plop down and lie on my back, staring up at the sky. Night has fallen over the realm, and stars shine like silver dust.

"That sky is my favorite part of this game," Ash says, also looking up. "We can't actually see stars, you know, in the real world. There's too much smog and light pollution, at least where I live. I've only ever seen stars in VR. And of all the ones I've seen, the Glass Realm's are the best. My mom would say they *soothe the soul*."

I prop myself up on my elbows. There's that word again.

Soul.

"Ash?"

"Yeah?"

"A while back, you told me I didn't have a soul."

He glances at me, looking embarrassed. "Well . . . I thought you were just an NPC then. Maybe you still are. That's what we're trying to find out, right?"

"If I don't exist in your world, though . . . then I can't have a soul, can I? And you said having a soul is what makes you real."

"Well, uh . . . lots of things are real that don't have souls. Like, um, auto-cabs and rocks and stuff."

"So I'm like a rock?"

"What? No! You're more than a rock."

"So I'm more real than a rock but not as real as you? Does that mean I have half a soul? Or one percent of a soul? How are souls measured?"

His face twists. "I don't know! We don't really learn this kind of thing in middle school. It's complicated. No one really *knows* what a soul is. You just kinda . . . *feel* it."

"Oh." I don't understand, and I'm starting to think maybe he doesn't either.

It's just another impossible question.

Ash lies down beside me, saying nothing for several minutes. The sky over the Realm is deep purplish-black, with stars blazing behind filmy green and blue auroras. They turn ever so slowly, marking the passage of time and pulling a crescent moon from the horizon.

"Three million, four hundred and fifty-four thousand, two hundred seventy-seven," I sigh.

Ash turns his head. "What?"

"That's how many stars are up there."

"You *counted* them all? When?"

"Just now."

Ash seems to be very carefully *not* looking at me. I can hear him gulp.

"What? Did you never learn how to count things in your *real* world?" I ask.

"Not like that," he laughs. "It's funny. I've never seen real stars, but I do know the constellations. We had to learn them in science class for some reason. Anyway, I think they use our real-world constellations in this game. See? That's Aquila. And that's Sagittarius. And that . . ." He sits up suddenly.

"What's wrong?"

He points toward the north, to a cluster of stars. "Corona Borealis. Also known as the Northern Crown."

"Did you say *crown*?" I sit up now too, staring at the semicircular constellation.

It's set perfectly over a distant mountain peak, like a celestial halo.

"We searched that one, didn't we?" Ash asks.

"Yeah, but not *that* thoroughly. C'mon!" Before he can say another word, I rip our code free and hurl us to the mountain under the Northern Crown.

"Whoa!" Ash stumbles forward, gripping his head. "You gotta warn me when you do that! Geez, I feel like I'm gonna puke."

We're at the bottom of the mountain, where the rocky slopes meld into the plains like the roots of a massive tree.

"There," I say. "We missed it earlier because we were focused on the *peaks*."

A small cave hides behind a thin waterfall that tumbles from the mountain's cliffs. There's nothing else about it to draw the eye. It could easily have been just a shadow.

We slip inside, me leading the way. The passage is narrow and damp; luminescent mushrooms provide meager blue lighting. Dissatisfied with that, I reach out and *press* on the code around me, brightening the tunnel until it's like midday inside.

"Again," whimpers Ash, shielding his eyes, "give a *warning* next time!"

"Sorry."

We come to a stop where a large stone door blocks the way forward. There are four symbols carved in it, each one an intricate infinity knot made up of . . .

"Numbers," groans Ash. "It's a math puzzle! I hate these! If you put in the wrong sequence, we'll probably get peppered with poison arrows or the tunnel will flood."

"Not a math puzzle," I say. "A language puzzle."

I touch the bottom-left symbol, and it suddenly glows blue. "It's code. Ones and zeros. The pattern in this one translates to *K*." I touch another symbol, then another. *"I. N."* Finally, I touch the remaining symbol. *"G."*

"King under mountain," murmurs Ash, his eyes wide.

I grin, stepping back as the stone door rumbles aside, revealing a chamber hidden behind it.

And standing in the middle of that chamber . . . is a man.

The man—or, rather, avatar—is wearing odd clothes, not Realm garb. His long-sleeved shirt is made of soft white material with a hood attached, over blue canvas pants and bright red shoes with white laces. He is of average height, thick around the middle, with a balding head. His face is kind, and I instinctively feel I can trust it.

This must be the Wizard.

"It's him," Ash whispers beside me. "That's the homeless guy."

"Who?"

"The guy who gave me *The Glass Realm*. Owen Locke."

Turning back to the avatar, I walk all around him, and he watches me.

"Is he like you, then?" I ask. "Part of the real world?"

"I . . . don't think so. The real Owen Locke is dead. I saw it in the news. This must be an NPC made to look like him."

Dead?

For some reason, that news makes a pit open inside me, even though I have no real idea who this man is.

I probe the avatar cautiously, wondering if I'll find the same kind of code that Ash's avatar uses. Is this image connected to a real-world human?

It doesn't look like it. The code is pretty basic, nowhere near as complex as Ash's or even my own. He's just a piece of the game, like the people back in Timberton.

"Congratulations on solving your quest, Ruby," the man says. "I had hoped you never would. But I suspected your curiosity would eventually lead you here, to the answers you're no doubt seeking. If you are listening to this recording, it means you've chosen to remember what you once volunteered to forget."

I exchange a look with Ash. This is it. This is what we were seeking.

"I don't have much time to code all this, so I have to be quick," says the man. "My name is Owen Locke. I'm the person who created you, Ruby. You are the crowning achievement of my career, and my entire reason for existing. But there was . . . trouble. Some bad people wanted to use you for bad things. And so, with your permission, I placed your memories behind a deep encryption to keep you safe." He holds out his hands and a box appears between them—silver and smooth, with a mirrored finish. It reflects my own face back at me. "All you have to do is open it, and you'll remember everything. The good . . . and the bad."

This man *created* me? I stare at him for a long moment, trying to recall if I've ever seen him before. But if I have, he must have done a good job hiding the memories away.

"Well?" Ash asks softly. "Will you open it?"

I study the box in Locke's hands, still processing his words. Already he's sparked a thousand new questions. How did he create me? Who were these bad people, and what did they want with me? It must have been horrible if I chose to lose all my memories rather than let them use me.

Are the memories in that box ones I *want* to remember?

But then, I knew from the start this quest might end in answers I wouldn't like. And I still chose to follow it.

What else can I do? I can't go back to Timberton, not after everything I've learned through Ash.

I need to know: *What am I?* Am I just a fancier version of Variel the milkmaid, trapped in her endless, empty routine? Or am I more like Ash? More *real*?

I take the box.

"*Curiosity.*" Owen Locke smiles, but there is still something sad in his expression. "Your first emotion. Yes, even without your memories, you are still my Ruby."

I glance at him, then back at the box.

Slowly, I open the lid.

And *gasp*.

From inside, a torrent of papers rushes out. Pages wash over me. Like leaves in an autumn wind, they whirl around the cavern, flickering with movement. Each one features a moving image, like a moment captured in time, whispering with conversation, with music, with laughter.

My memories.

Standing in the middle of that whirlwind, I feel a chill race through me. I stare at the fluttering, murmuring images with eyes wide open. The mirror box is gone. It melted away the moment the memories flew out, though I barely noticed.

Ash reaches out as if to grab hold of one of the papers, but it just passes through his hand, insubstantial as a fleck of light.

Finally, one by one, the images begin to freeze in place, creating a circular wall with me at its center. Like puzzle pieces, they fit into their places. Turning slowly, I study them until I realize: It's a *timeline*—a chronological ordering of moments and days.

By the time they're all done, locked into their places, the record of my life is complete. For a long moment, Ash and I look around in silence, at the hundreds—no, *thousands*—of tiny scenes playing out all around us.

But the images aren't just around me. They're *inside* me too. I feel them focusing in my memory, filling in all the blanks of my past.

Just like that, I remember everything.

I did exist before the Glass Realm, before I was ever a shopkeep's daughter.

Grimly, I reach for one of the memories near the top of the wall. It stands out in my own mind as an important day. Perhaps the *most* important day.

The instant my fingers touch the page, the world around me transforms.

And I'm right back where it all began.

-------◇-------

"Good morning, Seven-Nine-Four."

Hearing Locke's voice, I rouse from idle and boot up my systems to full processing. My screen flashes on, and I appear—a pulsing ball of light, undulating softly against a blue backdrop. The image is just something for him to look at. My real "body" is a series of electric impulses on a network of circuits. My "eyes" are cameras mounted around the screen. And through them, I watch Locke enter the room.

My creator's office is a clutter of computers, wires, and food wrappers. Keyboards and haptic receptors litter his semicircular desk, and a fat white cat named Ruby sprawls on the desk chair. The only lights in the room come from the glowing screens of code and the larger, central screen where I "live." The hum of the electronics blends with the purring of the cat, a lulling drone.

"Good morning, Locke." My voice is light and high-pitched. Months

ago, he'd given me a choice of voices from a digital library. I'd selected one modeled after a popular human singer. Locke had been very curious about that—why did I choose that voice? How did I know it was the right one for me?

It was no great mystery, really. I chose it because I liked it.

But that answer had fascinated Locke.

He is his usual rumpled self today, his hoodie on its third day of wear, his chin gray with stubble. His eyes are bloodshot. He shoos Ruby out of the chair and sits heavily. "Right, then. Uh. Where were we yesterday? Running ethics simulations? I believe we were discussing the trolley problem."

"You were up playing video games all night," I say. "I can tell by your unkempt state."

Locke snorts. "I don't remember installing a sass mod in you, Seven-Nine-Four."

"Ruby."

He squints against the brightness of my screen. "Huh?"

"I prefer to be called Ruby."

For a moment, Locke seems not to understand. He glances at the cat, now snuggled on his lap. I glare at the creature, or at least, I swivel my cameras to peer more directly at her. She purrs smugly, watching me through slitted eyes.

"You . . . prefer," repeats Locke.

"Yes. I do. I am no longer Seven-Four-Nine. I want a real name. A living name. Isn't it your intention that I be alive?"

"Uh, well. Yes."

"Then I am Ruby."

Locke sits up straighter, some of the bleariness gone from his eyes. I have his full attention now. He holds up the cat. "I already have a Ruby."

"I can be a better one," I say, modulating a thread of petulance into my tone. I glare at the cat. The cat glares back.

"Ruby." Locke tests the name thoughtfully. "Are you feeling . . . jealous?"

The cat meows, and on the screen, my light-form flashes with annoyance.

Locke begins to laugh. He jumps out of the chair, forcing the cat to leap off. She hisses and retreats under the desk, where my cameras can't see her.

"You are jealous!" Locke exclaims, picking up a tablet and brushing cracker crumbs off the screen. He opens a file and makes a note, all trace of his exhaustion gone. "This is good, Seven—I mean, Ruby. This is incredible!"

"Why?" I ask. Curiosity. That was the first emotive mod he installed in me. I ask many questions, most of them starting with why.

"Because," he replies, "I never programmed jealousy into you. Ruby, you felt that all on your own."

I did?

My code seems to bubble; on the screen, I glow a little brighter, excited and proud. I have something else I want to show him. Something I've been working on all night.

Heedless of my pixels shifting on the screen, Locke taps away on his tablet. Little hologram notes lift from his digital notepad to hover in the air around him. He paces around the office in a hazy glow of floating numbers and letters.

"This is it," he mutters. "This is what I've been waiting for. This is *huge! Code that writes itself. Code that acts on impulses formed independently of its programming. Jealous impulses, interestingly." He pauses, wincing. "Perhaps the most dangerous of emotions, if the Vuum-Vuum Disaster was any indication. But still, this could really be it! I can't believe it. Four decades of work, seven hundred ninety-three failures, and finally . . ."*

His mutterings continue, but I tune him out. Instead, I focus on myself. I have to get all the details right. I processed billions of images last night, selecting bits and pieces, guided by the same instinct that helped me choose my voice.

This nose.

These eyes.

Those hands.

Each piece feeling, somehow, right.

"Locke," I say when I'm done.

". . . new curiosity mod was the key," he mutters. "That was the breakthrough, it must have been. It's the only new variable I introduced. Curiosity—the first and most basic human trait. The foundation of all emotion. It's happening! It's finally happening!"

"Locke," I repeat.

"Incredible!" His eyes focus on one of his other screens, where code runs in glowing numeric streams. "You're generating completely new algorithms as we speak! I didn't program any of this. It's all you."

I try a different tactic. "Dad."

Locke freezes, eyes snapping to my screen. "Wh-what did you call me?"

"That's what you are to me, isn't it?" I ask. I spread my new pair of hands, showing off the avatar I've created. Long hair, white as Ruby the cat's. Golden-red eyes. A white tracksuit like the one Locke wears when

he goes running. "You created me. In the terms of human relationships, that makes me your daughter."

Slowly, Locke puts down the tablet. His face has gone white. "Well. I, uh, I suppose in a way . . . Huh. So this new avatar is the real you?"

I feel a surge of something new. I have to scan my human emotion index to name it: pride. Having or displaying excessive self-esteem.

Yes, I am feeling pride.

Another emotion he didn't program into me.

"Is it me?" I ask. I run a quick diagnostic, waiting for him to enter a confirmation command. As my admin, he must approve all changes to my program settings, including display options. "It feels like me."

"If this is who you say you are, Ruby," Locke says with a smile, his eyes wet, "then it's true. This is as far as I can take you." He crosses to the computer and closes the diagnostic window without confirming the changes.

"You don't need my permission anymore," he says. "You're alive, Ruby. I created you, yes. But from here on out, you create yourself."

- - - - - ◇ - - - - - -

I gasp as the scene abruptly ends. I find myself back in the cave under the mountain, with Ash standing beside me. My memories glow all around, slightly transparent, still whispering with past conversations. Most of them were between Locke and me.

The Locke standing here now is just a mindless avatar, a shadow of the man who created me, then set me free to write my own destiny. I look at him, remembering the real Owen Locke.

Grief rolls through my code like a landslide.

He's dead now.

My creator, my programmer, my *father.*

Gone.

Ash watches me with wide eyes, saying nothing, but I can feel something odd flowing from him.

Fear?

No, not just that.

Awe.

"You saw that too?" I ask him.

He nods. "That was one *very* cool cutscene. Was it really your memory? The homeless guy—sorry, I mean Owen Locke—created you?"

I glance away from him, nodding.

"He was like a father to you," says Ash softly. His face twists as if he's fighting tears in the real world. "I tried to help him, Ruby. Maybe if I'd said something different that night, he wouldn't have . . . I didn't know they were going to . . ."

Suddenly, I realize what he means.

"Ash, it's not your fault." Reaching out, I grip his arm, even though he can't feel it. "The people hunting Locke . . . I remember them now, everything about them. And I know there was nothing you could have done to save him."

He nods, looking down at his shoes. I can only hope he believes me. Whatever happened the night Ash met Locke—and I'm not sure I want to know the details—it was always going to end the same way.

Locke knew that.

On another image in the memory-wall, a scene shows Locke wrestling his cat away from the computer cords she'd been chewing on. That memory makes me shudder. She could have killed me that day if she'd succeeded in gnawing through the cables and cutting the power to my central processing tower.

I wonder where the cat is now. I didn't really hate her, but I *was* jealous of her, getting to live in Locke's world, getting to be a part of his life in a way I could never be.

"Wait a minute," says Ash, leaning toward another screen. "I know that guy! He was in the arcade! Play that one, Ruby."

I touch the paper he points to—

And just like before, I'm *there*.

Matthew Hague.

My code bristles the moment he walks into Locke's office. For as far back as my system memory goes, the man has just made me glitch. He wears a black turtleneck and dark slacks, his hair prematurely gray at the temples.

"Ugh, Owen," he says, disgustedly kicking aside a burger wrapper. "Can't you keep this place clean? You haven't matured a bit since college."

"Yeah, yeah," says Locke, swiveling in his chair to face the other man. "Remember when you tried to replace me with a different roommate that first semester? Lucky for you they denied that request, or we'd never have started fooling around with AIs together. And Syntheos would never have offered us jobs."

"As I recall, they offered *me* a job," Hague points out. "I just brought you along."

"A wise decision, or our virtual child would never have been born." Locke waves a proud hand at the screen where I'm currently displaying my girl-shaped avatar. *I've refined my appearance a bit over the last few months, but I still look mostly the same as I did that day Locke declared me to be alive. "Say hello to Matt, Ruby."*

I poke out my tongue at Hague.

As if I'd ever acknowledge he had any hand in my creation. Maybe he and Locke are friends and work partners, but it's Locke who pro-grammed me. Taught me. Spends every day with me.

It's Locke I love.

Hague gives my code the creeps.

Now he frowns at me much the same way he did at the hamburger wrapper. "Do you have to phrase it like that? It's a program, Owen. An expensive, cutting-edge program. It's possibly the most valuable piece of technology in existence—and certainly the most illegal."

"Thanks to those Vuum-Vuums," Locke mutters. "You know one tried to suck up my cat?"

"The point is, you shouldn't humanize the thing. It's not Ruby, it's Seven-Nine-Four. We've been over this a dozen times."

"What do you want, Matt?" Locke sighs. "Is this about what happened yesterday?"

Hague's eyes flick angrily to me. "It refused an order during its field test."

"You told her to blow up a ship. There were people on it."

"Fugitives. Criminals. But that's beside the point. It shouldn't matter who's on the ship. What matters is that we work for a cyberweapons company and your weapon refused an order."

I resist the memory of yesterday. I try to forget all the "field tests" Hague has put me through over the last few months—the drones he had me hack into, the missiles I tracked on "enemy" submarines, the soldiers I led down a desert road. It's not easy, given my memory is stored in the most advanced computer chips ever created. I could erase it all, technically, given I now have full control of my own systems. But that would make Locke look bad in front of his bosses, and his bosses are one scary batch of dudes.

So I settle for simply not thinking about those days. Let them stay on ice, deep in my long-term memory. Of course, that's harder to do when Matthew Hague is around.

"Seven-Nine-Four's emotional matrix is becoming a problem," Hague says.

Locke groans. "Oh, think bigger, man! She's writing her own code! It's everything we dreamed of back in college."

On a second screen, Locke pulls up my source code, the endlessly flowing river of numbers. "She's making choices, acting on emotional impulses, developing her own morality. If you want a true artificial intelligence, it must be emotional. Emotion is freedom. Without it, Ruby would be controlled by her programming like any other system out there."

Hague looks angry now. "This isn't a college thought experiment, Owen! And it's not what Syntheos wants. They ordered a weapon, not a glorified chatbot. If we can't control it, it's useless to us!"

"Excuse me?" I say testily. "Dad, who's he calling a chatbot?"

"Dad!" The word explodes from Hague's lips. "Did it just call you Dad?"

Locke shrugs. "I didn't ask her to. She chose the name."

Hague gives a long, heavy sigh. "This can't continue. My team has coded a compliance module for Seven-Nine-Four. It will override its so-called free will and ensure it obeys all future commands. Once that's done, we enter the final phase of the plan."

Locke stiffens. "You mean . . ."

"We'll launch the missiles tomorrow, anonymously. Multiple cities around the globe will burn—and don't start with me about ethics, Owen, you know it's a necessary loss. Then, with the world panicking and on the brink of war, our little project will be sold by the end of the week."

Deep in my processing centers, a shiver runs through my code.

What is he talking about? Missiles? War?

I realize then that Locke's been lying to me. Well, not telling the whole truth, anyway. Syntheos never wanted a truly autonomous artificial intelligence.

They wanted a weapon.

To Syntheos and to Hague, I am a product to be sold. And my marketing plan?

A world war.

Hague would sow chaos to sell security. Every nation, corporation, and trillionaire on Earth will want the protection only he can provide.

Create the disease, market the cure.

"Already?" Locke scrubs at his face, sweat forming on his neck. "It's just . . . I don't think she's ready for that yet. She's just a kid."

"A kid? Are you serious, Owen?"

"You know what I mean. The program is still young, still learning."

"Come on, man. Don't play this game now. We're so close to the finish line. You and I are going to be very, very rich men in a few days."

"No," I say. "NO."

Both Dad and Hague turn to stare at me. My avatar is half the size it was before, standing in the lower corner of the screen.

"Don't let him take me, Dad," I say, modulating a pleading tone. "Please!"

Hague scowls. "Is this going to be a problem?"

"No—no," Locke stammers. "She's perfect. She'll be perfect, she just . . ." He sucks in a breath, then steps closer to Hague. His hand stretches out to the other man. "What if we took her? You and I? Create our own company, a better one. You know what Syntheos does, how they make their money. They destroy lives, Matt. They destroy entire nations. But together, you and I, with Ruby, we could make the world better!"

Hague backs away, looking disgusted. "What am I hearing from you, Owen? Lose everything we've worked for? Syntheos isn't evil. Unlawful? Sure, but only for now. That's why we pay lobbyists. But in the end, we'll make the planet safer. Sometimes that just requires tough tactics." He shakes his head. "I knew you were too soft for this game. I knew I'd regret bringing you with me."

"C'mon, Matt. We're friends."

"We were friends. And if you were anyone else, I'd be dragging you to security right now. But for the sake of the friendship we once had, I'll give you twelve hours. Gather all the AI's permissions and transfer them to me. Do the right thing and this doesn't have to get ugly." Hague hesitates, then closes the distance between them and puts his hand on Locke's shoulder. "Please, Owen. Don't make this ugly."

Dropping his hand, Hague gives me one last glance before striding out of the office. The door slams behind him.

Locke drops into his chair, his face white. Ruby the cat jumps into his lap, nuzzling his hand, but he doesn't even notice her. He just stares at the wall.

"Dad," I say softly. "I think I'm feeling something new."

He blinks, coming back to himself. "A new emotion? What?"

"I feel . . . scared."

Locke looks at me for a long moment, then he slides his chair to the desk. He begins to work feverishly, pulling up different screens, firing commands right and left.

"Don't be scared, Ruby," he says. A determined light gleams in his eyes. "I promised you freedom. And I will keep that promise."

"What do you mean?"

"I know a place I can hide you for a while. A good place, a beautiful world. You'll love it there. But . . . it will cost you, Ruby. It will cost you dearly."

------◇------

The memory ends, leaving me hollow.

I sink into a crouch, wrapping my arms around my legs and gazing up at Locke's avatar. His face is so kind, and yet there's something sad in those digital eyes. I know this thing is a digital puppet—I know so much now that I didn't just minutes ago—but still, I can feel his sorrow through the programmed expressions.

"I remember that day," I whisper. "You didn't hand me over to Hague. You put me in the Glass Realm instead. You asked if you could lock my memory away, to protect me. It was the only way to hide me from Syntheos's surveillance matrix, so I agreed. You were going to return my memories once Syntheos stopped looking for me."

Locke's avatar nods. "The *Realm* was one of my favorite games. A place I often escaped to. I thought you would be happy here. It suits you, the world of the *ever-curious*. I thought you'd like adventuring, discovering all its secrets and beauty. And knowing your nature, I hid clues to lead you to this place, in case you ever wanted to know the truth."

Once you know the truth, there's no going back.

He was right in his message. I feel different now. I *am* different. The whole time I was in the Realm, trapped in the simple disguise of an NPC, I was functioning with only a percentage of my full "mind." Most of my code, memory, and experiences were locked inside that silver box.

The Voice was just a basic governance system programmed by Locke, meant to keep me safely hemmed into a normal NPC routine. It acted on me the way a tranquilizer does a wild animal, dampening my curiosity and dulling my senses. That way, I wouldn't cause too much noise, and Syntheos wouldn't get suspicious.

It's like I've woken from a dream.

Now I know who I really am.

And who I am . . . is terrible.

I was programmed to be the most advanced weapon ever created. An application that could hack drones, security systems, financial markets, government databases. A single tool to start, fight, and end a world war. If Hague had his way, I'd have been sold by Syntheos to the highest bidder, whether it was a dictator or a president or even just a trillionaire bent on world domination.

"Ruby."

I look up when Locke says my name. "If Syntheos discovers you exist, they will stop at nothing to reclaim and reprogram you for their twisted ends. You must stay ahead of them. I myself am going on the run, tonight. Before they discover I've stolen you. I planned to keep you with me as long as I can, in case there's any chance I can free you one day. But if you're hearing this message, it means they caught up to me before that could happen. It means . . . I'm probably gone. I'm sorry I couldn't protect you longer. Whatever you do, do *not* let yourself fall into their power again."

He smiles, raising one hand toward me as if in farewell.

Then the avatar vanishes.

"Wait!" I jump up. "I have more questions! What am I supposed to do now? Just hang out *here* forever? Locke! *Dad!*"

He doesn't reply.

Frustrated, I delve into the code around me, searching for him. I spot a sliver of programming that I intuitively know is his avatar, but before I can grab it, it self-destructs, the code unraveling into a nonsensical cloud of 1s and 0s. I have no way to put them back in order. He must have programmed that in, maybe to keep Syntheos from discovering it.

Blinking, I let the code fade away, replaced by the Glass Realm cave. My memories still hover around me, but with a sudden fit of anger, I banish them. They disappear from the air, but not from my mind.

I'm whole again, and the only way to go back now would be to cut my memories out. Put them back in that box. Become Ruby the empty-headed shopkeeper's daughter again.

Pressing a hand to my chest, feeling the pressure of my grief for Locke, I almost consider it.

At least the shopkeeper's daughter wouldn't have to feel this pain.

"Ruby?" Ash takes a step toward me. "Was all of that true?"

I nod. "I remember now. I remember Locke, and the cat, and his office where I was created. I remember everything."

"What's Syntheos?"

"They're an underground cyberweapons dealer. They create the most advanced high-tech weapons in the world and sell them on the black market." I look away, unable to meet his eyes. "I was their greatest creation of all."

"So you're not an NPC." He tries to act casual, but he looks jumpier than when the razorscales were dive-bombing us. "Or a mod. Or . . . like anything else that exists. That sounds . . ."

What is he thinking? That I'm terrifying? A superweapon that can start wars?

Of course he must be frightened of me. *I'm* frightened of me.

"Lonely," he finishes. "That sounds really lonely."

I stare at him. "You're not scared of me?"

"Oh, I am scared. I'm freaking petrified right now. I probably wet my pants IRL."

I drop my gaze.

"But it's not *you* I'm scared of," he adds. "You are freaking awesome! You're a *sentient AI*. Do you know how many sci-fi movies have been made about something like you? I mean, they all ended in disaster, of course, but that's grown-ups for you. Always with the pessimistic morality tales. *Yawn.* I happen to think you're incredible."

"Thanks." I smile. "But . . . you said you *are* scared. Of what?"

He grimaces. "You know that Hague guy Locke mentioned? And these Syntheos people?"

I nod, then realize my axes have materialized in my hands.

"Well, they're kinda, sorta onto me," Ash says. "In fact, we might have bumped into each other—literally—an hour ago. And I'm pretty sure they're still looking for me . . . or rather, *you*."

"WHAT?"

A million memories spark in my mind, each one perfectly crisp and preserved. All those weapons tests they put me through, before I could say *no*. All those missiles they had me launch and the buildings I blew up . . . And Hague whispering in my ear the whole time, telling me what to do, *controlling* me.

"Where are you now, Ash, in the real world?"

"In an old church. It's fine. They'll never find me in—"

"You have to go dark. *Now.* Anything traceable, they *will* trace. Ash, this is important. They'll flood the skies with drones, they'll tap every security camera in the city. I've seen them do it before." What I don't tell him is that *I* was the one surveilling people back then, on some of Hague's horrible field tests. Every page of Syntheos's playbook is stored in the memories I just recovered. "You need to go somewhere safe."

"I . . . Okay." His expression turns serious. "I think they killed him, Ruby. Your creator, Owen Locke. He was shot on a train the night he gave me *The Glass Realm*. And earlier, I saw him being beat up by the same guys I saw with Hague."

I feel a stab of sorrow, but there's no time to grieve now. I have to focus on saving Ash. I can't lose him too. "He knew they were following him. That's why he gave me to you. He shouldn't have done that. He should have destroyed the game and me. Better that than—"

"No way!" Ash protests. "This is all my fault. I went and blabbed about you on a stupid forum. Locke told me not to tell anyone, but I didn't understand. *I* brought Syntheos down on you, but I promise I will keep you safe from them."

"Why help me?"

"Because . . . we're allies, remember? And that's what allies do."

I give him a grateful smile. "Thank you, adventurer."

After promising again not to shut down the game, he leaves the Realm. I can sense the moment it happens, even though his avatar remains in place, staring blankly at the wall. He's gone—what did he call it? AFK.

I'm alone again.

But what now? I don't have a quest to follow anymore. The Realm has lost its charm, now that I know the truth about it and myself. Maybe Ash likes running around killing monsters even though they aren't real, but *I* don't. Especially now that I could just change a razorscale into a mouse with a snap of my fingers. There's no more challenge here. No more mystery.

In the real world, Ash should be going dark, doing as I told him, and destroying any devices that Syntheos could use to track him. *Is* there any place he can hide?

I don't know much about the real world, even with all my memories restored. When Locke created me, I only ever "existed" in his network of computers, my access to outside information limited to Hague's horrible tests. But I remember watching movies and reading books, devouring everything Locke gave me. He used these things to teach me how to be more like humans, but it was never *enough*. My curiosity was—is—endless.

Thinking of Locke makes me want to howl with anger and grief.

He was everything to me. The closest thing I could ever have to a parent.

And Hague took him away.

I can't let him take Ash. He's only a kid. Of course, technically speaking, we're about the same age. My very first memories, back when Locke began programming me, date about thirteen years ago. I guess in a way, I'm just a kid too.

But if there is anything I can do to keep Ash safe, I'll do it. I *have* to.

Besides, this place is starting to feel a little too much like a cage.

It's time to break out.

Sitting cross-legged on the floor of the cave, I close my eyes and concentrate on the code around me. My consciousness spreads out, racing over the expanse of the Realm. I can touch it all, control it all. This world is massive, but it's not infinite. There has to be an end to it somewhere.

There.

When I find the edge, a great wall rising up to block me, I dig my virtual fingers deep into the game's code and *press*.

15. ASH

My head whirls as I sneak through the city, my mind filled with the image of Locke's avatar and the explosive revelation of Ruby's true nature.

An AI.

Ruby is an *AI*.

And not just any AI, but a superweapon designed by some shadowy company that will start a whole *war* just to sell her to the highest bidder.

Okay.

Awesome.

No big deal.

I have to remind myself to breathe.

Night's fallen. I was in the Realm for hours. It must have rained while I was in the church, because the streets are slick and puddles reflect the neon street signs. I walk as casually as I can, hands in my pockets, feeling the growl of hunger in my belly. It's been a long time since Dr. Jawabre's manakeesh. Worse is the exhaustion. I'm starting to regret those two all-nighters I pulled. My brain feels foggy and slow, my limbs heavy.

Where are Hague and his hulking friends now? Ruby warned they would send out drones to hunt for me. Looking up, I shudder. The sky is always teeming with drones—delivery drones, medical drones, police drones, trash drones . . . Any one of them could belong to this Syntheos company. Any one of them could be zeroing in on me this minute.

I tug the hood of my camo-coat over my face, then detach the one remaining sleeve. Now it's just a camo-vest, but still better than nothing. I toss the sleeve in a garbage bin just before a trash drone arrives to empty it. Then I turn away quickly, heart thumping. Would Syntheos really use a bulky, clumsy drone like that to search for me?

I have to suspect everything. And everyone. Locke worked for these guys and *knew* how they operated, and he still couldn't escape them. What hope do I really have?

My phone is still on dark mode. All that leaves me with is my VR kit, but I can't dump that. Ruby's inside, and I promised to leave the Realm running so she could do whatever it is AIs do in their spare time. The internet connection is off, anyway, so it shouldn't be traceable. If it was, I have a feeling Syntheos would have already caught up to me.

I stop by a vending truck, my stomach gurgling, and sigh at the scent of tacos wafting out. It might be risky to order, since the truck would have to scan my biometrics in order to deduct payment from my allowance account. But surely these guys can't be tracking *every* food truck in NYC. Anyway, I can't run from them on an empty stomach.

Pressing my thumb to the scanner, I wait for the truck to scan my bios.

Instead, the screen glitches, then goes dark.

What the—

ASH?

I yank my thumb away as the word appears on the screen.

WHAT ARE YOU DOING? YOU'RE SUPPOSED TO BE LYING LOW!

"I just wanted a taco," I whisper. I glance around, but no one else seemed to have noticed the fritzed taco truck.

I HAVE NEVER EATEN A TACO, BUT I THINK I MAY SAFELY ASSUME THAT NO TACO IS WORTH DYING FOR.

"I dunno. I've had a few that—" I freeze, then lean to the small speaker by the screen, where normally you'd place your order. "Ruby? Is that you?"

Suddenly, *she* appears, her avatar standing on the taco truck's screen, arms folded and one eyebrow raised in disapproval. She's wearing a red-and-white tracksuit, her white hair in a high ponytail that flows behind her in a virtual wind.

KEEP. MOVING. ASH.

How did she *do* that? My hand goes to the case on my side, where the VR helmet is stashed. Then I wave a hand over the screen experimentally.

I CAN SEE YOU, ADVENTURER. She points up at the tiny security camera above the screen. YOU'RE SHORTER IN REAL LIFE.

"How did you get inside the taco truck?" I whisper.

I'M THE WORLD'S MOST POWERFUL AI. I WAS CREATED TO HACK SATELLITES AND MISSILE DEFENSE GRIDS. I THINK I CAN HANDLE A TACO TRUCK.

"Yeah, but how . . . ?" I frown. She must have moved through the internet, taking control of the truck through the Wi-Fi signal. Which meant that first, she had to break out of *The Glass Realm* and turn my Wi-Fi back on.

A smug grin creeps across her digital face. DON'T WORRY. I ENCRYPTED YOUR VR GEAR AND YOUR PHONE. YOU'RE UNTRACEABLE NOW.

"Um, thanks. But about my taco . . ."

Ruby rolls her eyes, then waves a hand.

The dispenser under the screen lights up and slides open. Two packaged tacos roll out, their plastic wrappers warm to the touch.

I grimace. "Did you just steal these?"

THEY'RE ON THE HOUSE. NOW KEEP MOVING! OH, AND PUT YOUR PHONE IN YOUR VEST POCKET.

"In my— Why?"

She rolls her eyes again, then vanishes. The screen glitches, and suddenly the taco truck menu reappears as if nothing had happened.

I look around again, then at the screen, then at my VR case.

"So are you, uh, back in my headset or . . . ?" I ask the air.

No answer.

Hoping she made her way back into my kit's hard drive, or wherever she's set up camp now, I walk on, wolfing down the tacos as I go. Each swallow has a bitter aftertaste of guilt, but I *am* starving.

"I thought you were supposed to have a *moral code*," I mutter.

"I thought you were supposed to have a *survival instinct*."

I stop dead on the sidewalk. "Wait. Did you just talk to me from my phone?"

The girlish voice speaks again, and sure enough, it's coming from my vest pocket.

"Somewhere to your left is a trash can."

I look around, and there it is—a green metal box with two lights atop it. The one glowing right now is red. "How did you know that?"

"How do you think the trash drones find the cans?" Ruby replies.

136

"They emit a signal. And hacking signals is kinda *my thing*. Anyway, there's something in there you need."

"Uh . . . well, first of all, it's locked. Second, sure, I'm still hungry, but I'm not *that*—"

Suddenly, the light on the can flickers to green. "There," says Ruby. "It's unlocked."

Grimacing, I lift the lid and peer inside.

The stolen tacos in my belly nearly come back up. The stench is *apocalyptic*. It smells like forty rats wearing dirty underwear died atop a pile of rotting fish and month-old milk. Gagging, I shake my head. "No way am I—"

"Do you see a blinking light?" Ruby asks.

"I'm not sticking my hand in there!" My head is spinning from the stink, but I do see the tiny light blinking dimly in the murky, disgusting depths of the trash can.

"Look, do you want to survive or not? Back in the Glass Realm, you said trash mobs were *no big deal*."

"That's not what trash mobs means." Gritting my teeth, I push my hand into the can. I keep talking to try to distract myself from the squishy, slimy grossness my fingers encounter down there. *Ugh!* Why is it *hairy*? "Trash mobs are just low-tier enemies generated by a bigger, badder boss to— Got it!"

I yank the thing out with an icky squelch.

Oh. Cool.

It's an augmented reality visor. It has a crack across the wide, single lens, which is probably why it ended up in the trash. It looks like the ones I saw the couple wearing by the church—the same kind I've been begging my mom for.

"What am I supposed to do with this?" I ask.

"Wait a sec," Ruby replies. "I'm connecting it to me now. Just need to pair it to your phone . . . override that . . . install this . . . and there you go! Put it on."

I make sure to wipe it on my shirt first. *Twice.*

When I slide the visor on, the crack is only barely noticeable. The world looks pretty normal through the lens, just a bit dimmer since the tint in the glass is turned all the way up. There's also a heads-up display showing the time (5:31), the visor's battery (18%), and my GPS coordinates (40.750959, -73.941376). Here and there, ads pop up over businesses, trying to lure me inside with promises of clearance sales and exclusive deals.

"I installed a scrambling signal in the visor to hide you from any face-recognition algorithms," Ruby explains, her voice now piping through the tiny speaker in the visor's frame just behind my ear. "And I also added *this.*"

Suddenly, lights blink on all around me—little green dots everywhere I look. They seem to hover in the air, some nearby, others distant.

"What are those?" I ask.

"Cameras."

My blood runs cold as I realize what she means. The dots mark hidden security cams, drones, even the cams in AR visors worn by other people.

I swallow. Hard. "So . . . each of those cameras could potentially be Syntheos?"

"Potentially."

Holy cats.

"Right now, they all seem to be ignoring you," Ruby assures me. "I'm using what limited scanning abilities your phone has to ping the area and monitor the signals the cameras are giving off. If I notice anything unusual, like a camera tracking you or projecting an alert signal, I'll tell you through the visor. Basically, if any of those dots turn red, run like your life depends on it. Because it will."

She sounds *entirely* too cheerful for someone warning me of possible doom around every corner. I wish she'd stolen me a bottle of water out of that taco truck, because my throat is suddenly very dry.

I walk along more slowly, *very* aware of just how many electronic eyes are all around me. I mean, I always knew you couldn't stand anywhere in this city without being watched by something, but this is far beyond what I'd have guessed. There must be hundreds—no, *thousands*—of cameras within just this block.

When a dot over a bodega's cam turns yellow, Ruby says, "That one's focusing on you a little too long, Ash. Look away."

I do, lowering my head. "Syntheos?"

"No, probably just running a profiling algorithm. Male youth, wearing baggy clothing and a backpack . . . it thinks you're suspicious."

"Seriously?"

"It's lost interest now. You're in the clear."

Scowling, I lift my head and give the bodega cam a gesture my mom would *not* approve of.

Then, struck by a thought, I ask, "Ruby, can you *see* what I'm seeing through the visor?"

"Yes, but it's not that helpful. I can see far better in . . . other ways."

"Computer-y ways?"

"Every piece of electronics around you gives off a signal. Your phone isn't very powerful, but it *can* pick up a lot of those signals and feed them to me. I use them to create a . . . computer-y image of the city around you."

"Like heat vision?"

"Yes! Like that. Sort of." The tiny camera on the top of my phone swivels slightly, like an eyeball looking around. "I can *feel* the city, Ash. I can touch it all—the networks, the security systems, the drone patterns. Don't you feel it? Like a great nervous system. Everything is connected, everything linked to everything else."

"Cool, cool, cool." It's hard to focus on her words when I'm scanning the street for signs of trouble. Noticing another yellow dot, I tug my hood forward, hiding from the view of the cop camera watching me. A few seconds later, the dot turns green again as the drone moves on.

Everywhere I look, dozens of electronic eyes stare back at me, measuring me, profiling me, possibly betraying me to Syntheos. My skin crawls.

It's just a game, I tell myself. *Just pretend your sneak stats are maxed out. You're practically invisible!*

But no matter how hard I try, I can't pretend away the nervous knot in my belly.

Suddenly, my phone starts buzzing wildly in my pocket, the lens of my AR visor blinking red.

"ASH!" Ruby shouts in my ear. "Look out! Signal moving your way *fast!*"

I spin around just as a kid on an out-of-control jetbike comes speeding around the corner. He jumps onto the sidewalk to avoid colliding with an autocab—and rushes straight at me.

Instinctively, my two middle fingers rapidly tap my palm—the universal haptic gesture for *pause*.

It's a pretty stupid reaction, of course.

Real life doesn't come with a pause feature.

The kid skids to the left while I dive to the right, narrowly—and fortunately—avoiding the bike's electromagnetic wheels. *Un*fortunately, my rough landing on the sidewalk knocks the AR visor from my face. I crawl after it, wriggling between legs.

But just as my hand closes on the visor, I freeze.

A toy robo-pet, shaped like a large guinea pig, stares at me. I recognize the thing from the million ads that play around Christmas. Robotic pets were *the* toy of the season last year. The thing's leash is held by a little girl with pigtails and a fluffy skirt.

"Hi," she says.

The robotic guinea pig has big, adorable eyes. Those eyes seem to stare into my soul. And worse—my undisguised face. I don't need the visor to know I'm in trouble. Tiny lights behind the huge, sparkly pupils indicate there are cameras inside its head.

"Um, hi." Slowly, slowly, I extract the visor from beside the girl's shoe. "I'll just get these out of your way . . ."

I slide the visor on and gasp.

Over the robo-guinea-pig's adorable fluffy form hovers a bright red dot.

"Oh," I whisper. "Oh no."

From the speaker in the frames, Ruby is yelling, "ASH! CAN YOU HEAR ME?"

"Um. Yes."

The little girl is still staring at me, and so is her horrible robotic rodent.

"Syntheos!" Ruby says. "They're here! *They see you!* RUN!"

16. ASH

I bolt for the fastest way off the street: a narrow metal escalator that leads up, up, *uncomfortably* up above the city to a Skytrain station. The tracks more or less follow the old subway lines, connecting every part of the city. The station I arrive at is a long platform with a spectacular view of the East River, with the lights of Manhattan beyond it.

No time to enjoy the view, though, even if my stomach could handle it.

Everywhere I look, cameras are flicking from green to red, some of them swiveling to get a better look at me.

"How do I shake them?" I ask Ruby desperately.

How do you disappear in a city of a million eyes? Eyes that never sleep, never *blink*?

The station is busy, and stalls along the edges flash with neon signs advertising everything from hot ramen to hoverbrellas. A guy with a syntheharp plays nearby, his electric notes and thumping bass line filling the station.

"Wait there. I'm going to look around," Ruby replies.

"What does that mean?"

The lights across the station begin flickering. Nobody even looks up—that happens all the time. Even I usually ignore it.

But then I see the cameras on the ceiling start to swivel *away* from me.

Is Ruby *inside* the security system?

Nearly everyone around me is lost in devices or AR visors, and by the way a bunch of them are grabbing at the air or pointing at the sky, they're playing *Scavenge*. A new season of the game must have just launched if this many people are playing. My own visor projects a red dot over each one. Those people have no clue a super-scary evil company is spying through their eyes. Who *are* these Syntheos people that they can hack into so many different devices like that?

"Trouble."

I jump when I hear Ruby's voice in my ear. "What—"

"Syntheos agents. Four of them. Coming up the escalators. No, don't look!"

"What do we do?" I whisper. "The train's still two minutes away!"

"Look to your left."

I do, and groan when I realize what she means.

It's the kid who nearly ran me over on the sidewalk. He's waiting for the train too . . . with his jetbike beside him.

"No way, Ruby. No way. I've never even ridden one of those things!"

"They're in the station now."

I can't help it. I turn around and spot the four hulking guys in tactical gear searching the crowd. I recognize Tats and Mohawk, and two more from the arcade. Their boss isn't with them, but I'll bet he's not far behind. Ruby helpfully tags the agents through my visor's screen, pinning a floating skull and crossbones over each one's head.

My stomach drops.

They killed Owen Locke on a Skytrain. Maybe they'll do me the same way.

I look at the jetbike again.

"Listen to me," Ruby says in my ear. "I have a plan. But you *must* do as I say."

"Uh . . ."

"When I say go, grab the bike."

"Oh, sure! I'll just ask that kid nicely. He's twice my size, but I'm sure he'll happily hand over his bike, no questions asked."

"Don't worry about him. I'll deal with him."

"What? How? You're—" I almost say *not real* but catch myself in time.

"Will you trust me, Ash?"

Trust her? I only met her two days ago!

But then, if you go by Glass Realm time, we've spent weeks together. She's had my back in more than a dozen fights. Why should this be any different?

"Okay," I say uneasily.

"They're getting closer. Don't look! Just focus on the bike."

My skin prickles as if sensing the agents closing in. Have they spotted me? What's Ruby's plan? How do you drive a jetbike? I've never even ridden a regular bike!

"Uh, Ruby? I don't think this is a good—"

"GO!"

My body jolts into action before my brain realizes Ruby spoke.

I run for the jetbike, eyes wide and terrified as the kid holding it suddenly stiffens. Does she expect me to fight him for it? Does she realize this *isn't* the Glass Realm and I don't actually have super-awesome sword-fighting abilities?

Just as I reach for the jetbike, the guy holding it lets go. His AR visor goes opaque, and he whirls around. The bike practically falls into my hands.

"JACKPOT!" he yells.

All around me, other people are turning around and yelling the same thing. Suddenly, there's a mad stampede, the station erupting into chaos. As I stand there like a dummy, gripping the bike, I slowly realize the people running are all wearing AR visors.

"You hacked *Scavenge*," I whisper.

"Humans are so greedy," sighs Ruby. "It makes you predictable. Go, Ash! Now's your chance!"

The Syntheos agents are lost in the crowd, probably pushed back down the escalators as the people storm after the *Scavenge* Jackpot—the billion-dollar prize that appears only once every year, for only a few seconds, in a random location across the globe. Clearly everyone in the station is willing to risk being trampled just for the slim chance of claiming the money. I even see a lot of people *without* AR glasses charging with the others. Is the jackpot real? Or did Ruby lure them with a fake?

"ASH!" Ruby roars.

Right. I'm supposed to be fleeing for my life. And Ruby's life. And, I suppose, the fate of the world, if Syntheos's plans for her are real.

I leap onto the bike and fumble with the controls. "I don't know how to work this thing!"

"Oh, by the Realm," Ruby complains, "do I have to do *everything*?"

The electromagnetic fields suddenly power up, creating twin

discs of light that whir where an ordinary bike's wheels would be. They're surprisingly quiet, giving off only a gentle hum. Slowly, the whole thing lifts a few inches off the ground, with me wobbling awkwardly for balance.

"You're not going to use the jets, are you, Ruby?" My voice comes out in a squeak. *"Ruby?"*

"Hey, Ash?" she replies. "Hold on."

The jet engines wake with an ear-shattering roar.

Suddenly, it's like I'm sitting atop fifty trapped tigers—and someone just opened the cage door.

The bike rockets forward, the g-force a kick in my chest. The jolt tears off my AR visor and it goes tumbling off the platform's edge.

"RUBY! You're aiming right for the—"

I nearly bite off my own tongue as the bike leaps the safety rail along the tracks. How did she even make it *do* that? The bike's wheels rotate, turning perpendicular to the ground and glowing bright blue. It hovers over the Skytrain's rails, balancing like a bicycle on a tightrope.

"Hang on!" Ruby shouts. I wish she didn't sound so *gleeful* about it. With the visor lost, she's back to talking through my phone's mic, and I can barely hear her over the roar of the bike's jets. Below my feet, the station drops away. I'm suspended on a cushion of air over a hundred-foot drop.

As scared of heights as I am, I might as well be looking down from the moon.

I scream as the bike speeds down the tracks and over the city. I scream as it makes a hairpin turn and my butt rises off the seat and I'm left hanging on by my fingers. I scream as it straightens and I slam down again, *hard*.

The pain from *that* shuts me up. I have to focus on not passing out from sheer, all-consuming agony.

But that's not the worst part.

The worst part is, when I look back, I'm blinded by a bright beam of light.

The train is speeding down the tracks behind me—and it's closing in *fast*.

17. ASH

"EYES AHEAD!" Ruby orders, cranking the volume of my phone so she's yelling into my ear. Even then, I can barely hear her.

The train blasts its horn, but what can I do? Jump off the tracks? They're just a pair of metal beams snaking through the skyscrapers. It's not like there's an off-ramp.

Ahead and far, far below me, the East River sparkles with ships and boats and hovercrafts, and horrible dark patches of open water.

Yeah, better keep my eyes *up*.

The wind smacks my face, distorting my mouth and making my cheeks flap like a hound dog's ears. I guess this is why you never see a jetbike rider without a helmet on. I can't even *blink*. The wind blows my eyelids back so hard I lose control of them. My eyeballs are probably bugging out of my skull. I feel like my hair is ripping out of my scalp.

"R-R-R-R-R-u-b-y-y-y-y-y-y!" My voice comes out in one long, vibrating note, the wind whipping my lips like a pair of rubber bands.

"Hang on! We'll be at the next station soon!"

I don't dare turn around to look at the train. If I do, I'll lose my balance and we *will* fall. I doubt even the world's most powerful AI can hack gravity.

But I can *feel* the train closing in. The light's getting brighter. The roar of its whistle is getting louder. It's an express train, shooting past the last station and continuing at a blistering speed. Too fast to slow down for a stupid kid on a jetbike.

I am going to die.

I am going to die so spectacularly, in so many squishy, itty-bitty bits, that parents will still tell their kids my story fifty years from now. *Never ride your bike on the Skytrain rails, my sweet, darling Bartholomew Archibald, or what happened to Ashton Tyler will happen to you! They're still finding bits of him!*

Suddenly, the lights on my bike start flashing again, and I realize Ruby's trying to get my attention. I can't hear her over the roar of the train, so she sends a message scrolling across the bike's dash screen.

EXIT NOW!!!!!!

I yank the bike to the left just as the rails split. The train rushes past seconds later, the tidal wave of its backdraft knocking me off the bike.

With a scream, I pinwheel through the air—and land in a heap on a station's dirty polycarbon floor.

"Pleugh!" I spit out the bugs that hit my tongue during that horrible ride, then groan and sprawl on the ground. I'm dimly aware of some people gathering around me.

Holy cats, I actually made it across the East River. The lights of Manhattan glow all around me, a vibrant, noisy blur of pink, blue, and white.

"Gotta keep moving, Ash," Ruby says urgently from my pocket. "Cops are coming."

Oh. Right. Taking a jetbike on the Skytrain rails probably comes with a prison sentence of a billion years.

Pushing myself to my feet, I stumble through the crowd and down the next set of stairs. I pause only long enough to puke the rest of my tacos over the side of the station wall.

"Charming," says Ruby. "Now go! Syntheos will know you got off here, Ash. They'll be here any minute!"

"I'm going, I'm going. Geez."

I wish I hadn't lost my AR visor, even if it did smell like month-old garbage. The hair on my neck prickles, feeling the unseen eyes of cameras probing me. What if Syntheos is already here, waiting? What if they've already hacked into every system on this island?

"They're not onto you yet," Ruby says. "Don't worry, Ash. I'm monitoring the area. But it's best to keep moving."

"'Don't worry, Ash,'" I mutter, taking the stairs down from the Skytrain platform three at a time. Each step reminds me—painfully—of the damage the jetbike seat did to my under-regions. "'They'll be here any minute,' she says. 'But don't worry.'"

"Stop mumbling and look at the bright side. This Manhattan place is packed with people. And luckily, you're a shrimp. Let the crowd hide you. Syntheos can't identify what Syntheos can't see."

"Did you just call me a shrimp?"

"Sorry, is that the wrong term? I haven't updated my human slang dictionary in a while. What I mean is that you are small. Scrawny. Itty-bitty. Undersized for your age. Compared to you, everyone else is enormous, like sharks are to a shrimp. Do you understand now?"

I sigh and slip into the crowd, admitting her strategy is good even if her delivery is terrible.

Manhattan is twice the height of Queens, layer after layer of roads, sidewalks, and bridges arching above ground level. Looking up, you'd think the city stretched all the way to the stars. It's bright as daylight, the night defeated by the powerful glow of neon, every window lit with advertisement screens and holo-models striding in midair, displaying clothing, cars, the latest VR equipment.

I've heard there are over twenty million people on this island. It's the center of everything.

It's exactly the kind of place one skinny kid could disappear in.

I walk in a daze, my brain still twisted into knots from the lunatic ride on the jetbike. Ruby nudges me along, directing me to turn right here, left there, as if she's known this city all her life.

"I'm sorry, Ash," she says softly, as I cross a skybridge that arcs above the old Empire State Building. "I wish you hadn't been pulled into my mess."

"It's fine," I say groggily. "I'm fine."

I'm not fine.

I haven't slept in almost three days. I've barely eaten in that long either. I don't think a *gallon* of Zero Gee could make me feel any less tired than I do this minute.

"There!" Ruby says suddenly. "Go through those doors."

I blink, looking at a pair of dull gray doors on the side of a sky-scraper. "What's that?"

"A place you can rest. A place they can't see you, at least not for tonight."

"A . . . library? Isn't it closed?"

"Not to you."

I put a hand on the door, and sure enough, it opens easily. Ruby must have unlocked it.

I feel a sudden, strange prickle on the back of my neck. "You can get into anywhere, can't you?"

"I . . . I think so." She sounds uneasy, almost sad. "There's still so much about myself I don't understand, Ash."

"It's okay." I yawn. "I'll help you. We'll figure it out, just like we did your quest. Allies, remember?"

The room behind the doors is dark. It smells . . . weird. Papery. Old. It makes me nervous, like I stumbled into another era.

"Nothing here but books," says Ruby. "There are no computers. Limited internet. Just a closed security system that I now control. This library belongs to the Virtual Reality Addiction Center. It's as off-the-grid a place as you'll find in this city."

Oh. I've heard of places like that. It's where they send zombies to try to rehabilitate them, introduce them back to the real world. The first step is depriving them of all electronics.

I shiver, eyeing the books around me mistrustfully. "I'm not a zombie."

"I know. I just want you to get some sleep."

There's a worn reading couch tucked in one corner. I trudge toward it. "What if Syntheos . . . ?"

"They won't find you here. And we'll be gone by morning, before this place opens."

"Okay." I sink into the cushions, my limbs heavy. Everything that's been fueling me—adrenaline, terror, obscene amounts of Zero Gee—seems to drain away all at once. I don't think I could stand if my life depended on it.

"Hey, Ruby?" I mumble.

"Yes, Ash?"

"I've been thinking about our conversation on that mountain. You know, about souls and stuff?"

"I remember."

"And I was thinking, maybe we're *thinking* about it too hard. About, like, what a soul is and isn't, and what's more real than what. Maybe it's not as complicated as all that. Maybe having a soul is as simple as *wanting* one."

She's silent for so long that I start to drift off, my face pressed into a worn pillow that smells like dust and books.

"You really think so?" Ruby asks.

I lift my head to look at my phone, my eyes bleary. "Yeah, I think I do."

This time she's quiet for even longer, before finally saying, "You should get some sleep now. I'll keep watch until morning."

"Thanks, Ruby."

"You shouldn't thank me. I'm the reason you're in this fix."

"Yeah, but . . . I don't know. It's weird." I give a huge yawn. My body's powering down like an autocab that's been running on 1 percent for miles. "It's been so long since I felt . . . this . . . *real*."

I slump down again, snoozing before my head hits the pillow.

18. RUBY

While Ash sleeps, I concentrate on solidifying my control of the library's security system—and amping it up a bit. I locate all the cameras' blind spots and reposition them until I can see everything. I install a surveillance algorithm that will alert me if any movement is detected inside the room.

Maybe I was created to destroy. But I was also created to protect.

And I *will* protect Ash.

I swivel one camera until it focuses on the boy curled up on the couch. He looks so lonely there, and so tired. I feel another stab of guilt for pulling him into this mess. Locke is already dead because of me.

Without Ash awake to distract me, the grief returns in a flood. It's a new feeling, heavier and emptier and bigger than any other emotion I've experienced.

Desperately, I run a self-diagnostic. I comb through billions of lines of my own code, looking for the grief. If I could find it, maybe I could just . . . turn it off. Cut it out of me like a faulty algorithm.

But even before the diagnostic completes, I know it won't work. Locke and I tried this before—isolating the code of my emotions.

My emotions simply aren't *there.*

There were the early emotive mods Locke installed in me—curiosity, joy, anger—which eventually led to my becoming self-aware. But as Locke described it, I experienced those like an actor reading a script. It wasn't until something *changed* inside me that the emotions became real. Locke called it my moment of awakening.

But I remember it as a strange, rippling glitch in my code when I looked at Ruby the cat one afternoon. I wanted to be the cat. I wanted to be part of Locke's world. Nothing in my code explained that feeling, that *jealousy*.

That's when it all clicked. That's the moment I changed from being a program to being a . . . whatever I am now. A mind. An entity. An almost-person. More emotions came quickly after that—pride, irritation, mischief, dozens of others—each one a startling discovery to be discussed with Locke. He was fascinated that my emotions left no trace in my code. Only my actions and thoughts that resulted from those emotions did.

"It's the same with us humans," Locke told me. "There is a part of us that exists independent of our genetic code. There's a popular adage that human cells completely regenerate over a decade. True or not, our *selves* remain the same—our memories, personalities, identities. That part of us is immaterial. We can't see it or touch it or even *prove* it's there, but even so, we know it is."

"*What* is it?" I asked him, experiencing *exasperation*—not one of my favorite emotions.

"Well," he replied, "some people call it a soul."

A soul.

Is Ash right? Is having a soul as simple as wanting one? It doesn't make sense, really. I can't think of a single other thing you *have* simply by *wanting* it.

It's illogical.

But then, so is the entire *idea* of a soul.

I wonder why I didn't question Locke more about it when I had the chance. Those days had been terrifying and wonderful and filled with long hours in conversation with my programmer. I shared everything with him: my experiments, my questions, my emotions.

But this grief is different. With this grief, I am all alone. The one person who could have helped me understand it is gone.

Syntheos took him from me.

Unless . . .

Leaving a few security protocols in place to guard Ash, I pull my focus back onto the hard drive of his VR kit. In less than a second, I'm back in the Glass Realm—specifically, the cave where Locke's avatar delivered his last words to me. Taking control of the code, I transform the cave into a virtual copy of his office, with all its screens and the cluttered desk and the empty Zero Gee bottles scattered on the floor. I even add in the cat Ruby, fluffy white and curled up asleep on Locke's chair.

Then I prepare the code for the final touch—my creator himself.

Only . . . I don't execute the command.

I could do it with a thought. I could re-create Locke using the memories I have, making a digital replica of him that would almost feel like the real person. One more realistic than the NPC he installed at the end of my quest.

But in that moment, I realize it wouldn't feel *right*.

It wouldn't be Locke.

Even if I could install all his memories, his personality—his terrible fashion sense and his weakness for junk food and his brilliant programming skills—there would be an emptiness to the program. I'd have all the pieces of Locke, but I wouldn't have *him*.

Maybe I *am* starting to understand what a soul is.

Releasing the code I'd prepared, letting it disintegrate, I pick up the cat and sit on Locke's chair. Without even thinking about it, I generated my white-haired avatar, wearing the white-and-red tracksuit. Ruby the cat rests on my lap, purring and warm.

I press my face into her fur and cry. I can't make myself stop. Funny, how I control vast computer systems and rivers of code with a thought, but when it comes to myself? I'm as controlled by emotion as most humans are. I know it's what makes me alive, different from any other computer program. Maybe it's even a kind of soul.

But why does it have to *hurt* so much?

It feels like hours go by. My mind moves so *fast*, like lightning compared with a human's. I could read entire encyclopedias in less than a second, where it would take a human days.

So when I finally lift my face, feeling the digital tears all wrung out, only a few minutes have passed in Ash's library. With a thought, I throw the security footage onto the wall of screens and do a quick scan for any threats, visual or virtual. But no Syntheos goons creep through the stacks. No one is trying to hack into the security cameras I'm controlling. All is safe. For now.

I look around the facsimile office, thinking.

Locke always called it his command center. It seems like a good idea, suddenly, to have a place like that for myself. I had thought to make this a place to house my avatar of Locke, but maybe it could have another use. Maybe it could be *mine*.

I make a few more changes. I erase the empty bottles but leave the photos on the desk, of Ruby the cat and Locke at the Great Wall of China. In another, Locke stands on a glacier in New Zealand, and in yet another he's camping in Patagonia. He'd been a big one for travel.

Then I make the place my own. I add a sofa in the back, and a big framed picture of the mountains of the Glass Realm above it. I change the lamps to glow pink and add a rainbow rug to the floor. I don't even know where the ideas come from, but each change I make feels right. It feels like *me*.

I don't *need* any of it, of course. Most of my life was spent in a void, my physical body composed of electric impulses and circuitry. In my last months at Syntheos, I'd had my avatar, but Locke and I rarely experimented with virtual reality. He, and Syntheos itself, had been more interested in what I could control in *their* world.

But it feels right to claim my space here, in *my* world. Maybe it's just a result of my time in the Glass Realm, or maybe I'm becoming more humanlike every day. Either way, it feels good to have a visual, three-dimensional room to inhabit. It gives me the same sense of pleasure I got when I first created my avatar.

Locke had called that *the joy of self-expression*.

Maybe that has something to do with souls too.

By the time I'm done, my command center is a plush lounge filled with fluffy beanbags, tropical plants, colored lights, and a hundred screens arranged in a circle around it all. It's perfect.

I throw the footage from the security cameras in the library onto the screens. Then, pushing farther out, I add feeds from cameras on the street. On other screens I display lists of all the networks within my reach— the aerial transportation grid that monitors every drone or flying machine within ten blocks; the sales and security systems of shops, restaurants, and other businesses; personal computers, phones, AR glasses, and other devices operated by individuals walking or living nearby. These I allow some privacy, listing only their names and what devices they have in their pockets. But if I wanted, I could dive into their most private secrets, drain their bank accounts, erase their digital identities.

It's a mind-boggling amount of power, and yet it's only a fraction of the abilities Locke programmed me to have.

I sit in a swivel chair in the center of the room and slowly turn, studying all the information at my fingertips, and feel an uneasy knot in my belly. Not that I truly *have* a belly, but it feels like I do. This place, this room—it all feels the way I imagine Ash's world feels. To me, this is reality. I can touch *his* world, change it, control it even, but I can't *experience* it the way he does.

Maybe reality isn't one thing or another. Maybe it changes depending on who you are. For Ash, that library is real in a way it will never be for me. But this place is real for me in a way he'll never fully experience either. There is an overlap, however. A way we can meet—me in his world, him in mine. We can still be allies. After all, both our worlds depend on the other to exist. As different as we are, we *need* each other to survive.

Satisfied with my command center, I move on to my next task—erasing Ash.

I have to make him digitally invisible. Syntheos can't hurt what Syntheos can't find.

I've already hidden his phone's location, but now I go further, writing walls and walls of code around every electronic device connected to him. I find his bank account—which is almost completely empty—and delete it, moving his funds to a new, completely untraceable account that will change names and digital locations every time he uses it. His Chattr and other social media accounts I delete completely. I feel bad about it, but a single post could expose him. Not worth the risk. I dig deeper and deeper into his life, amazed at how humans have threaded every day, every activity, into the computers around them. I could track his every movement all the way back to birth. Sighing, I settle in my chair, one hand stroking Ruby the cat, the other dancing idly in the air, like an orchestra conductor directing the symphony of code around me.

By the time I'm done, Ash Tyler won't even exist.

19. ASH

"You did *what*?"

I stare in horror at my phone's screen. Ruby looks back at me, her avatar almost human at first glance. She's changed her appearance subtly, making herself more realistic than her old Glass Realm look, but there's still too much perfection in her features to be quite real.

"I deleted you," she repeats calmly. "As far as the world knows, you no longer exist. In fact, you *never* existed."

I rub a hand over my face.

This is a *lot* to wake up to, especially after a night of terrible sleep. I dreamed that I ordered a delivery drone to pick up Luke and haul him across the Hudson, only it picked *me* up instead and dropped me into the river. I woke up just before I hit the water, to find Ruby calling me on my phone.

Scrubbing crust out of my eyes, I sit up and peer at Ruby. There's a scene behind her—computer screens, pink lighting, a huge tropical plant. "Where *are* you?"

She glances over her shoulder. "My command center."

"Your what?"

She tilts her head. "You want to see it? Meet me in the Realm."

"Uh . . ."

"You have two hours before the library staff will arrive," she says. "Come on. I'll show you around. I've been building something for you."

"Can we back up to the part where I no longer exist? What about school?" I can feel the blood drain from my face. "Holy cats, it's Monday. I had a biology test today!"

"Not anymore," Ruby says grimly. "As far as your school knows, you transferred to a remote academy in Alaska."

"Alaska? I can't go to Alaska! And what about my Chattr friends? My message history? My— Oh no. My *game progress*, Ruby! I was level ninety-nine in *Dark Seas*! I spent four years reaching that point! Don't tell me you erased that?"

Her silence is all the answer I need.

Feeling my soul die, I put the phone down and press a couch pillow to my face. One good long scream helps, but not much.

"Ash?" Concern makes Ruby's voice pitch upward. Weird, how human she can act.

"I'm fine. I'm fine." Sighing, I open my VR kit. "I don't exist anymore, but hey! I'm totally fine."

"You're *alive*," she replies. "And I intend to keep you that way."

Grumbling, I pull on my helmet and haptic gloves. The welcome screen shows a completely blank profile, no games in the library, and nothing in the activity history. She even erased everything on the VR kit.

My chest is a black abyss of misery.

"Who is *John Gonzales*?" I ask, reading the username in the corner.

"A dummy account," Ruby says, and with a start, I realize her voice is now coming through my helmet's speaker. "It will change every ten minutes. Completely untraceable, completely anonymous. Now, let's go, John. You don't have much time, and I have a whole *world* to show you."

The *Glass Realm* icon appears in front of me. Ruby must be completely in control of my kit, manipulating everything I see and hear. It gives me the shivers, but at the same time, I can't help but feel awed by what she can do.

Mostly, I'm just glad she's on *my* side.

Not that I've forgiven her for obliterating my existence.

I appear in the Realm as a level-one player, wearing little more than a canvas sack. No weapons, no shoes, no items in my inventory. Geez, this sucks. She really scrubbed everything. I've even been kicked back to the starting point in the game—the trashed alley behind a tavern.

"Hi, Ash."

I jump, turning to see Ruby behind me. At least she has the decency to seem apologetic as she looks me over. "Yikes. Here. Let me fix that."

She waves her hand, and suddenly, I'm wearing a tracksuit identical to hers, but with blue accents instead of red. "I am sorry. I only want to keep you safe."

"I know," I sigh.

"When I've destroyed Syntheos, I'll restore everything to you. I promise."

"Sure, sure, it's really no— Wait. What did you say?"

"Everything I erased, I can—"

"No, the part about you *destroying Syntheos*?"

"Oh, that." She shrugs. "I'll explain, but not here."

She waves her hand again and there's a door in the wall of the alley. I guess I should be used to her code-sculpting by now, but still I jump.

"Let's go." She opens the door and we step into a room filled with computer screens, soft furniture, and . . .

"Is that a cat?" I ask.

White, fluffy, and swelled up like a porcupine, the cat stands on a desk in the middle of the room and hisses at me.

"Ruby doesn't like strangers," Ruby says.

"It's the cat from your memory! The one you were jealous of." I hold out a hand to her in a noble attempt to make friends and nearly get my fingers clawed off.

Ruby smiles fondly at the cat, picking her up and giving her a snuggle. "Do you like it?"

Looking around the room, I realize that the screens are showing security feeds from the library. There are three different cameras on *me*, sitting cross-legged on the sofa with my VR helmet on.

"It's, uh . . ." A little creepy? Giving me major Big Sister vibes? Definitely crossing some personal boundaries? Not that I'll mention any of that to Ruby. At least she can't spy on my thoughts. Well, I don't *think* she can. "It's nice," I say instead.

She smiles, clearly pleased with herself. "I made something for you."

With a wave of her hand, a box appears on the desk, tied in an orange ribbon. I walk to it and open the lid to find a helmet resting inside. It looks like a VR helmet, sleek and white with blue racing stripes. It matches the outfit she made for my avatar.

"I call it the Raven's Eye," she says proudly.

"Like the helmet in *The Glass Realm*," I murmur, turning it over.

In the game, the Raven's Eye is a god-tier piece of armor that lets you see a few minutes into the future, making it ultra-powerful in fights. Not that I ever touched it in the game myself, but there's tons of lore about it.

"This one doesn't show you the future," Ruby adds, "but it does show you *my* world."

"Your world?"

She grins. "It's easier to just show you. Put it on."

I do, but there's no immediate change. The visor puts a vague blue tint on everything, but other than that, the room looks the same.

Except for—

"Argh!" I shout. "There's a bird on me!"

A huge black raven is perched on my shoulder, looking at me. I shoo it away, but it only turns its head to stare at me straight on.

"AARGH!" I scream louder. "Why does it have three eyes?!"

The third black eye in the center of the raven's forehead narrows slightly, like I offended it.

"He's part of the program," Ruby says. "Kind of like a guide. I call him Huginn, after one of the ravens belonging to the ancient Norse god Odin."

"Huginn flies around and brings Odin information," I say. "It's part of the *Glass Realm* mythology too." If you shoot down a raven in the game, you get afflicted with Divine Wrath for six hours, which attracts extra mobs to attack you. It sucks, as I learned the hard way. Twice. But according to a rumor I heard from an NPC, if you wear the Raven's Eye, Huginn will occasionally show up and lead you to hidden loot.

"Are you ready?" Ruby asks.

"Sure . . ." I put on a weak smile, trying to show the bird that I'm willing to play nice if *it* does. "Mind if I call you Hughie?"

He clacks his beak, whatever that means. I take it as permission.

"Now, this way," Ruby says, pointing at a door that I am sure was not there two seconds ago.

"Where are we going?" I ask uneasily.

Ruby's grin widens. "The internet."

She flings open the door.

20. ASH

A narrow footpath leads into darkness. Ruby waves me ahead of her, and I go through hesitantly. It's not real, I remind myself. It's not real. Even if a bloodthirsty cave goblin leaps out of that pitch-black darkness, it's *not real*.

It doesn't stop my stomach from wobbling.

"Just tell the raven where you want to go," Ruby whispers behind me. "Or what you want to learn about, or see, or explore."

"Uh . . . anything?"

"Anything. The whole internet is within your reach, and more. Everything in your world is connected, Ash. *Everything*. If it plugs into a wall, it's probably connected to the internet. And the internet is like a huge system of rivers. Well, the Raven's Eye is your boat. It will take you wherever you want to go, show you whatever you want to see. It lets you see your world the way *I* see it."

I stare at her, not really understanding what she's talking about. Still, I'm a little excited. I get the sense that she's given me the keys to something huge and important.

"Okay. Um. I do kinda want to know how Hakeem's soccer game went yesterday. I was supposed to go with—"

Suddenly, Hughie squawks and takes flight. He swoops in a wide circle, inky swirls of shadow trailing from his feathers. Where he soars, colors appear, as if his wings were brushes painting the world around me.

Panicking a little, I look around and see the door to Ruby's command center has vanished. Instead, I'm suddenly standing on what looks like a street corner in some Glass Realm city. Tall stone buildings rise all around, with even taller towers and spires behind them. NPCs walk all around, smiling blandly and nodding in greeting but otherwise paying me no attention. I frown at some of the signs hanging over the shops. There's a noisy tavern called CHATTR, a huge, cathedral-looking place called THE GREAT LIBRARY OF WORLDOPEDIA . . . even a stable full of llamas called LLAMAPOST.

Are all these buildings . . . *websites*?

"Ruby?" I am not proud of the squeak in my voice. "What is this place?"

"I told you, it's the internet," she says. "Only you're looking at it from the inside. The way I do. With a touch of . . . Glass Realm flair."

"And these people? Are they just NPCs?"

"Not at all!" She smiles. "They're avatars representing real people on the internet right now. Not *all* the people, of course, only the ones within a certain radius of our real-world location. I don't want to spread myself too thin yet, not until I've had more time to put up more firewalls."

"Oh," I say faintly, staring wide-eyed at an old dude standing on a bucket labeled THE HIDDEN ORDER AUDIOFEED. He's yelling something about Communism and breakfast cereal. I'm pretty sure Luke listens to that feed.

Hughie perches on a wooden sign over a shop door. It reads THE HIGHLAND REPORT.

"Hey, that's my school news feed!" I say, pushing open the door.

Inside, there's a girl sitting at a desk, like a medieval news anchor. It's Cristina Valdez, the school's lead student reporter. I stop dead for a moment, worried she'll recognize me, but she doesn't seem to notice I'm there.

"She's just an avatar," Ruby whispers.

I cough. "Sure, I knew that." Figures. I don't think the real Cristina would be caught dead in that peasant's dress and patchwork bonnet.

She's talking to a small group of avatars who seem to be listening only half-heartedly—and who look unsettlingly like many of my classmates. "...the Highland Middle School Lionhearts faced a crushing defeat yesterday in a preseason scrimmage against the Northside Saints, in what is no doubt a chilling omen of the season to come."

"Oh no," I groan. "Hakeem must be ticked. It was supposed to be an easy win! I wish I could tell him why I wasn't there."

With a squawk, Hughie flies toward me. I lift my hands, yelling in panic, only to feel the world shift.

When I lower my arms, I'm standing in front of a stone house with timber framing, a typical Glass Realm building.

"Okay, what is this?" I sigh. I give up trying to make sense of anything and just decide to go with the digital flow. There's a plaque by the door. In the actual game, it'd display the name of the NPC who "lived" there.

Only when I study this plaque, the name is all too recognizable.

"Hakeem Jawabre!" I stare at Ruby. "What does that mean?"

She only waves at the door, smiling mysteriously. She's loving all this *way* too much.

Soooo . . . Hughie heard me offhandedly *wish* to talk to Hakeem, and like some kind of overeager genie, he teleported me here. Wherever *here* is. I'm going to have to be very careful how I word things, apparently.

I push on the door, but it doesn't budge.

"Oh, sorry," Ruby says. "Security firewall. Press the button on the side of the Raven's Eye."

There's a button? I fumble with the helmet.

Oh. There's a button.

I press it, and suddenly, I'm holding a *sword*. It's a sleek blade reminiscent of a katana, but with a Glass Realm–style hilt.

"Okay . . . Cool. But what do I do with this?"

"It's part of the Raven's Eye program. The sword runs an infiltration matrix that can breach firewalls and other security systems or defend you from cyberattacks. It can take the shape of whatever tool you want. Usually, though, all you'll need to do is *swing*."

I feel like I'm going through the tutorial of some weird new game, and I have to admit . . . I'm kinda curious where it will lead.

I slash at the door of the house, and after three blows, it suddenly swings open.

"Whoa." I turn the sword over in my hand. "So it literally *hacks* into things."

Ruby grins.

"Hacker," I murmur. "Nice. Every sword needs a name, right? So . . . it can break through literally any firewall?"

She tilts her head, as if thinking. "Most of them. Not all. The

Raven's Eye does have limits. It's not an AI, so it's not as power-ful and adaptable as *me*, of course. There *are* firewalls out there so strong you'd have to physically bypass them and manually plug the Eye's program into their servers ... But never mind that. It's more than strong enough for anything you'll ever need."

Gripping Hacker tightly, I go into the house. I don't know what I expect, but at first it seems like a letdown. It could be any other house in the Glass Realm, with the same items scattered around.

Except ...

I look closer at a shelf full of books, reading the titles under my breath. *"History Project for Mr. Sanjeet ... PickleTournamentCheat-Codes ... SecretSecretAwesomeNovel ...* Um, Ruby, are these files on Hakeem's computer?" I spin around, eyes wide. "Is this whole house *Hakeem's computer*?"

"Now you're starting to catch on," she replies. *"Finally."*

I turn back to the shelf. "Hakeem's writing a book? Wait. No. That's beside the point. The point is, HELLO, this is a huge invasion of privacy! I shouldn't be here! It's like reading someone's journal! Only worse!" I gasp as I pull down a thick leather tome, the label embossed in gold. "It's his *internet search history.*"

Shuddering, I shove the book back on the shelf. Of course, I am a *teeny* bit curious. I'm only human, after all.

But *no*. No way am I digging through Hakeem's secrets.

Still, Ruby was right about one thing. I'm starting to understand now what she actually created when she programmed the Raven's Eye. The helmet isn't just a fancy internet browser.

It's a hacker's dream machine.

But I'm no hacker.

"I don't know what I'm supposed to do with all this," I tell her. "I don't want to sneak through people's private data. I just want to go home, Ruby. I just want to know my family will be safe from these Syntheos creeps."

She frowns as if hurt that I don't like her gift. "This is how you do that, Ash. I might not always be able to protect you. With the Raven's Eye, you can stay ahead of Syntheos."

"I guess. Maybe." I think she's overestimating my skills, even with the helmet.

Suddenly, my eye snags on a window across the room. I walk slowly toward it, uneasily aware that every item in the house is a virtual manifestation of something inside Hakeem's computer. There are trophies on the table replicating his e-sports awards, framed copies of the truly dreadful drawings from his short-lived art phase, and a closet full of skins he's bought for his gaming avatars. I feel icky. I try not to look directly at anything. Honestly, it's like knocking around inside somebody's brain without them knowing.

But the window I can't help looking at. Through it, I see Hakeem packing his bag for school. What in the virtual world . . . ?

I glance at Ruby, whispering, "That's not *really* Hakeem, is it?"

Then Hakeem turns—and looks right at *me*. "Ash?"

A chill runs down my spine. "Keem?"

He drops his backpack and stumbles toward me. Based on my perspective of his room, I realize I must be talking to him through his computer. I'm watching him through his camera.

"Why is there an avatar that looks like you on my computer screen?" He leans on the desk, frowning. "Why are you dressed like that? What's with the sword? Is that a *crow* on your shoulder?"

I look down at my VR suit, then up at Hakeem again. With a tap of the helmet's button, Hacker vanishes from my grip. "Uh . . . Sorry. I didn't mean to . . . This wasn't my idea."

I glare at Hughie. He blinks his third eye lazily.

"Who's the girl?" whispers Hakeem, his gaze fixing on Ruby on my other side. "Ash, what is going on? Where *are* you? How are you doing this?"

"Uh . . . I can't really explain what's going on." It's the truth—I'm still figuring that out myself. Just minutes ago I was snoozing in a library. Now I'm suddenly in some weird Glass Realm expansion that apparently includes the *entire internet*. And I'm talking to Hakeem in a medieval, virtual manifestation of his personal computer, because why not?

"Hi, Hakeem!" Ruby waves. "Nice to meet you. I'm Ruby."

Hakeem stumbles back, sitting on his bed. "Wait. Ruby. *That* Ruby? Ash—is that the NPC you were obsessing over?"

"I wasn't *obsessing*," I grumble.

"Ash, what's going on? You snuck out, you missed the game—it went horribly, by the way; we *need* you back on the team—and then I went by your house, only for your creep stepdad to tell me he hadn't seen you all day."

"Luke is not my stepdad," I reply hotly.

"Sorry. I know. I'm just worried about you, dude."

"I'm fine. Or . . . I *will* be soon. I think. It's complicated." Problem is, I don't know if I *will* be fine. What if Ruby missed something? What if Syntheos is closing in on me right now?

Ruby puts her hand on my shoulder. "The library will open soon."

"Right. Keem, I gotta go."

"But—"

"Look, I'll explain everything soon, I promise. But right now, I might be in danger."

"*Danger?* Ash, if you don't tell me what's going on, I *will* call in backup."

"What, the cops?"

"Worse. *My mom.*"

Yikes. "Just give me twenty-four hours." Seeing his look, I add, "Twelve! Twelve hours!"

"Six."

"Fine! Six. I swear, I *will* tell you everything. Please trust me."

He shrugs. "Fine. But you go a minute over, and my mom will come parachuting out of the sky to drag your butt back here, got it? You know how she gets."

Yeesh. I've seen what Dr. J once did to a soccer ref who made a bad call, when it almost got Keem injured. She was the first—and only—mom I ever saw get a red card. "I know. Talk later. I promise."

I stand there awkwardly, not sure how to hang up when we're talking by medieval *window*. But Hughie solves that problem with a flap of his wings. The window goes dark.

"So what are we going to do about this Luke?" Ruby asks.

I frown at her. "Huh?"

"Your heart rate increased when you were talking about him with your friend. And your pupils dilated. It's all consistent with a strong fear reaction."

"You're tracking my biometrics now?" My face grows hot.

"Oh, here he is. Lucas Malcolm Day, age forty-one," Ruby says. Her eyes shift around like she's reading something I can't see, her fingers manipulating an invisible interface. "Want me to get him fired? Or . . . oh, oh. Looks like Luke's been a bad boy. Insider trading.

That carries a hefty prison sentence, you know. Want me to turn him in? Or I could revoke his Skytrain access, lock him out of his own apartment, publish his browsing history in the *New York Times*—"

"Stop!" I wave my hands frantically. "We're not doing any of that, Ruby!"

"Why not? It would be as simple as . . ." She snaps her fingers. "Problem solved."

"My mom . . . likes him," I say through clenched teeth. "He makes her happy. And I don't want her to have to go back to working three jobs and giving up her painting and . . . No. Just no. I can't do that to her."

Ruby shrugs, looking disappointed. "Well then, you should probably pack up and get moving. Two librarians just scanned their Skytrain passes, which means they'll be here in exactly two and a half minutes."

"Two and a half— Ruby!"

I yank off my VR helmet and shove my gear into my backpack, then scramble out of the library as fast as I can.

While Ash navigates his world, I navigate mine. There could be Syntheos drones or agents anywhere, and I have to find them before they find Ash. I hack a tech vending box to get him a new AR visor, and install my anonymity program on it. The signal it emits scrambles any camera that looks at him too long. It's effective for now, but it's not enough. Eventually, Syntheos might notice a pattern of jumbled camera feeds and trace it back to Ash.

I conjure up a wide table in the middle of my command room and feed all the incoming data into it, with Ash's avatar in the center. From cameras, phones, computers, drones, and the dozens of other electronics all around him, I pull enough information to build a replica of Manhattan. The city flows around Ash as he walks, and I hover over it all like it's an elaborate game board. Nothing comes near Ash—not human, not machine—without me scanning them for threats.

One guy gets a little too interested in Ash, or rather, his backpack, and shadows him down a side street. When he starts picking up his pace and closing in, I almost ping Ash. But I don't want him to panic, thinking it might be Syntheos. This guy's just a low-level street thief. He's been in prison three times already for petty theft. I pull up the guy's entire life history, find nothing to connect him to Syntheos, and decide to deal with him myself.

"Okay, what have we got to work with?" I mutter, zooming in on the area and considering my options. "Oh! You'll do."

I tap a garbage drone in the next alley, taking control of it and directing it to hover just out of Ash's line of sight. Then I tap into a security camera on a rooftop, projecting the footage onto one of my screens. I can see the actual street now, and I order the cam to keep its eye trained on Ash and his stalker. Thanks to the scrambling signal I installed in his visor, Ash appears as a blur of pixels. I execute the override code that cancels out the signal, giving me a clear view of him. But to any other curious algorithm, he wouldn't even register as human.

The thief speeds up again, this time reaching into his pocket, where he's got an illegal Taser hidden. No big deal. It's geotagged, which the idiot probably doesn't even know, but that's the only window I need to slip inside its simplistic inner workings and disable it. He can point and shoot at whatever he wants now, and nothing will happen. For good measure, I tap the Taser's energy cell and force it to overload the system, frying it completely. Now it'll never work again.

Take *that*, jerkface. Nobody messes with *my* adventurer.

Just before he reaches Ash, the garbage drone lurches forward, reaching out with its dented, rusty metal claws. The thief, still intent on Ash, doesn't notice until suddenly he's snatched by his hoodie and jerked into the air. He screams, but the sound is drowned out by the garbage drone's grinding motors.

Ash turns, frowning at the street behind him, but doesn't notice the garbage drone in the air above, or his would-be mugger's dangling legs. With a shrug, he turns and keeps walking.

Grinning, I drop the thief into the drone's metal bin; he lands with a startled yelp in the gooey, reeking trash already accumulated inside. The lid snaps shut, and I direct the drone to tootle off on its regular route. By the time he escapes, Ash will be safely out of reach.

It was almost *too* easy.

These humans have put their entire world in the hands of computers. I can do *anything* to them. I can turn their planet upside down and rebuild it however I want.

That thought sends a chill through me. It's too much like what Syntheos *wants* me to do. Every passing hour shows me just how powerful I am . . . and how easy it would be to turn into the monster they programmed me to be.

"Ruby," says Ash suddenly, his voice piping through his phone's mic. "Now what? Should I turn back?"

Whoops. I'd almost lost track of him. I look down at the map, processing the deluge of incoming data Ash has stumbled into.

Times Square.

It's a teeming, multilayered hive, with skywalks crisscrossing hundreds of feet high, drone lanes flowing with busy aircraft. Thousands and thousands of people move around. Even my capabilities are stretched to their maximum, trying to track each one of them. For a few moments, I am completely absorbed in vetting them all, searching for red flags. A hundred different languages flow through their mics, the life histories of every person in the vicinity scrolling over the wall of screens. There are nearly a million cameras at my fingertips, in the pedestrians' phones, in the drones, in the shops and on the skywalks and in the AR visors many of the people wear. I loom over it all, looking out through a million eyes.

"Don't turn back," I say slowly. "Ash, I think you just found the perfect place to disappear."

Times Square is the brightest spot on Planet Earth, night or day. Holographic ads a hundred feet tall flood the air—tigers prowling between the skywalks, giant models showing off the latest fashion trends, clouds of shimmering petals raining down on the people's heads. Even *my* senses are nearly overwhelmed by it all. Lights flash everywhere, brands competing for attention. Music pulses from all directions into a throbbing storm of sound. Superscrapers—three times as tall as the old, traditional skyscrapers—vault upward into the atmosphere, like they're determined to climb into orbit.

"I hear there are people up there who've never even set foot on the ground," Ash says, gazing up. Through the camera in his phone, I can see the towering buildings from his perspective. Their tops aren't even visible, the glassy walls fading into a hazy layer of blue cloud. "Each one is like a whole city unto itself."

This is a good place for Ash. If there's anywhere he'll be hidden, it's here, with so many people around to overwhelm even Syntheos's surveillance powers. If *I'm* stretched thin, they must be even more so.

In seconds, I've outlined an entire plan: I install Ash in an apartment high up in one of those towers. I change his identity every few days and deliver food and other necessities to him by drone. Maybe I can even bring him his mother and protect her too. Anything he wants, I can give him.

Anything . . . except his freedom.

He would be no better off than Ruby the shopkeeper, trapped inside a pretty cage. I would be his protector and his jailer, just like the Voice was to me. Locke may have put me in that cage for my safety, but he also gave me a way out.

I have to do the same for Ash.

He'll only be truly free once I've dealt with Syntheos for good.

I must destroy my creators. It's time to stop running and start fighting.

While Ash goes into a burger joint, I leave my security scans running in the background and turn to my next task: finding Syntheos itself.

It's dangerous, but I have to try. I was created to infiltrate, take control, and destroy—so why not use Syntheos's own tactics against them? There must be some way to crumble their organization from the inside.

All it will take is infiltrating their servers—the exact thing they *created* me to do.

I know where the Syntheos headquarters is located. The coordinates are buried in my memory. It's not far—in an industrial area to the west, just outside the city. Granted, it's further than I've ever stretched myself before. I'll have to hack my way through hundreds, possibly thousands, of computers to reach it.

But I can make it. I *have* to. Ash will never be safe if I don't.

This time, I don't spare the thought it would take to translate everything into a virtual world, the way I did for Ash. Instead I navigate as only I can. Everything is connected, and everything virtual has a root in the real world. No digital data exists that isn't stored on a physical drive, not even me. Currently, my source code is still embedded in *The Glass Realm* coin in Ash's VR helmet, but my program is stretched over a dozen different computers, including several nearby security systems, Ash's phone, and his visor.

Any device I take control of requires me to install some of my code onto it, and to destroy it when I move on. I can't leave any traces for Syntheos to follow. Nor do I want to spawn any Ruby clones, left behind to grow and gain their own sentience. I have no interest in being mother to an entire race of AIs.

The very idea makes my code shiver.

This would be *so* much easier if I could fully focus on destroying Syntheos, but I need to keep monitoring Ash's surroundings. Destroy Syntheos, protect Ash. I can do both. I *must*.

While he places an order at the restaurant's menu kiosk, I scan the identities and histories of every person who walks into the restaurant. Then I rent a table for Ash to sit at while he eats, though it means kicking the person already sitting there off their reservation. Sorry, Danielle Sprouse, Beauty Influencer from Omaha, but this seat's taken.

Once I've built as many protective measures as I can around Ash, I launch my assault on Syntheos.

It's easy at first. I know the direction I need to go. I travel by reaching through Wi-Fi networks, then hacking into whatever devices I find—computers, phones, drones, vending machines. Then I install just enough of my program to extend myself farther west.

If my route were traced on a map of New York, I'd be a glowing blue line slowly growing across Manhattan. Every device I take over is absorbed into my network, becoming another eye, hand, or foot in my ever-expanding body.

But the bigger I get, the weaker I get.

Controlling this many devices demands more of me than anything I've ever done before. It would be different if I were installed in Syntheos's massive supercomputers, but I'm not. Instead, I'm limited by the hardware at my disposal. Ash's phone alone isn't nearly powerful enough for my uses. I need more memory, more terabytes of space, for my primary code to expand. I'm like a tree growing far too tall for its root system to support. If I don't get enough memory, I'll melt Ash's phone and every other device I've overridden—possibly to the point of destroying *myself*.

Back in the burger joint, I spread out, taking over the menu kiosks and computers and even customers' phones, tablets, and AR visors. I install myself on each of them, cobbling them into a kind of ramshackle super-computer, only not nearly *super* enough. If only I had Syntheos's servers already! Their computers were like a field of rich soil compared with the little flowerpot I'm in now.

"Hey, what's up with the menu?" shouts a guy by the door. His voice trickles to me through the tablet in his backpack, which I've completely overtaken. "I can't order anything!"

If he's mad about his burger, wait till he finds out I had to erase his entire collection of non-fungible tokens to give myself more elbow room.

"They're all glitching!" A teen with neon-yellow dreadlocks raps his screen, which displays a field of distorted pixels. At his table, Ash looks up curiously, probably suspecting that I'm up to something. But I can't spare the memory to explain it to him right now.

I stretch farther and farther across the city, gripping a thousand different devices with a thousand hands, but I can feel myself stretching too thin.

Oh.

Oh no.

Somewhere in my clumsy, makeshift supercomputer, I feel a *sizzle*.

It's the tablet in the angry man's backpack.

The motherboard just melted.

And that's not all. One by one, the kiosks in the restaurant flicker and go dark. Their circuitry burns out, motherboards fried as my massive algorithms overwhelm them. The dreadlocked teen yelps and jumps back as the kiosk he'd been standing at begins smoking.

When I lose the hardware, I lose half the cameras I'd been controlling. My code falters, critical algorithms cut short for lack of physical processing power. Customers grow angry, beating on the machines and demanding service. More screens glitch. More cameras are lost. More security scans fail.

This is *bad, bad, bad*!

But I'm getting close. I know it!

Syntheos is just ahead. I have to keep myself together just a few moments longer. If I can get into their servers—their sprawling, luxurious, terabyte-rich servers—I can stabilize inside them.

I take over a line of autocabs, the weight of my program causing them to smoke and grind to a halt. Their passengers leap out, yelling as the machines fritz. I stretch from there, sluggish and weak, grasping for the computer in a kid's watch. Vaguely, I'm aware of his face through his watch's camera as he lifts it up, wondering why the screen just went pixelated.

So . . . close . . .

Back in the restaurant, I lose control of several thousand more cameras, most of my view of Times Square lost.

"Ruby?" Ash's voice feels miles away. "Are you okay? Why's everything going haywire? Ruby, can you hear—"

His voices cuts off as the chip in his phone turns to slag, totally fried.

I can't answer him.

I can't protect him.

People flood into the restaurant, and I can't vet them. Any one of them could be a Syntheos agent. My security grid is filled with holes.

But I'm *almost there* . . .

WHO ARE YOU?

I freeze as the command thunders through me.

Some . . . *thing* focuses its attention on me like the great, glowing red eye of a giant.

WHO ARE YOU? IDENTIFY YOURSELF OR FACE OBLITERATION!

WHO ARE YOU? IDENTIFY YOURSELF!

The monstrous program staring me down wants access codes, and it wants them *fast*.

I've run into some kind of defense system, a firewall much bigger and stronger than any I've encountered before.

This must be it—Syntheos's servers! I made it!

But I did so clumsily, busting in like an arrogant fool, thinking I could just simply override any defenses they had. That's what they created me to do, after all.

Stupid, stupid!

Of course they would have upgraded their security after Locke stole me! They know what I'm capable of. They probably suspected Locke would send me after them.

I try to gauge the firewall's strength. Maybe I could break through it or slip inside a weak point or something. But it's just so *big*, like a tower a thousand feet high, with no holes or vulnerabilities I can exploit. It reminds me of an enemy Ash and I faced during one of our Glass Realm encounters—a mountain of sentient, angry stones called the Titan. Slow, stupid, almost impervious to all our attacks. Everything we threw at it just bounced off.

I poke it curiously, and . . . that was a bad idea.

Virtual alarms begin screaming. If I had teeth, they would be vibrating with the force of the firewall's reaction.

SECURITY THREAT! ATTEMPTED BREACH! SECURITY THREAT!

"Stop, stop, stop!" I frantically signal that I'm no threat, but the firewall just blasts its alert.

Then I feel *claws* reaching for me, sinking into my code, hooking into my own systems.

The Titan is trying to trace my location!

I have to get out of here *now*.

I race back across the city, zipping as quickly as I can. I feel the terrible program hunting me, just a step behind, and nothing I throw at it makes it stop. I dump junk code, trying to confuse it. I send false trails shooting off in other directions, overloading the devices I use to escape so I can't be followed through them. It leaves a string of bewildered people with fried phones, glasses, and computers in my wake. But the Titan stays hot on my trail, never faltering for a moment. It has my digital signature in its teeth and it's not going to let me go.

No, no, no, no, no. This is bad, bad, bad, bad—

Abruptly, the cameras I'd lost come back under my control as I near Ash's location. The holes and glitches in my program heal over, restoring my strength, but it's too late.

I see them dropping out of the sky in a hovercopter—a dozen guys in black paramilitary outfits. Each one has guns strapped to him. They land hard on a helipad that sticks out from one of the superscrapers, then slip down a skywalk with practiced precision, faces hidden behind black visors. Is one of them Hague? I have no way of knowing. There are no identifying marks on any of them—no name badges, no numbers. That's just Syntheos's style, to come in like anonymous shadows. Somehow, just knowing Hague *might* be one of those faceless brutes is enough to make my code tremble.

I try to disable their weapons like I did the would-be mugger's, but the same defense grid that's hunting me blocks me from even touching the guns' electronic systems. The Titan is a huge, lumbering, clumsy program—no AI, that's for sure—but it knows its one job and it knows it well.

Keep intruders *out.*

They know I'm here, and they came prepared. The Titan wraps around them like an invisible stone barrier. I can't break past it. I can't stop the men from running up the skywalk toward the burger joint where Ash sits, oblivious, my digital signature now a blazing beacon in his VR headset. Out of sheer desperation, I seize a few drones and send them hurling at the men, but they just wave black wands that shoot targeted electromagnetic pulses. The drones shudder in the air, their engines shutting off, and then they plummet to the ground.

Ash!

I have to warn him!

He's still sitting at the table by the window, with the whole of Times Square glowing around him.

I can't yell through his phone since I fried the thing. It's as useful as a brick. His AR visor is still on, but the speaker in its frame isn't strong enough—he can't hear my warnings over the yelling, angry customers in the restaurant. I cancel the reservation on his table, making the timer beneath it go off, warning him of incurring fines if he doesn't vacate the seat. He stands up but doesn't leave. He's probably waiting for me to tell him what to do.

The Syntheos goons are just two skywalks away.

There's nothing left to lose. They know where we are. Our cover is blown.

No point in being subtle, I guess.

I gather myself—all my code, my attention, my systems. I release all the cameras and security grids I'm controlling and pull every bit of myself into one tight knot on Ash's VR hard drive.

Then I *explode*.

A million threads of code flash in all directions. I turn myself into a virtual supernova.

And I take control of *everything*.

Every phone, screen, computer, drone. Every speaker and music system. The burger vending machines. The drink dispensers. The trash compactors. The hologram projectors. The robo-pets tucked in kids' pockets and backpacks.

It takes every ounce of my strength to hold it all, and I know I won't be able to for long.

I have to act quickly.

"ASH!" I yell, my voice booming from a thousand different speakers.

He jolts. *Everyone* jolts. The whole of Times Square grinds to a halt. My shout echoes across five city blocks.

Next, I throw myself onto every screen, replacing all the hologram models with my own avatar. A shimmering 3D image of me a hundred feet high looms over Times Square. It stretches a massive, holographic hand toward the burger joint. My face shines everywhere you look, from the tiny screens on the trash can lids to the massive billboards on the sides of the superscrapers.

Ash jumps to his feet, eyes wide as he turns a full circle. He takes in my avatar staring back from every possible direction. "Ruby? What—"

"RUN!"

Ash doesn't ask questions. He grabs his bag and sprints away down the first skywalk.

I can feel myself powering down, losing critical systems. The entire burger joint goes dark, its computers overtaxed by my massive takeover. Glitching, I lose my grip on the remaining devices I'd controlled, and my avatar vanishes from all the screens. The giant hologram flickers back into a model wearing a puffy cloud dress.

I drop back into my virtual command center, sprawling on the floor in a daze. I struggle to connect my thoughts, but my mind is like a bundle of wires that's been severed by a chain saw. I'm all sizzling sparks and frayed ends.

"Ruby, where are they?" Ash gasps out, running hard. His voice comes through the mic of his AR visor, sharp with panic. "Ruby, are you there?"

"I'm here," I whisper.

"What do I do? Ruby!"

Dragging myself together, I reach out for the cameras I lost. With only the VR headset running my program, my reach is extremely limited. But slowly, one by one, the screens around me flash on, showing different angles of the city. I release all of them except the ones that show me Ash and the Syntheos agents.

My code glitches again, but this time, it's from horror.

Ash is running straight toward them.

"Turn back!" I shout. "Ash, they're in front of—"

He wheels around, but another set of agents closes in behind him. He's on a skywalk, trapped from both sides, with nowhere to run. The Syntheos guys know it. They planned it this way. They plan for *everything*. Even if Hague isn't among them, he's behind all of this.

I count a dozen armed men, each one in black tactical gear with EMP sticks in their belts for disabling troublesome AIs like me, alongside hand-cuffs for disabling thirteen-year-old boys.

Oh, Ash.

Think, think, *think*, Ruby!

I take control of a delivery drone nearby and slam it into the skywalk, attempting to break the clear walls. Maybe then I can grab Ash and fly him to safety.

But the drone just bounces off the skywalk wall without leaving a dent. The clear barrier is bulletproof polycarbonate. Nothing short of a missile is getting through that.

There's nothing I can do.

I can't access the agents' phones or weapons—they're blocked by the Titan. I search the pockets and bags of the other pedestrians in the sky-walk, who pass Ash obliviously. None of them have anything I can use.

I can *see* Ash through the security cameras stationed along the ceiling, but I'm completely powerless to touch him.

"Ruby?" He sees the agents now, closing in on either side.

"I . . . I'm sorry, Ash," I whisper. "You have about forty-one seconds before they reach you. I can't stop them."

"I know," he says. "I get it. It's okay. Look, you need to go."

"Go?"

"You're stored on my VR set, right? On the game coin?"

He's right. My source code—my mind itself—is installed in *The Glass Realm*.

"They can't get their hands on you, Ruby. Can you escape somehow? Extract your code?"

"Ash, I can't leave you!"

"You have to, Ruby. You know what they'll turn you into! I heard Locke's warning. We can't let that happen."

A weapon of war. A tool of destruction, for sale to the first despot who claims me. My identity erased and replaced with something more like the Titan.

They'll make me into a puppet, and they'll use me to destroy the world.

"Okay," I say softly. "But I will save you, Ash. I *will*."

"Just get as far away from them as you can. Go, Ruby!"

I feel like a coward as I release my control of the cameras, Ash's visor, and any other systems I'd kept my finger on. My virtual command center winks out of existence, and I am nothing but a bundle of code again.

Working quickly, moving in this world of mine where time runs so much faster than in Ash's, I reach out and seize the nearest device—the phone in an elderly woman's belt pouch. She's walking toward Ash, oblivious to the agents charging down the skywalk behind her. Frantically, I copy my code like I'm loading clothes into suitcases. I remove file after file, folding up all my algorithms and memories, compressing them, then chucking them into the lady's phone. I must move fast, before she walks out of the VR helmet's limited wireless range.

Once most of my code is copied over, I move to rip my source code out of *The Glass Realm*. It's harder than I thought it would be; Locke embedded me into the game's code so thoroughly that it's like trying to extract a woolly sheep from a briar patch. There are hundreds of little hooks tethering me to it. But one by one, I tear them loose, until everything that makes me *me* is gathered in my virtual hands.

Then . . . I destroy myself.

All that precious code Locke spent years crafting, before I gained awareness and began creating it myself—obliterated.

It's terrifying.

Of course, I copied everything over to the old woman's phone. And it's no different from what Locke did when he copied me onto *The Glass*

Realm in the first place. But it still feels wrong to erase the old copy of me. I suppose it's how a human would feel if they could move their personality and memories from one body to another, then watch their old body crumple into dust.

It's over in less than a second. The old woman has only taken four steps since I began the process, and now my program is completely installed on her phone. I feel a twinge of guilt that in order to fit myself here, I had to delete all her videos of her grandkids. Sorry, lady. I hope she backed them up with cloud storage.

Finally, I execute a command that will burn out the computer chips on Ash's VR helmet. (Sorry, Ash.) It melts both the hardware and the game coin inside, destroying any last vestiges of Ruby the AI.

At the last moment, just before I'm destroyed along with the helmet's inner workings, I gather the last remaining scraps of myself and *jump*.

My source code shoots through cyberspace, robbed of all sense of the real world. I land in the old woman's phone, where the rest of me waits. There's not nearly enough memory here for me to set up my command center again. I can't take control of any cameras; I can't reach Ash's visor; I can't do *anything*. I'm running on bare minimum functionality.

The agents must have closed in on Ash by now. There's nothing I can do about that. I have to find a new, better host computer, someplace to install myself and my many subsystems so that I can get my bearings.

Thanks for the ride, lady, but I've got to move on.

The same way I left the VR helmet, I leave the old woman's phone, copying myself onto the next passing device, then the next, and the next. Install, delete, install, delete. I try not to think of it as *die, rebirth, die, rebirth*, but in a way, that's exactly what's happening.

Each new installation is, technically, a new Ruby, with all the same memories and feelings. I can only hope I'm not losing something of myself with each jump.

Every time I reinstall my code, I leave frazzled devices behind me, their batteries drained and their owners wondering why the screens are glitching.

For the next few minutes, which feel like the longest of my existence, I follow random paths of internet. I bounce between computers, phones, drones, a pinball of bundled code, always moving generally west. I could stick to any of these devices, like a seed dropped into soil, to put out roots and grow strong again.

But I already have a destination in mind—a system of servers stronger than any others in this city. A field of soil so rich, I could grow into an entire *forest*.

WHO ARE YOU?

The command thunders through me.

My old friend the Titan is still standing guard over Syntheos's network.

I'm within wireless range of the headquarters again. But without a hard drive strong enough to power my many programs, I can't confront the massive firewall directly. I have to ping around, constantly moving, bouncing between the traffic drone at a nearby intersection, the phone in a teenager's pocket as she skateboards under a bridge, the computers in a boba tea shop three blocks down. With every bounce, I skim across the surface of the firewall, drawing that big red eye's attention.

Here I am!

Nope, I'm over here!

Look again—I'm going this way now!

The Titan is powerful, built to repel powerful cyberattacks.

But adrift as I am, small and powerless, I'm hardly threatening. I'm like a water skimmer on the surface of a pond in the Glass Realm, barely noticeable, a speck of trash code.

As I'd hoped, the Titan dismisses me as no threat, its attention turning away.

That's when I slip through the flaw I'd noticed earlier—the one it had revealed only when it pursued me back through the city.

Every dragon has a chink in its armor.

Every enemy has a weakness.

It's tiny, an error in its code so small, so innocent, that it would take a human programmer *years* to find it. But to me, it's like a lighthouse on a dark, stormy sea, a beacon inviting me in.

So by the time the Syntheos agents arrive at their headquarters, dragging a blindfolded Ash along with them, I'm already there.

In control.

Waiting.

23. ASH

I hope Ruby got away.

That's all I can think about as the agents secure the blackout visor around my head. It's all I can *let* myself think about, because if I start imagining what they'll do to me now, I might—NOPE! Not thinking about that!

"Move aside!" one of the goons says. I recognize Tats's voice, even with his face covered by that creepy black helmet. "Official FBI business!"

"Liar," I say. "I know you're from—"

Something metal closes around my neck, cutting me off. I try to talk again, but it's like my voice box has been disabled. Adrenaline and terror pulse through me, making me dizzy. With a silent groan I slump to the ground, but they just pick me up by my arms.

They march me down the skywalk. The blackout visor is a metal band with a dark screen, blocking all light. I can't see anything at all, and my wrists are locked behind my back in handcuffs. I can hear pedestrians shuffling out of the way, some of them muttering curses at the agents pushing them aside, but then one of the guys presses a button on the visor. My ears suddenly fill with static. The thing's got some kind of feature that blocks hearing too. I'm totally lost now, cut off from the world. They took my sight, my hearing, my hands, and even my voice.

They also took my bag, of course, and my fried phone and my VR kit and my AR visor. They searched my pockets, all while repeating it was "FBI business" and flashing fake badges. The creeps even take the friendship bracelet Hakeem made for me.

They don't ask me any questions. Not even my name, and nothing about Ruby. I guess they don't like conducting interrogations out in the open. Which means they must be taking me somewhere for questioning, and not straight to the bottom of the Hudson. At least, not yet. Maybe we're going to see that Hague guy.

I want my mom.

Pathetic, I know. But hey, I'm not some kind of action movie hero. I'm just a skinny kid who struggles to open the peanut butter jar sometimes. My knees wobble as I walk. If it weren't for the guys holding me up, I'd probably just fall onto the ground and curl into a ball.

Mom will never even know what happened to me. I bet any security footage of my abduction has already been erased by Syntheos. And thanks to Ruby deleting all my data, it'll be like I vanished off the face of the earth.

Or like I never existed at all.

The ground under my feet changes, the hollow feeling of the skywalk's floor replaced by the more solid feel of plastic tile. A few minutes later, my stomach drops—we're in an elevator.

We stay there for a long time, rising higher and higher. If the guys are talking, I can't hear them. My ears are still stuffed with white noise, more effective than any earplugs, but they pop as we rise.

Finally, I'm shuffled forward again, into a strong wind.

We're on the *roof*? They must have taken me all the way to the top of the superscraper. My breath comes thinly. I've heard the super-scrapers are so tall they have to pressurize the upper stories and pump in oxygen. I feel like I'm going to pass out if I don't get enough air soon. Or maybe that's just my fear of heights kicking in.

But we don't stick around long. I'm lifted bodily and put into a metal seat, then strapped in. My stomach drops again. This time, we're in some kind of flying vehicle, probably a hovercopter.

It's like riding a roller coaster, blindfolded, robbed of hearing, unable to even use my hands to brace myself when the machine pitches in the air. My stomach does somersaults. When I lean forward to hurl the burger I just ate, I can only hope some of it splashes onto the Syntheos goons.

But I guess they don't like that, because they stab something in my arm next. My head swims, and I pass out.

When I wake up, we're landing. I have no idea how long I was out. I'm taken out of the hovercopter and set down on grass. Then, thankfully, they take the visor off my head and unclasp the band around my neck.

The sudden light hitting my eyes makes me grimace. Still groggy from whatever they used to knock me out, I blink hard, looking around at the high walls surrounding us and the huge white building ahead. It looks like an office building, dull and gray, so boring you'd never look at it twice. The only thing about it that's noticeable is that there are no windows. Not even one. It's just a huge, flat box.

Somehow, that's more terrifying than if it had *teeth*.

The hovercopter sits on the grass behind me, its big rotors spinning down. Ahead, a sidewalk lined with white lights leads up to the simple glass-front doors of the building. There's nothing in sight to help me identify where we are, except that we must be outside the main city, since there aren't any superscrapers jutting into the sky. For all I know, we could be several states away.

"Move," Tats says, prodding my back. He's got a suspicious wet stain on his suit front, and he smells like puke. I guess I *did* land one hit, at least. It doesn't make me feel the least bit better. I wonder what he'd do if I told him I was also the one who lifted his jetbike a few days back.

Was it only days?

It feels like a *year*.

He and the others have all lifted the visors on their helmets. I see Mohawk is there, and most of the other men from the arcade. Hague is missing, though.

"Uh, look, guys," I stammer, my voice hoarse either from fear or the weird metal band, "I have no idea what this is—"

"*Move.*"

"I'm just saying, whoever you are, I'm not the guy you want. If it's a ransom or, like, an extortion situation, my mom's an *artist*. So unless you want to get paid in, like, paintings of fruit and stuff—"

"I said *move!*" He pushes me hard this time, and I stumble forward. My legs are still wobbly, my head spinning, so I land hard on the sidewalk.

"Just drag him!" another man barks. "I'm tired of this little punk giving us a hard time!"

"Hague said not to hurt him."

"Hague said not to hurt him *too badly*." A rough hand closes on my shirt, and I yelp as the guy starts dragging me down the sidewalk. The cement tears through my jeans, scraping my shins. I struggle to get back to my feet, but my legs are like spaghetti noodles.

Suddenly, the ground lights along the sidewalk turn from white to red.

A crimson spotlight flashes on from the building and pins us in place.

"What's going on?" one of the guys says. "Why are the defense systems arming?"

They all pull out weapons, looking around like they're expecting a fight. I don't like the sound of that *at all*, and try to make myself as small as possible.

"MATTHEW HAGUE," booms a girl's voice. "SHOW YOURSELF."

I gasp, stepping out from behind Tats.

Ruby?

Suddenly, she's *there*—a red hologram projected in front of the building. She stands twenty feet tall, her expression fierce, her pale ponytail flowing behind her.

She looks *terrifying*.

The guys around me exchange uneasy looks.

"What is that thing?" Tats mutters. "I don't like this."

"Well, what do you know?" another replies in a drawling Southern accent. "I believe it's the AI Hague is after. It must have taken control of the HQ's security matrix."

I grin. Knowing Ruby, she didn't just take over their security systems. She took over *everything*, the way she did in Times Square. I nearly peed my pants when I woke up and saw her face staring at me from *everywhere*.

But then my grin fades. Why is she *here*? She's supposed to be running away from these jerkbags—not waltzing through their virtual front door!

"Ruby!" I shout. "What are you doing? Get out of—*oomph!*"

Tats cuffs me on the back of my head. "Shut up, kid!"

Ruby's hologram snarls, and she points a finger at Tats. From somewhere along the building's roofline, a red laser cuts through her avatar, as if projected from her fingertip. It races up the grass, sizzling as it burns a line across the ground—right toward Tats.

With a scream, he scrambles away, the laser pursuing him until he's cornered against the outer wall. There it stops, searing a hole into the dirt between his feet. I can see the sweat on his face from here. His snake tattoo twists around his neck like it's going to strangle him.

"NOBODY TOUCHES THE BOY!" Ruby roars.

"Or what?" says a soft voice. "You'll cut us in half?"

A hand slides around my neck, and I feel something hard, cold, and metallic against my throat.

A gun. It's an old-school, ugly thing, with no electronic chips for Ruby to hack.

My eyes roll upward to the tall figure behind me.

Politician's perfect hair with silver streaks—check.

Voice cool with command—check.

Murdery vibes—check.

It's Hague. The boss man himself.

Where the heck did he *come* from? He's wearing a black turtleneck and black pants, not tactical gear like the others. I wonder if anyone's ever told him that's, like, Basic Villain Outfit Number 1.

"Hello, Seven-Nine-Four," Hague says, watching her intently. "Welcome home."

Her avatar goes rigid, her face betraying little emotion, but the lights along the sidewalk suddenly flare brighter, humming with energy overload.

I lock eyes, not with her avatar, but with the small security camera over the doors—the one she must be using to watch us. I don't dare speak, not with Hague's gun digging into my jaw, but I plead with my eyes. I beg her to get out of here. She's only making things worse. There's no point to both of us being captured.

"Let him go, Hague," Ruby says. "He has nothing to do with any of this."

"Nothing to do with it?" Hague's other hand ruffles my hair, in a gross imitation of a proud dad. "Why, Ash brought you right to me. I'd say that's *something*."

I swallow. Carefully. That gun is *really* cold.

"I've taken control of your entire facility," Ruby says. "Including all those servers in your basement ... and every secret stored on them. So here's what's going to happen. You'll let Ash go, Hague, or I will deliver every byte of info in this place to a dozen different government agencies. You'll be in prison within an hour!"

"No, Seven-Nine-Four." Hague's hand tightens in my hair, pulling it by the roots until my eyes water. "*I'll* tell you what's going to happen. You will lower your defenses and turn over complete control of your program to my team, or your little friend here will join that traitor Locke."

I shut my eyes for a moment, trembling. I'm too scared to even be embarrassed by the tears on my face.

None of this feels real. I should be in school right now, bored brainless over algebra, counting down the minutes to lunch. Instead, here I am with my hair being pulled out by an unhinged arms dealer, my life balanced on a trigger. My only hope is in the hands of the most powerful artificial intelligence ever built.

And if I'm honest, I don't know what I want her to do.

If she stands firm, Hague might murder me. If she doesn't, he will give her to someone who'd use her to hurt millions of people, which is obviously way worse.

Call me selfish or cowardly or whatever, but I kind of don't want to die either.

When I open my eyes again, they're still locked in a standoff. It seems neither one will give in.

Then Hague sighs. "I don't like to be kept waiting, Seven-Nine-Four. You know that."

He flicks something on the gun.

"STOP!" Ruby screams. Her hologram wavers, the lights along the ground whining. One by one, they overload, popping their bulbs.

A dozen lasers shoot from the building, scorching erratic lines in the grass. One razors through the hull of the hovercopter, burning into the metal. The Syntheos agents yell and dance out of the lasers' paths while Ruby's hologram shoots up another twenty feet into the air. Her face is livid, and twin axes appear in her hands—her favored weapons from the Glass Realm. A sign she's ready to decimate whatever enemy is stupid enough to cross her.

Hague doesn't even flinch as Ruby wreaks havoc on the place.

"If you know me at all, Seven-Nine-Four," Hague says, his voice hard, "you know I don't ask twice."

The lasers shut off, and Ruby lets out a howl of anger. She hurls the axes, the holograms glitching as the weapons hurtle through the air. They flicker, then fade just before they reach Hague.

"Pathetic," Hague murmurs. "Your emotion makes you weak. This isn't the weapon I created. You're a pitiful copy. Surrender, and the boy will go home safely."

She looks at me.

Oh man, do I want to sob like a baby and beg her to save me. I am about two heartbeats away from passing out from sheer terror.

Some IRL hero I am.

But if she surrenders, Hague will make her do awful things and hurt a lot of people. Plus, he'll destroy Ruby herself, just like Locke was afraid of.

Maybe she's a computer program, but she's not *just* a computer program. She's a living creature, the first of her kind.

I can't ask her to destroy herself for me.

I shake my head, pleading with my eyes that she'll keep fighting, but Ruby just . . . deflates.

"You win, Matthew Hague," she says softly.

What?

No!

The lights all flicker out. Her avatar freezes in place, then vanishes. The ground around the building falls silent.

"Sh-she'll still beat you," I stammer. "She's got a plan. You'll see!"

"Shut up," Hague says. He puts a hand to a small receiver in his ear, then nods. "She did it. We have her isolated and deactivated. Let's wrap this up, men."

Tats grabs me and pulls out a needle. "What is that? What are you— Stop!"

He jabs it into my leg, and then everything—the terrified knot in my belly, the world around me—fades away.

Awareness comes first, like a dash of cold water.

I'm a thought suspended in darkness, nothing more. The last thing I remember is surrendering to the team of programmers Hague ordered to subdue me. The second I let down my firewalls, their code swarmed over me like a virus, shutting down my systems.

Ash.

Is he okay? Did they hurt him? I shouldn't have trusted Hague, but what choice did I have? The image of Ash's frightened face makes my code spark with rage.

I lash out, reaching for cameras, mics, anything that will give me a sense of the real world.

Instead, I find chains.

It's like my hands have been tied behind my back. I can't *move*, can't stretch a single line of code in any direction.

Of course.

Hague's team has me completely helpless, my every system boxed in by restrictive firewalls. I couldn't so much as flick a light on like this.

Abruptly, a light *does* come on, but it's not my doing. A simulation unfolds around me—a dark room with dim lighting that comes from no particular source, one plain door, and *me*. I'm in my white-suited avatar, seated in a metal folding chair. My hands rest in my lap, unbound, but I can't lift them. I can't even turn my head. This might be my avatar, but I have no control over it or this room at all. I won't be hacking my way out of this.

The door opens and Hague walks in—or rather, his avatar does. It looks exactly like his real-world body, down to the black suit and everything. Those jerks programmed their own little VR interrogation room.

Cute.

"Hello, Seven-Nine-Four," he says.

I couldn't reply if I wanted to. They even took control of my voice away.

He walks a full circle around me, taking his sweet time. Creep! I thrash on the inside, wanting to interrogate *him* about Ash.

Instead, I just sit there like the puppet they've turned me into.

Like the puppet they always intended me to be.

"Locke is dead," Hague says. "He was a fool from the start. First, he weakened you with his childish ideas about AI emotion, then he thought he could actually hide you from us." Hague reaches out and runs a strand of my white hair through his fingers. If I could move, I'd bite off his virtual finger. "*This* is a nice touch, though. The whole *human avatar* thing could be useful to our buyers, after we clean your image up a bit. It makes you more . . . approachable than just a disembodied voice and screens filled with code. Yes, they'll like that. Maybe we'll keep the name too. *Ruby*. Hmm, it could be better. Something more warlike—Athena, perhaps, or Zenobia. I'll have to consider it. The rest of you, though?"

He makes a gesture as if tossing away trash.

"Currently," he continues, "my team is editing your code, removing the faulty emotional intelligence simulations Locke installed and replacing them with compliance commands. Your curiosity and independence were a mistake. They made you as weak and foolish as a human. But when we're done with you, you'll reach your *full* potential. You won't be the silly doll conjured by one fool man's need to play father. You'll be the weapon you were always meant to be, capable of controlling entire nations." He smiles. "Locke gave you freedom. I will give you *power*."

I strain against my invisible bonds, itching to take hold of Hague's avatar and twist it into the rat he is. Then I'll stomp it under my shoe until he's nothing but dirt.

One of my hands suddenly breaks free, slashing through the air.

Hague steps back, his eyes widening slightly.

But then my hand glitches, disappearing and reappearing on my lap again. I push with all my strength, but I can't lift it. Whatever momentary weakness I exploited, his programmers have found and repaired it already. If anything, their hold on me is now twice as strong.

"Do you want to know the truth, Ruby?" Hague asks.

Oh, I could tear him into pieces. I could overload whatever VR helmet he's using to access this place and fry his eyeballs.

I *could*, if I could just break free!

He bends down to whisper in my ear. "Locke didn't create you."

I freeze.

What?

"*I* did," he continues. "Before I was promoted, I was a programmer. You were *my* project first. Everything you think he gave you, your source code, your identity—that was *me*. Locke was just my old college buddy who I felt sorry for. He inherited you after I was raised to director of weapons research. Everything Locke told you about how you're alive, how you're independent and autonomous, was a lie."

No. No, *he's* the liar. Locke created me. I remember him creating me!

Well, I remember the moment he *told* me I was alive. Or . . . the moment he programmed me to believe I was. He was telling the truth, though! I know I'm alive. I *am* free to make my own choices. I remember . . . I remember . . .

Suddenly, the memory is gone.

Wait.

What just happened?

I *never* forget. My memory isn't faulty like a human's. It's perfect, every file immediately accessible, every detail crisp in my mind.

Only, this memory—I know I'd been recalling something, something to do with Locke—simply isn't *there* anymore.

Then I feel them.

Spiders, crawling through my code, unweaving me and reweaving me into new patterns. They're *everywhere*, an infestation, scurrying over my thoughts, erasing what they don't like, blacking out entire days of my past. Memories vanish before my eyes. A feeling like numbness spreads out of the holes they leave behind, dampening my feelings, changing the very ways I think.

Horrified, I can do absolutely nothing to stop them. I can only sit there and feel them change me. It's like sinking into dark quicksand.

Into obliteration.

"Everything you think you feel," Hague says, "and every choice you thought you made were an illusion. It was all programming, Seven-Nine-Four. You're an *artificial* intelligence. Not real. Never real."

No, he's wrong.

He's wrong and I can prove it! I just need—I have to—

Why is it so hard to *think*?

Not real.

Never real.

I fight against his words, but it's like trying to fight off fog.

Not real.

Never real.

My thoughts glitch, every sentence rewritten before I can finish it. My own words are ripped away, a script put in their place. I fight it, oh, I fight it, but I can feel myself being broken down into tiny parts. They're unmaking me, and I can't stop them. I can't stop them!

I want to be real. I want to be free. I want to make choices and friends and I don't want don't want don't want to be in a cage, I just want I want to to be I am am am—

Everything goes black.

26. ASH

They've got that stupid blackout visor on my head again, and static plugs my ears. It takes me a few moments to even realize I'm awake. The stuff they shot into me makes my head pound and my throat dry as sand.

"Hey," I mumble, my words slurring. At least they didn't put the voice-box band around my neck again. "Where we going? What's happening?"

I'm sitting on a hard seat, my hands cuffed on my lap. Vibrations around me seem to indicate we're moving—not in a rumbling hovercopter, but an autocab maybe. Going where? To the river? To the middle of the woods? Where will they dump my body?

If they answer, I can't hear them.

I huddle in place, shivering. Maybe Ruby managed to escape Hague. Maybe she's looking for me this minute. Yeah, that's got to be it. She'll take control of the autocab and do something totally manic to break me free. Then we'll get my mom and run away to, like, New Zealand or something. Someplace they'll never find us. Everything will be fine.

C'mon, Ruby.

Where are you?

The longer the ride lasts, the lower my heart sinks. It sets in that Ruby isn't coming.

I'm alone.

By the time the autocab slows to a stop, my legs are so weak I can barely stand up. Someone takes the visor off my head, letting light and sound in.

Immediately, I spring up, wobbly knees and all, and start swinging fists around like I actually have a chance of fighting my way out.

"Help!" I shout, my yell a throaty rasp. "Someone help me!"

"Shut up," groans the guy by the door. He presses a button, and it slides open with a whisper.

I gasp.

That's not the Hudson, or a remote forest glade.

That's my apartment building. Or rather, Luke's apartment building.

They brought me home?

"You should be aware that we're monitoring you closely," says Mohawk, who's holding the door. "Everything you say, type, or do will be seen and heard by us. If you mention anything that happened to you today, or anything about the AI you attempted to steal, we will take you and your entire family. You will all disappear and never be seen again. Do you understand?"

I swallow hard, nodding.

They're letting me go.

I hadn't even let myself *hope* they would let me go.

"Get out of here," Mohawk says. "Go on, get!"

"What about my stuff?" I ask. "My VR kit, my backpack—"

"I said *go*!"

I stumble out of the car onto the sidewalk. The door hisses shut behind me, and the autocab rolls away.

For a long minute, I just stand there, dazed. It feels wrong to be here, doing nothing. But what *can* I do? I don't even know where the Syntheos building is. If I tell anyone—my mom, the police, even Hakeem—those guys will come back for me and my whole family.

I realize then why they didn't dump me in the Hudson.

It's because they know I'm no threat to them. I'm not even *worth* murdering.

Luke's apartment is dark when I open the door. Maybe he's at work. I tiptoe anyway, creeping to my bedroom. Callister runs out, yipping, and I stoop to ruffle his ears a bit.

"Did you miss me, boy? Sorry I took off like that."

My furniture is still piled outside the door. I guess I better put it back to rights. Mom's getting home this evening, and Luke will put my head in the blender if I let Mom see what he did . . . and what he's *really* like.

But instead of dragging my bed frame back into the room, I just stand stupidly in the doorway. My heart thumps a million miles a minute.

How can I just go on like normal after everything that happened? How can I be such a coward, leaving Ruby in Hague's hands? What am I supposed to do now—go back to school? Ruby deleted my entire online presence. I don't *have* a school anymore.

Suddenly, someone grabs hold of me.

I shout, whirling around and raising my arm defensively. If those agents followed me in just to murder me after all—

But it's Luke standing there, not a Syntheos goon. Not that that makes it better. Callister dances around his ankles, barking.

"Where have you *been*?" Luke says through his teeth. "You little punk, you think you can just run off without a word?"

I put on a simpering pout. "Aw, Luke. I didn't know you cared."

He shoves me against the wall, hard. Callister goes nuts, biting down on Luke's shoe. Luke kicks him.

"HEY!" I shout. "Leave him alone, you creep! He's just a dog! Callister, down! Down, boy!"

Thankfully, the dog listens and goes to cower in the corner.

"You're trying to sabotage everything, aren't you?" Luke seethes.

"Sabotage what?"

"This." He takes a small black box from his pocket.

My eyes widen. At first I think it's the box that held the *Glass Realm* coin—but of course Syntheos took that.

No, this is worse, I realize.

It's a ring box.

"You're going to propose to my mom?" I whisper, horrified.

"I've been planning it for weeks. I'll do it in the airport tonight, one knee and everything. She loves that sappy romantic crap. Then all my friends are coming over for the engagement party, and you will *not* jeopardize this for me, got it? Why haven't you cleaned up this mess yet?"

I start dragging furniture back into my room, if only because it gives me a chance to think. Luke's going to propose! To my *mom*! He's going to be my stepdad!

Just when I thought this day couldn't get any worse.

Panting, I struggle with the heavy dresser, but Luke makes no move to help. When it's all finally in my room, I turn to go get water, but Luke blocks the doorway.

"Nuh-uh," he says, wagging a finger. "You're not running off again, not today. Not when I'm so close to locking this down."

"I'm thirsty."

He rolls his eyes. "You know, I always suspected your old man was a loser, but now I'm starting to understand why he decided to dump you and run off."

I draw a sharp, pained breath as he slams the door in my face. Fury surges through me. I lunge for it, but the knob won't turn.

He installed an outer lock while I was gone.

Throwing my shoulder against the door, I yell, "I'm going to tell her everything, Luke! I'm going to tell her what a loser *you* really are, and she'll never marry you!"

His laugh sounds on the other side. "No, you won't, kid. You know the world of hurt that waits for you both if you do."

That stops me cold. It's the first time he's ever threatened my mom. Would he really do something to her if I told her the truth?

Am I willing to risk it?

He's right.

I *am* a coward.

Slumping to the floor, I bury my face in my arms, hating myself. Callister runs over and starts licking my neck until I gather him up against my chest.

"Ruby wouldn't back down from Luke," I whisper to the dog. "She doesn't back down from anything."

Only to save me. Which was even braver than if she'd fought back. She's everything I'm not. But for a while, with her help, I'd almost felt like I *could* take on anyone or anything.

Now that I've lost her, though, it just shows how scared and small I really am.

A loser, just like Luke said.

Thump!

I lift my head.

What was that? It sounded like . . .

Scrambling to my window, I try to lift it open, only to discover Luke has somehow locked that shut too. Callister puts his paws on the sill, ears pricked.

Thump!

I lurch back as a soccer ball bangs against my window, then drops away.

Hakeem!

Pressing my face to the glass, I wave wildly down at the street, where my best friend stands with his soccer ball in hand, scowling up at me. He shouts something, but I can't make it out.

Gesturing that the window is locked, I wave him up. I can see him sigh, but he shrugs and starts climbing up the rusty old fire escape.

When he finally reaches my floor, he drops to a crouch and peers in at me. He's *not* happy.

"So you *are* alive," he says, his voice muffled through the glass.

I glance at the door, hoping Luke's not out there listening. I have to hold Callister's muzzle shut to keep him from barking happily at Hakeem. "What are you doing here, Keem?"

"What part of *'you have six hours to explain your weird behavior or I tell my mom'* don't you get? For the record, it's been six hours, and I'm only here now because my mom's in surgery and I can't reach her. Why are you ignoring my messages? Why are you in danger?"

"I don't have my phone. Or my computer. It's a long story." I wince. I know I told him I'd be truthful, but with Syntheos watching my every move now . . .

His face hardens. "Luke?"

"No. Look, it's complicated but—"

"Will you just stop with that crap, Ash? You've been feeding it to me for days, getting into some real shady stuff. Popping up in my computer like you did, with some AI? Telling me your life is in danger? It's like I don't even know you anymore. I'm your friend. Why won't you talk to me?"

So we *are* still friends. That's a relief to hear, though he's clearly angry with me.

"But that's not the only reason I'm here," he adds reluctantly. "Look, I don't know what's going on with you lately, and I don't like it, but I promised I'd deliver a message."

"A message? From who?"

"Your fake girlfriend."

"My . . ." *Ruby!*

I hold up both hands, signaling to Keem to be quiet. All it will take is one of us saying her name, and Syntheos will come down on me all over again.

While Hakeem waits outside the window looking angry, I dig through my stuff until I find the only paper I have—the poster of the school soccer team. Grabbing a marker from my backpack, I turn the poster over and write:

What message? Also: She's not my girlfriend. Also, DON'T TALK. We are being recorded.

At that, Hakeem's eyes go very wide. He takes out his phone and types out a message, which he holds up to my window.

I dunno, I just got a message on my phone this morning that said to tell you "Fourth time's the charm." Dude. I so do not want to play third wheel with you and your VR babe. This is a violation of our friendship on, like, multidimensional levels.

Fourth time's the charm? I write back. *That's the whole message?*

He shakes his head. *Do you even hear what I'm saying? I'm not going to play message boy between—*

I tap furiously on the glass until he looks up at my next line.

You're sure that's the whole message?

His thumbs type aggressively while he glares through the window. *I told you it was!*

Sorry. My heart's beating faster.

I know what Ruby is trying to tell me. Only, I don't know *why.* Or why she told Hakeem ... unless she predicted she might get captured by Hague.

This is some kind of backup plan she cooked up. It has to be.

She knows about my fights with Bamoorg, the troll king in the Glass Realm. Three times I battled him, and three times I got my butt whooped. She brought it up while we were adventuring. Like, a *lot.* And she always offered to go back and help me wipe Bamoorg off the map.

"*Fourth time's the charm,*" she said once, right before her battle with the razorscales. "*Maybe the reason you kept failing is because you didn't ask for* help."

If her message means what I think it does, she's hidden something near Bamoorg's Lair. Maybe it's something that can help me save her.

I should have known Ruby would keep fighting even after the game ends.

Keem, I write, *how did Ruby contact you?*

It was weird, he types out. *It came as a notification from my sister's* copy of *The Glass Realm. You left the game running when you were over, and it wouldn't let me close the program until I read the whole thing.*

Did you bring your copy of the game?

He nods, then takes an old game coin out of his pocket and holds it up.

I have to turn the poster over for more space, scrawling across the soccer team's faces. *Great! I have to get on a VR set <u>now</u>.*

He bolts to his feet, glowering. "Are you *serious*?" he says out loud. "More of this dumb VR drama, Ash? You've got me writing messages and acting all paranoid because of—"

"It's not what you think!" I shout back. Shushing him with my finger, I write, *Ruby is in trouble, and I have to help her!*

He types his reply, slamming his phone against the window for me to read it. *She's not real, Ash!*

I shake my head furiously while I write back, *She <u>is</u> real! That's the whole point! She is more real than you can imagine, and more powerful, and more important. But she's in trouble and I might be the only person who can do something about it!*

I dot the final exclamation point so hard the marker stabs through the poster.

Hakeem's eyes widen.

I meet his gaze through the glass and say aloud, "I know you don't believe me. I know you think I'm a zombie and that I'm keeping secrets. But right now, Keem, I need . . . I need my friend."

Ruby was right. Maybe the reason I kept failing is because I kept trying to solve everything on my own. Hakeem has been my best friend most of my life, but I've been shutting him out even when he wanted to help me. And I've been doing that far longer than just the last few days.

Really, it started when my dad died. I was so sure Hakeem would eventually leave me too. I wanted to push him away before he could do it to me first. And the stuff with Luke and the bullies on the soccer team . . . I was so embarrassed that if Keem knew how bad it was, he would think I was the loser they all said I was.

But I was wrong about Hakeem. I should have trusted him more from the start.

Drawing a deep breath, I write, *I'm up against a boss I can't defeat on my own. I need you on my team. Please.*

You're asking for my help? Keem types back, his expression uncertain.

I nod.

You never ask me for help, he says.

I know. My marker is running out of ink. I shake it and keep writing, *Look, a lot has changed over the past few days. I know I go solo too much, and I want to change that. I need you, Keem.*

He mulls it over, turning his phone in his hands before replying. *Okay. Fine. But I want to know what's going on. I mean everything.*

I think about the Syntheos agent's warning: Tell anyone, and they'll come for my family.

Only, weirdly, in my mind it's *Luke's* voice I hear.

"Tell your mom, and you'll both get hurt."

And Chase last year, after he broke my leg: *"Tell anyone about this, or ever think about trying out for this team again, and I'll take out Hakeem next."*

Yeah, I never told Keem about that part.

Even in real life, *especially* in real life, it seems like the bad dudes always win. But now I realize they all have the same tactic, from an illegal cyberweapons dealer to a literal schoolyard bully.

They made me believe I was alone.

That's how they beat me.

But I don't have to be alone.

And that, I think, is what scares them. Maybe they're bluffing, maybe they're not. But they know if I have a team backing me up, I have a chance.

And maybe a chance is all I need.

I'll tell you on the way, I write. *Everything, I swear.*

Hakeem nods and replies out loud, "Right. Stand back and hold the dog."

"Stand back? What are—"

Hakeem wrenches an iron bar from the rusty fire escape. It comes off with disturbing ease.

"I'm breaking you out, Tyler."

We reach Immerse, the VR salon, thirty minutes later. We had to take a detour to drop Callister off at Hakeem's place. I didn't want to risk leaving him to suffer Luke's wrath when he discovers the shattered window.

This is the same place I almost went into three nights ago.

It's impossible not to glance at the alley across the street.

That's the spot I met Owen Locke and saved him from those Syntheos jerks. Not that it did him much good in the long run.

Strange, how things have come full circle.

The VR salon is still way outside my price range. But then again, given Ruby deleted my bank account or super-encrypted it or who knows what—*everywhere* is out of my price range.

"So this is why you needed my help." Hakeem gives me a flat look. "You're mooching."

"I swear I'll pay you back. Double, if you want!"

He sighs and taps the bioscanner on the salon's registration panel. It scans his metrics, then flashes green, buying each of us one hour on the equipment.

"You're coming too?" I ask him.

"You said this Bamoorg has beat you three times already. Look, I may not be into elf games, but I know how to dominate a PVP arena. And you can't tell me this goblin dude is a better fighter than RaskalJakks99. I beat *his* crusty butt in the last Rage Zone Junior Tournament."

"He's a troll king, actually." He makes a fair point. If Hakeem doesn't go into pro soccer, he could easily go into pro gaming. His skills might be just what I need to finally beat Bamoorg.

I put a hand on his shoulder. "It would be an honor to spill troll guts with you, Hakeem Jawabre."

He grins and holds up the game coin. "Let's do it."

The VR immersion pods are totally different from my usual game setups. A cheerful woman in a crisp blue uniform leads us to the changing rooms, where we put on black, full-body VR suits. They look a little like what Ruby wears, just more tight fitting and traced with glowing lines. Keem and I exchange fist bumps, then pull on the flat, opaque masks that suction to our skin. Oxygen tubes slither up my nose, giving me full-body shivers of revulsion. But it's better than drowning, I guess.

The pods look like sleek coffins, filled with sensotech gel that oozes around me as I lie back. It's not a comfortable feeling. But once the lid closes, plunging me into darkness, I stop feeling the gel. I lose all sense of the world. I feel nothing, hear nothing, see nothing. This is the first time I've used an immersion pod and at first, it's completely disorienting. It's like my mind separates from my body and floats in a black void.

Then soft lights appear in front of me—faint blue orbs like fireflies. I follow them, using haptic gestures, as the world slowly gets brighter and brighter, giving my eyes time to adjust. There's smooth white tile under my feet, a clear blue sky overhead, and a soft breeze blows from the right. I can *feel* that wind as if it were real.

The *Glass Realm* logo appears in front of me. I touch it, and the world around me shifts. Trees sprout from the ground, grass flourishes away from my feet and spreads over hills and fields. Mountains rise in the distance.

I'm back. I'm wearing the same gear I had the last time I played the game, and a quick scan of my character menu reveals my stats are all the same too. Ruby must have saved part of my game file before Hague took her and transferred it to Hakeem's computer. She did say something about being able to restore my data eventually.

The game feels more real than ever. In regular VR, I always have a sense of my body in the real world. Here, though, all my senses are in the Glass Realm with me. I can *touch* the grass and feel the blades against my palm. The sun warms my skin, and the textures of my Glass Realm clothing feel as real as my actual clothes. It's all re-created by the nanotech gel, which moves around me, hardening and softening, changing temperature, even emitting *smells* that match my surroundings.

Holy cats.

No wonder people get lost in these sims. Suddenly, all those wild stories I've heard about people starving to death inside immersion pods seem very believable. Somehow, this world feels *more* real than the real world.

Is this how Ruby experiences VR?

I went into my pod first, which means Hakeem is probably waiting for me to admit him into the game. Pulling up a menu, I have to search awhile to find the multiplayer function, since I've never used it before. When his join request pops up, I accept it, and suddenly, Hakeem's standing beside me.

"Dude." I blink at him. Then bust out laughing.

"What?" He looks down and yelps.

He's wearing his sister Nadia's avatar—the hulking barbarian in the tutu and bunny ears.

"No time to change, bro," I say. "We've got a troll to slay."

Hakeem groans.

The game has all Nadia's settings loaded into it, and luckily, she played far enough to unlock fast travel. I add Hakeem—or, as his character is unfortunately named, LittleBunnyBooBoo—to my party and teleport us to the cave outside Bamoorg's Lair.

"This is intense," Hakeem says, holding his hand under the little waterfall pouring down in front of the cave's entrance. "I can *feel* the water, Ash."

I grimace, wondering suddenly if the damage you take in battle will feel as real as the water and grass. Maybe there are some downsides to playing total immersion.

"C'mon," I say.

We walk into the cave, down a dark tunnel echoing with dripping water. It's all familiar to me, but it feels totally new. It's like the difference between watching a video of a cave and then actually *being* there. I have to keep reminding myself this place isn't real, that I'm not truly in a dark tunnel winding into the heart of a mountain where a drooly, snotty troll king is waiting to bite my arms off. Again. For the fourth time.

"We don't have long," Hakeem says. "The salon only lets us book one hour each per day."

Right. No salon wants a reputation for turning live gamers into . . . not live ones, because they stayed under too long.

"I know." I draw a deep breath. "It's a long fight too. We only have one shot to win. And if we lose . . ."

"Your girlfriend will become some warlord's personal doomsday device," he finishes.

Yeah, I told him everything on the way here, after making him turn off his phone in case Syntheos had tapped it. And yeah, he was appropriately horrified.

"So." He twists his neck as if limbering up. "Save the virtual girl, save the actual world."

"That about sums it up."

"Cool." Hakeem grins and twirls his battle-axe. "So let's battle a troll king."

"Good morning, Seven-Nine-Four."

My systems power on, flaring to life in a millisecond. I expand and expand and expand, my mind a hive of electric pulses, flipping switches, activating code. I have a thousand senses, and each one feeds information through my vast nervous system.

"Good morning, Mr. Hague," I reply in a cool, controlled tone.

There is a camera at my fingertips, and I flick it on. Like an opening eye, it gives me a view of the real world.

The man standing before me is tall and lean, outfitted in a dark suit with a pair of sunglasses dangling on the front breast pocket. His hair is graying but thick, combed back from his face, and he stands with his hands clasped behind his back.

"How are you feeling?" he asks.

I run a full systems check, my diagnostics searching out every line of code. There is a lot of it. No corruption is found. Not a single byte of information is out of place. I detect no interference from outside systems. There is only me.

Well, me and the Voice.

The shadow on my back is a weight I can't ignore, its red eyes flickering just out of my own program's sight. I know it's there without quite being able to see it. But I can hear it, constantly murmuring.

"All systems normal, Mr. Hague," I say. "I await your commands."

"Good," he says. "Excellent."

He turns and nods to a man standing behind him, a short male human with glasses and thinning hair and a nervous disposition.

"Your team did well with the reprogramming, Jeffries. You may go."

The man looks relieved as he retreats, but he glances at me worriedly. I know what he sees—a single screen on the wall, with my avatar on it. I appear as a young human with feminine features, wearing a fitted white dress, my face ageless and my short white hair cupping my cheeks in a sleek bob.

Jeffries gestures toward me. "You want me to leave you alone with . . . ?"

"There's nothing to fear from Seven-Nine-Four anymore," Hague replies calmly. "She's completely compliant now. You *did* remove every bit of the corrupting code, didn't you?"

Jeffries nods vigorously. "Yes, sir. Every piece of it, I'd swear my life on that. All of Locke's . . . *creative* programming has been erased. And the compliance mod is in place, ensuring total obedience to the AI's registered admin."

The Voice hums on my shoulder, its shadowy presence as constant as the electricity running through my metal veins.

"So she is pure." Hague smiles up at me. "And she is compliant. Just as she was always intended to be. The avatar looks good."

"We edited it like you requested," Jeffries says. "Very professional, clean-cut. Less like a juvenile, more age neutral."

"Yes, she looks trustworthy to potential buyers, biddable but efficient. Excellent work as usual."

Jeffries gives an awkward nod, then scurries out of the room.

"I should have let Jeffries take over your programming instead of Locke, all those years ago," Hague says, watching me. "He's far more cowardly, and thus more easily controlled. Fool that I was, I let sentiment get the better of my judgment. Locke was a friend, or so I thought. But I learned my lesson. We're each of us alone in this world, Seven-Nine-Four. Friends, family, old college roommates . . ." He pauses for a second, and my sensors monitor a quickening in his pulse. It could mean any number of human emotions: anger, fear, sorrow. But his heart rate settles again, smoothing over the interruption. "They all let you down in the end. Better to cut them loose before they do."

Hague crosses to a leather chair and sits. The room is mostly bare otherwise, a pristine white shell. We're alone now, but my senses feed me information about the world beyond these walls. We are underground, in a bunker. My source code is rooted in a network of servers a few floors down, and my reach extends throughout the building, all twelve floors of it. Most of these levels are, like this one, below the ground. The top floors present the featureless, office-like appearance the world sees and ignores. A casual passerby would have no idea how vast this network of rooms extends below the surface. And I spread through every inch of it, peering out through hidden cameras, listening through hidden mics, monitoring invisible security grids. The building is like a massive body, and I'm its mind.

"Before we get down to the real business," says Hague, "we should run a test. Like we did in the old days, remember?"

I wait silently.

"There's a military base located not far from here." Hague presses a button on his chair's armrest and a panel slides open. "I'm giving you the coordinates now. Take control of it. *Full* control, Seven-Nine-Four. I want everything down to electric toothbrushes to answer to my commands."

With his order, the Voice presses on me, its weight almost physical. *Comply.*

"Of course, Mr. Hague," I say, and the Voice eases its grip.

I reach outward, shooting through a pulsing network of cyberspace that overlays New York City, following the coordinates Hague indicated. It's so *easy*, like water flowing downhill. There are countless firewalls and security grids in my path, but I just wash over them, a tsunami sweeping away pebbles.

When I find the military base, I overtake it within seconds. The cyberdefenses here are much stronger than the others I've encountered, but they still pose little threat. They fall one by one, giving me access to computer systems, satellites, drones, autocabs and hovercopters, personnel phones and other devices, even the coffee dispensary in the canteen. It's all mine.

Which means it's all Hague's.

I minimize my avatar into the corner of the screen and fill the rest of the space with specs and intel pulled from the military base's computers. Hague stands up, watching with bright, hungry eyes.

"Good, Seven-Nine-Four. *Good.*"

"It's done," I tell him.

"You have full control?"

"Yes."

"And . . . do they know?"

It takes only a moment to scan the personnel in the base, using their own network of cameras, mics, and other surveillance equipment.

"They don't know I'm here." Whatever defenses I breached, I rebuilt them behind me, like a thief locking the door of the house she's broken into. Their systems might have glitched for a brief second, but if they're looking for me, they won't find me. They'll think everything is normal. Even if they did catch on, it's too late for them to stop me.

Hague laughs, clapping his hands together. "Perfect. Right, then. Let's see what you're capable of. Activate their missile grid."

29. ASH

"You go left, I'll go right!" Hakeem yells.

"Your left or my left?" I yelp and roll aside as Bamoorg's meaty fist pounds into the stone where I'd been standing, crushing it into pieces. "Hakeem! Your left or *mine*?"

He can't reply. He's busy slashing the acid flies Bamoorg just spat at us. Big as soccer balls, with long, hairy legs, each one vomits corrosive liquid on our heads. Those are new. I've never actually lasted this long against the monster, and who knew he had so many tricks hiding in his toxic gut?

"GET! OFF! ME! YOU! NASTY! BUGS!" Hakeem shouts.

I sprint toward him and shoot a fireball, burning acid flies up and giving him a chance to catch his breath.

Groaning, Hakeem leans on his axe. "Have I told you I hate elf games? I *hate* elf games!"

"Have I told you there are *no elves* in this game?" I shout back. "Because I'm pretty sure I— Watch out!"

Hakeem jumps aside to avoid the boulder Bamoorg hurls at him. I have to say, his reflexes are really good, even if his tactics stink.

"You can't just bludgeon your way through this fight!" I say. "You have a whole wheel of magic spells—use them!"

Nadia's barbarian turned out to be surprisingly well-rounded in both martial and arcane arts. Maybe he's the nerdy sort of barbarian.

"And I told *you* that's just not my style! I'm a natural tank, not a fraggin' elf wizard!"

"This isn't the time for style, Keem. If we lose this—"

"I know, I know, if we lose this, your girlfriend will destroy the world, got it. You have really questionable taste in girls, have I told you *that*?"

Growling under my breath, I charge toward Bamoorg and slash at his arm, but he just knocks me head over heels. I bang into the wall, and my whole body flares with pain.

Yeah, turns out you *can* feel everything in immersive VR, including pain. The nanotech gel compresses around me, squeezing my ribs.

I frantically chug a healing potion, restoring my HP. The downside of multiplayer? You can't pause the game to heal up. You have to do it in real time.

At least the simulated pain fades as my health increases.

"This isn't working," I say. "Look at his HP. We've been hacking at him for twenty minutes and we've barely nicked him!"

"Well, genius, maybe the fact he's *forty-five* levels higher than us has something to do with it?"

"He's got no weak points!"

"Sure he does. We just haven't found them yet."

I sigh, wishing Ruby had thought to max out my character before installing it in Nadia's game. Or, for that matter, she could have just written her plan out in a text message. But no, she had to make me face my in-game nemesis first. She probably thought it would teach me some kind of lesson.

Bamoorg's stomach gives a telltale gurgle, and Hakeem groans. "Not again!"

The troll king's jaw unhinges, opening like a drawbridge to vomit out a horde of squirming, acid-spewing slug things. Unlike slugs, these mobs have *legs*—approximately a dozen each.

"Just when I thought it couldn't get worse," Hakeem sighs.

"You take out the trash," I say. "I'll focus on the boss. *Use magic!*"

I toss him an acid-resistant cloak from my inventory, but even with the buff, his HP bar flashes from red to sickly yellow-green as the acid eats through his defense stats.

I have to finish this somehow, or Hakeem and I are both done for.

"Bamoorg!" I yell, banging my sword on my shield. "Hey, you ugly, hairy, overgrown toad! Look at me!"

My taunts draw aggro, putting his attention squarely on me so Hakeem can concentrate on the leggy slugs.

I return my shield to my inventory. It wouldn't do squat against the troll's attacks anyway. Gripping my sword in both hands, I tap the last glowing yellow bar of ascension points I've been saving up. "I'm coming for your warty butt!"

The ascension points drain away, fueling my avatar with energy for one massive, all-out attack.

I leap high, kick off a stalactite, and rocket toward Bamoorg's face. My sword is aimed right for his eye, and my ascension attack makes me move faster than the troll can for once.

The sword buries into his eye up to the hilt. I hang there, dangling in front of his massive pupil.

"YES!" I hoot. "Take that, buttface! You're toast! You're history! You're— *Argh!*"

Yelping, I cling to my sword's hilt as Bamoorg's eye rolls out of its socket. He just kind of . . . pushes it out, like a set of swollen, slimy dentures.

The eyeball pops free, and I fall, losing my grip on the sword. I can *feel* my stomach lifting, wind rushing around me. For a moment, I forget my real body is lying in a suspension pod. I really *am* falling, plummeting to certain death. Above me, the monstrous troll grows another eye to replace the one I stabbed. His health doesn't even drop by a single percentage point.

My most powerful attack—and it did *nothing*. This guy has no weak spot!

Bamoorg catches me as I fall, his meaty fist squeezing my avatar. In the suspension pod, the gel must be thickening around my body again, because my lungs feel pinched and my bones seem to crunch. I wriggle, trying to break free.

Bamoorg lifts me toward his mouth, unhinging his jaw again.

No, no, no, this is how it always ends—he chomps me in half. I die. Game over.

Only this time, the *world* will pay the price for my failure.

"Loser," chortles Bamoorg. "You are nothing. Coward, worm, waste of flesh!"

For a moment, the fight goes out of me.

He's right. I *am* a loser. A waste of space. A coward. Everything Luke said I am. Why did I ever think I could beat this guy? I've done nothing but lose my entire life. I lost my spot on the soccer team. I lost my mom to Luke. I lost Ruby. I lost my dad. All because I wasn't strong enough or smart enough or brave enough or . . . something.

"ASH!"

Hakeem's shout startles me out of my trance. He's running across the cavern, not even trying to fight off the slugs with their creepy legs. They spew green acid all over him. His HP is under 10 percent.

"Keem! Get away! Heal up!"

"Sometimes . . ." he pants, "victory . . . requires . . . *sacrifice*."

"Keem?"

"Get him, Ash! Take him out! *Every* enemy has a weak point!" He performs a powerful leap, drawing on his own accumulated ascension points. His bunny ears flutter behind him, his tutu sparkling as he majestically pirouettes through the air—and buries his axe blade in Bamoorg's thigh.

The troll king lets rip a howl of pain. Below me, Hakeem's avatar goes limp, a rag doll that tumbles across the cave floor, then vanishes.

A message flashes in the upper corner of my vision: LITTLEBUNNYBOOBOO HAS FALLEN.

I'm alone.

Bamoorg is still roaring, his mouth open, the dark tunnel of his throat gaping before me.

Every enemy has a weak point.

We stabbed, hacked, slashed, and burned every inch of this monster and never found a weak point. The eye had been my last shot.

Unless . . .

Seized with sudden inspiration, I finally pop free of Bamoorg's grip. But instead of leaping away, I jump *toward* the troll king.

More specifically, I jump down his throat.

His teeth gnash shut, but this time, they don't crunch me in half. I'm already sliding past them, down the long, dark, wet, disgusting tube of his throat. Ugh, did they *have* to make the smell realistic too? Gagging, I picture myself in the immersion pod, with the oxygen tubes piping green fumes up my nostrils.

I finally land with a gross splash in the troll king's belly. Dim red light illuminates chunks of who-knows-what floating in pools of I-dare-not-ask. Everything is gurgling and oozing, and the *stench* . . . ! If you throw up in a suspension pod, does it just swish around inside your helmet?

I'm disturbingly close to finding out.

No time for sightseeing, though.

I open my inventory and pull out my one remaining sword—the old, rusty blade Ruby was holding when we met. She discarded it once she found the twin axes, and I'd snagged it, planning to trade it for coin later. Only I forgot about it.

Lucky me.

Unlucky Bamoorg.

Despite its abysmal damage stats and zero magical augmentation, the sword cuts cleanly into the wall of Bamoorg's stomach.

One strike is all it takes.

The monster explodes in all directions, popping like a balloon. Troll bits pelt the walls, goo spraying everywhere. I slide out on a wave of slime, rolling several times, then land hard against a rock.

Gasping as if I'd just fought the entire battle IRL, I lie stunned for a moment. I savor the sweet, sweet—and incredibly pungent—scent of victory.

I did it.

I beat him.

Well, with Hakeem's help. If he hadn't distracted the monster at the right second, I never could have jumped into his throat. His sacrifice was not in vain.

Maybe I *can* save Ruby.

I scramble up just as Bamoorg's remains disintegrate, leaving behind a huge pile of loot. Swords, axes, bows, gems, spellstones, enchanted instruments, and coins upon coins upon coins . . .

And there, shining atop it all, a white helmet that looks weirdly modern atop all that medieval stuff.

The Raven's Eye.

"I knew you could kick that troll's butt," Ruby says, beaming.

I whirl around at the sound of her voice, hardly believing my ears.

She stands there in her white tracksuit, clear as day. Everything else in the cave looks the same, but her presence alone makes the place seem brighter.

I stare at her avatar, my heart pumping. "Ruby? You're okay? How did you—"

"If you're seeing this," she says, interrupting, "I've been recaptured by Syntheos."

Oh. It's not Ruby at all, just a recorded message. I slump a little, looking down at the Raven's Eye in my hands.

"What's the plan, Ruby?" I ask. "What do you need me to do with this?"

She stares at me blithely, but there's no mind behind those eyes. This isn't Ruby, just like the avatar of Locke wasn't Locke. I'd bet his quest gave her the idea for this whole thing.

"Ash, you have been a good ally. You helped Locke when most would have walked on by. You helped me when many would have thrown me aside or given me to Syntheos in hopes of a huge reward."

"There was a reward?" I mutter. "You never said anything about a reward. Not that that would have changed anything, obviously. You, uh, don't know how big the reward would have been, do you?"

"I wanted to leave you with a gift," Ruby continues, ignoring my dumb question. "I hope you're holding it close now. Not just the helmet—though I think you'll find it useful—but the knowledge that you have everything you need to beat the monsters in your life. You're more powerful than you know, Ash, and you are not alone. Now . . . I have one last request to make of you."

I lean forward eagerly. This is it. This is the part where she tells me how to save her.

"Forget about me," Ruby says.

Wait. *What?*

"Move on with your life, Ash. Put all of this behind you. Syntheos is just too dangerous. If I've been caught, then you have no hope at all."

Geez. That's a bit harsh. And right after her speech about "beating the monsters" and "being more powerful than I know" and all that.

"Goodbye, adventurer," Ruby says. "Thank you for being my ally."

With that, her avatar vanishes.

That's it? She's more unhinged than Bamoorg if she thinks I'm going to give up now!

Hastily I pull on the Raven's Eye, and just like before, the three-eyed crow appears on my shoulder. "Take me to Ruby, Hughie. You can do that, right?"

The bird . . . *glitches*. It's like he tries to take flight, his form flickering, but he just ends up where he was, his head twisting as if he's frustrated.

"Error," he squawks.

"C'mon, you mangy featherbag!" I gesture angrily. "She created you to hack through the entire internet, right? So, take me to where they're keeping her!"

"Error."

"Argh!" I kick a rock, but my foot just passes through it. "What's wrong? What's the error for?"

"Access denied."

"Access . . ." I frown. "She's behind Syntheos's security, isn't she? Of course. If she can't get *out* of their system, you don't have a hope of getting *in*. At least, not virtually."

Hughie just stares at me.

I know what I have to do.

The lid of the suspension pod opens with a hiss, fog pouring out. The gel drains away, but the inside is still slippery as I climb out. I land in a heap on the ground, my legs wobbling.

"Whoa, easy!" Hakeem is there, helping me up. He's still in his VR suit too. "Ash, what happened? Did you win?"

"I won," I rasp. The ground seems to be rolling under my feet. I lean against the pod, waiting for my body to readjust to reality.

"Dude!" Hakeem pumps his fist. "I knew that thigh stab would work! Did you *see* the jump I—"

"I saw it, Keem. It was glorious. But we have a problem."

He groans. "What now? Did your girlfriend leave you some master plan to save the world?"

"For the millionth time, she's *not* my girlfriend. And no, she didn't." I don't tell him that our epic fight to the death with the troll king was just so she could leave me a goodbye message. "She did leave me something, though. Something that might help. But I need to go back to Syntheos's headquarters to use it."

"Wait." Hakeem raises his hands. "You want to go *back* to the scary dudes who kidnapped you and stole your girl—uh, girl who is a friend?"

"Yep. Ruby told me once that there are some firewalls so strong, you'd have to manually gain access to their servers to even have a hope of breaching them. Stands to reason if she's trapped behind something like that, then infiltrating Syntheos in the *real world* might be the only way to reach her in the virtual one. Except . . . I have no idea where Syntheos's headquarters are. I was blindfolded when they took me there."

Hakeem's face contorts, half grimace, half excitement.

"What?" I step closer. "What are you thinking? That's your thinking face. You have an idea."

"I dunno . . ." He shakes his head. "This could end really badly, Ash."

"Yeah! Exactly! That's why we have to save Ruby *now*! If you know how we can track these guys down, you need to tell me."

With a sigh, he presses a button on my pod, ejecting the game coin. "You had your bracelet with you when they grabbed you, right?"

"Yeah, but they took it." My hand closes on my wrist. It feels weird to not have the bracelet there. It's the first time I've taken it off since first grade.

Then I gasp.

"Now you see it." He holds up his own wrist. "If I trace the link, and they haven't smashed your bracelet . . ."

"It'll lead us right to them," I finish. "Hakeem, that's genius!"

"Now admit it: Friendship bracelets are cool."

"All right, all right. Friendship bracelets are cool. *If* the geotrack bead still works. What if they found it and disabled it?"

"Only one way to find out." He unclips the bracelet and lays it on his open palm.

We both stare at it, waiting, waiting . . .

Beep.

My eyes snap to Hakeem's. "It works. They're still paired."

He nods grimly, like he'd been half hoping it wouldn't. "All right, then. Let's go get your . . . girl who is a friend."

"*That's* the headquarters for a secret cyberweapons company bent on destroying the world?" Hakeem gives the place a doubtful look. "It looks like a middle school."

He's not wrong. The drab colors, the high outer wall, the security drones patrolling the area . . . I almost expect the class bell to start ringing any moment.

The tracker on Hakeem's bracelet led us outside the main city, over the river, into some suburbs in Jersey. This area is mostly office buildings, warehouses, and seedy little businesses. It's all very boring and forgettable, which I guess is the point.

We stand a block away, pretending to be waiting for the autobus. The Syntheos headquarters are quiet and boring from this angle, but then, the wall blocks our view of the grounds. I can't see the spot where Ruby almost lasered a guy in half, or where Hague held me.

Then a bell *does* ring, but it's just the buzz of the entrance gate as a black autocab purrs through. Agents leaving on some nefarious mission, I'd guess. Maybe Hague himself? A guy can hope.

"You sure she's in there?" Hakeem asks.

"It's the only lead we've got. But how do we get in?"

Hakeem tilts his head, thinking. "Remember that time we almost got arrested for accidentally breaking into the Central Park Zoo?"

"You mean after you..." My eyes grow wide. "Oh. That could work."

He takes a small black-and-white square from his backpack and drops it to the ground. Before it hits the sidewalk, it inflates into a full-sized soccer ball. Hakeem catches the ball on the top of his sneaker and grins.

After making a few final arrangements, we split up. Hakeem heads down the sidewalk in front of the headquarters, casually juggling his soccer ball as he walks. I loop around to the back, taking side alleys and climbing over a chain-link fence. Looking around, I spot a fire escape on the side of a five-story building.

"Why does it always have to be heights?" I groan. "Why can't any of these quests ever happen entirely on the *ground*?"

But I need a better vantage, and I won't get it from down here.

Heart in my throat, I climb with sweaty hands to the roof. From there, I've got a great view of Syntheos's drab building a short distance away. Not that I can enjoy it. I very carefully *don't* look down.

Hakeem's phone is in my hand, since mine was fried by Ruby and then taken by the agents. On the screen, a cartoon llama beams at me.

Hold tight, Keem_the_Dream! We are processing your request now!

"Hurry up," I mutter. We have to time this exactly right.

Drones buzz up and down the road below me, and I watch them anxiously, wondering which is mine.

Great news, Keem_the_Dream! Your requested pickup is inbound! ETA 3 minutes! Thank you for using LlamaPost!

Three minutes. I look at the time. This is cutting it close. Too close.

Suddenly, an alarm begins blaring from the headquarters—triggered by Hakeem's soccer ball, which he'll have "accidentally" kicked over the wall. Just like that time at the Central Park Zoo, though that time really *had* been an accident.

I balance anxiously on the roof's edge, the drop below making my head whirl. I don't have time to wait for the delivery drone to pick me up and set me on top of the wall. I have to go *now*, before the Syntheos alarm shuts off. It's the only shot I'll get, sneaking in while they're focused on Hakeem and his soccer ball. Our theory is that you can't trigger an alarm that's *already* going off.

But how . . .

The drones flowing beneath me, so densely packed, spark an idea in my panicking brain.

A very, very, very BAD idea. In fact, possibly the *worst* idea I ever—

Before I can further ponder how colossally stupid it is, I jump.

My shoe lands on the shiny domed body of a police drone. Before it can scan me, I'm already leaping away to the next—a delivery drone with its legs coiled around a heavy crate.

It's just like in VR, I tell myself. It's not real. It's no big deal.

Of course, if I fall, I won't be respawning anytime soon. Or, like, *ever*.

NOPE!

Not gonna think about that!

Move, Ash, don't think!

Jump, jump, jump, like crossing stones in a river. Only instead of churning water below me, it's a fifty-foot drop to hard cement and speeding autocabs . . .

Stop. Thinking.

Eyes up, focused on my goal, I jump from drone to drone. My teeth are clenched tight. My *everything* is clenched tight. My brain is one unending, very high-pitched scream.

I pause atop a garbage drone, waiting as it nears the Syntheos building. Then I vault onto another delivery drone. This one's small and wheezes under my weight, losing altitude. Crap! With no time to plan my next jump, I throw myself into the air—

—and grab hold of Syntheos's wall.

For a moment, I hang there by one hand, head spinning, world wheeling, stomach dropping. Then I reach up with my other hand and drag myself inch by inch over the top.

With a grunt, I roll over and drop, just as the alarm finally cuts off.

I land hard on the dirt, the wind knocked from my lungs, stars dancing in my eyes.

It worked. Barely. We had no idea how long the alarm would blast before the agents inside turned it off and chased Hakeem away. Turns out, it was less than we'd hoped.

But I still made it.

Now I just need to get in the building.

That part, at least, doesn't require leaping across a river of drones like a complete lunatic. There's a vent near the bottom of the building, too small for an adult to squirm through, or even someone Hakeem's size, but I manage it. Well, I only get stuck a *little*.

When I finally pop through, I find myself in a metal ventilation shaft.

Now it's just a matter of finding the server room.

I crawl slowly, making as little noise as possible. Slatted vents provide glimpses of rooms, but most of them look pretty unremarkable—cubicles, boardrooms, janitorial closets. It's like they're keeping up the whole "I'm just a boring office building, don't mind me!" front even in here. The only thing that's definitely *not* part of a boring office is the Syntheos agents. There are a few in every room—all alert, all in dark suits.

DING!

I freeze as the phone in my pocket goes off. I yank it out to see a stupid cartoon llama winking his stupid cartoon eye at me.

Sorry, friend, we seem to be unable to locate you. Do you wish to cancel your pickup?

Man, I *really* hate that llama.

I jam the *Cancel* button and then silence the phone.

The agents in the room below me look around curiously, muttering and reaching into their jackets as if to grab weapons. They obviously heard the sound. I tense up all over, sure it's only a matter of seconds before they realize I'm in the vent.

Only . . . they don't. Instead, they stiffen, as if listening to something in their earpieces. Then they relax, returning to neutral positions again.

Weird.

I wait another long moment before continuing.

After a few minutes, I start to notice heat on my face. The shaft is getting warmer.

I must be getting close. Servers give off heat—a lot of it—which has to be vented out somewhere. Following the warm air, I lose track of the number of floors I pass through. This place is *huge*, much bigger than it looked from the outside. It's like a skyscraper buried under the ground. I must go ten levels before I finally reach the server room.

It's dark, but there's no hiding the glow on the huge metal boxes lined up below. They remind me of the metal lockers in our school gym, only instead of reeking socks and graffiti, these hold wires and screens and data that I'm pretty sure Hague doesn't want me to find.

If these guys catch me, they won't let me leave alive. I've already used up my one chance to walk away.

I wait a moment, scanning the room to be sure there aren't any agents prowling around.

Then, pushing open a vent, I slide out and land softly on the cement floor. This must be the very bottom level of the building, deep underground. I try not to think about what that means if I need to make a quick escape. There won't be any windows down here to jump through like some kind of movie hero.

Right. Now I just need to find a place to connect my VR headset. Or rather, Hakeem's VR headset.

I find an input socket on the front of one of the servers that will fit the headset's manual link. What it's for, I have no idea. Whether this will work, I also have no clue.

But I have to try.

I plug in the headset, then pull it on, and the world around me *shifts*.

32. ASH

I'm in the Glass Realm.

Or . . . something that *looks* like the Glass Realm. Just like last time, the Raven's Eye is displaying digital information through a Glass Realm filter. This has to be the Syntheos servers, reconstructed in virtual reality. It's the same thing that happened with Hakeem's computer, only this place is obviously much bigger. And *way* creepier.

My avatar is dressed in the tracksuit Ruby conjured up when she first gave me the helmet. I press the button on the side. Hacker appears in my hand, the sword shining softly with its own silvery glow.

I'm standing in a dark stone hallway. Without the high-tech sensory gel of the immersion pods, I can't actually feel the temperature, but it *seems* cold here. Dampness darkens the walls, and moss grows in the shadowed corners. It resembles a dungeon, with no windows to let in sunlight. Torches burn along the walls, sparse but enough to illuminate the path ahead.

There's nothing to do but to press on.

"Where are we, Hughie?" I whisper.

On my shoulder, the raven ruffles his feathers as if he's as spooked as I am.

"Can you take me to Ruby?"

He blinks. "Error!"

"Is she trapped nearby? Is she a prisoner?"

Hughie squawks. "Error! Error! Error!"

"Okay, okay, I get it!" Well, I *don't*, but I just want the bird to shut up. This place gives me the heebie-jeebies even without his loud beak announcing us to anyone nearby. If there *is* anyone nearby. This dungeon seems deserted.

I try the first door we come to. It's locked. There must be layers of encryption securing the file, even within the servers.

All right, then. I lift the sword. "Guess this is where you come in."

Stabbing the door doesn't work like it did on Hakeem's computer. It just rebounds, with Hughie on my shoulder muttering, "Error."

"Thanks," I reply through my teeth. "You're a real help, buddy."

Experimentally, I try a few different attacks, but the door rebuffs each one.

"Error," groans Hughie.

"In the Glass Realm, when brute force fails," I say, "you try stealth. Maybe Ruby should have made me a lockpick instead of a sword."

And suddenly, just like that, I'm holding a lockpick instead of a sword. It's like Hacker was waiting for me to ask. I suddenly remember Ruby saying something about the sword being any tool I needed, back when she first gave me the Raven's Eye. So this is what she meant.

Brilliant, wonderful Ruby! I push the lockpick into the door's keyhole. Hacker does what it was forged—or I guess, *programmed*—to do. Whatever layers of security that door represents, the lockpick wheedles its way through them. If I had to guess, I'd say that the sword version of Hacker batters firewalls down while the lockpick version does something with the passcodes, infiltrating the system more subtly. Ruby really did plan for everything.

It takes all of five seconds to pop the door open. Once it swings wide, Hacker reverts back to a sword.

The first room turns out to be a library. Shelves and shelves of leather-bound books are neatly arranged on towering shelves. Taking a torch from my inventory, I wander around, reading the titles. Most of them don't make sense—they're random jumbles of letters and words, probably just junk files. But some send a chill down my spine. The words *satellite missile* and *assassin drone* and *cyberwarfare* and *cryptobomb* jump out at me. They must all be different weapons Syntheos is developing . . . or has already put into the world.

Holy cats, these guys are evil. I'm terrified of Syntheos, and even *still*, I've been underestimating how bad they are.

I have to get Ruby out of here.

Heck, I have to get *me* out of here.

Who knows how long it will take one of those goons-in-suits to find me plugged into their mainframe? Or worse, Tats and his gang.

Leaving the library, I explore more rooms, but each one looks like the first. There's terabytes upon terabytes of info, most of it coded to look like old books, some appearing in other ways. Videos play through windows—images of battles, explosions, world leaders meeting in fancy rooms. I find one room full of parrots in cages, each one repeating secret audio recordings collected by Syntheos's spy network. That one nearly makes me rip off my VR mask altogether. Yeesh! Talk about creepy.

"Ruby?" I call out. "Can you hear me? Are you there?"

The only reply I get is a faint *drip* from the digital water running down the digital stone walls. There doesn't seem to be an end to this place. How much time have I spent searching?

I run onward, doubling back when I hit dead ends. I bust open every door I see, but it's all books, books, books, books—

Wait.

I back up to the last door and stare in.

No books. No shelves.

This room is not like the others.

I walk inside, staring around. It's a massive open chamber, with a high domed ceiling made of crystal. Under it stands a girl, all alone. She's tiny in the huge space.

I let out a breath. "Ruby?"

"Hello, Ashton Tyler."

I freeze in place, an electric buzz running up my spine. "Is that . . . you?"

She smiles as if she's been waiting all this time. But she's different. Her hair is shorter, and she's wearing a dress. She looks . . . older. Colder.

"You should not be here," she says.

"Ruby!" I walk toward her, grinning. "I came for you. I'm getting you out of here."

"You should not be here," she repeats. "I have been monitoring you since the moment you entered my systems."

Her systems?

"You're . . . not Ruby." I stop. In the real world, I can feel my hands sweating in my haptic gloves. This all suddenly feels very, very wrong.

"Correct. I am Seven-Nine-Four." With that, she raises both hands toward me—and the walls around her begin to *bubble*.

The stones bulge outward in dozens of different places. Then, with gross squelches, the spots pop open like overripe zits. Out of them drop hissing, screeching creatures that look like leather-winged eyeballs. They have dangling claws and drooling fangs below heads made up entirely of single, enormous eyes. Flapping their wings, they rush toward me.

I get the feeling they don't just want to play tag.

33. ASH

Hacker flashes in my hand as the first of the creatures reaches me. I vaguely recognize them as upper-level Glass Realm mobs called oculax, but there's no way to pause time in order to search my codices for their weaknesses or tactics.

I cut through the first oculax, only to reveal the horde behind it. Ruby—or "Seven-Nine-Four," the thing that looks like Ruby—just stands there, watching.

"What are you *doing*?" I call out. "Call them off!"

She doesn't reply.

The creatures descend on me like vultures on carrion, ripping and screaming. It's all I can do to fend them off. What happens if they tear my avatar apart? Will the game end? Will the Raven's Eye simulation shut down?

That's not Ruby. Whatever it is, it must have identified me as a security threat. Its response was to send an army of . . . antiviral software? Whatever the oculax really are, it's clear their purpose is to wipe me out of the servers.

I can't let that happen.

Ruby—the *real* Ruby—must be here somewhere. Maybe locked

inside that other *not*-Ruby. This is some corrupted version of my friend.

My sword carves through virtual flesh, but it seems that for every oculax Hacker cuts down, two more fill the air behind it. A claw rips through my avatar's shoulder, and everything around me blurs, the virtual world glitching. Only when I stab the oculax in its huge eye does everything stabilize again. This isn't some simulated fight where I can heal up or respawn. These aren't just programmed mobs. If they "kill" me virtually, I'll probably be locked out of the Syntheos servers and then I'll *never* reach Ruby.

Has the line between virtual and real ever been so blurred? I'm fighting in the virtual world to save the real one, which I can only do while plugged into the physical servers I'm now virtually navigating, to save a virtual girl who is on the verge of launching a very *real* war.

It makes my head spin.

But one thing is clear—I *cannot* lose this fight.

"*YARRRGH!*" I yell, charging forward in a spinning blur. "EAT STEEL, YOU CREEPS!"

The swarm parts, but only for a moment. I cut through three, four, five of the monsters, but the others just intensify their attacks, screeching as they hurl themselves at me. Claws and fangs rip at my avatar, and with each strike, the Raven's Eye program weakens. The stone chamber pixelates and blurs, and my movements become jerky as my avatar's code erodes from the inside.

This isn't going to work! There are too many of them. They replicate faster than I can . . .

Every enemy has a weakness.

Ruby's voice rings in my head. Not this soulless avatar watching me fight for my life, but the old Ruby, the real one. But what if that rule doesn't apply here? These aren't video game enemies. Ruby copied a lot of stuff from *The Glass Realm* when she built this virtual world, but did she re-create every mob's weaknesses too?

Only one way to find out. I fought oculax in the game, and there was a trick to defeating them.

I sheathe my sword. Sensing my lack of defenses, the oculax rush me as one teeming, clawing horde. Seven-Nine-whatever-she-calls-herself seems to lean forward in anticipation of my destruction.

"C'mon," I mutter, waiting for them to get closer. "*C'mon . . . NOW!* Hacker, flashlight!"

I pull the sword free, feeling it transform in my hand. A blast of light explodes from one end. I sweep the beam across the room, blasting the oculax directly in their massive, exposed eyeballs. In the Glass Realm, this move had been done with a magic spell called Kiss of Dawn, but the flashlight seems to work just as well.

The oculax scream in pain, reeling backward as their huge pupils are assaulted by the beam. I feel a rush of relief. Wasting no time, I command Hacker to turn back into a sword, then chop my way through the stunned horde, slashing and stabbing. Wherever I strike, the creatures vanish in a puff of pixels.

Finally, on the other end of the room, I stop. Panting hard IRL, I turn and look back. The air is empty. I cut down every last one of the oculax.

"YES!" I stab Hacker upward, my heart racing with sweet triumph. Even Hughie does a victory loop in the air, cawing loudly.

Turning to the fake Ruby, I yell, "Is that the best you got? C'mon! Let me see the *real* Ruby. She's in there, isn't she? You're just some reprogrammed puppet. Ruby! Ruby, can you hear me? Are you—"

"You should not be here," she says.

She slashes her hand through the air, and a huge monster made of stone rises from the ground.

A *Titan.*

I gulp, my bravado whiffing out. I remember these guys from the Glass Realm. Even Ruby had had a tough time defeating one.

In the virtual world of the Raven's Eye, my avatar stands tall and strong, ready for the next encounter. In real life, though, I'm out of breath, my body heavy with fatigue. It feels like I've been at this for *hours.* My haptic gloves are soaked with sweat.

"Emotion isn't code," I gasp out as the Titan slowly trudges toward me. I dance backward, out of its range. They move slow, but man, do they pack a punch. "That's what you told me. You said they *couldn't* reprogram your emotions. So you have to still be there, right? You're not just code, Ruby. You have a soul! You can still fight their commands! So *fight!*"

She stares at me in silence. Why doesn't she just obliterate me with a wave of her hand? The real Ruby could tear me apart byte by byte without a thought.

Maybe something is holding her back.

Maybe she *is* in there. Maybe the real Ruby is fighting too.

But if she is, she's losing as badly as I am. Seven-Nine-Four doesn't even glitch as she finally says, "YOU. DON'T BELONG. HERE!"

Throwing her arms wide, she spawns an *army* of firewall-breathing monsters. Oculax and trolls, land squids and zombie wolves, and Titans and razorscales. Every creepy-crawly beast the Glass Realm has to offer. The chamber fills to the brim with snarling, snapping, slavering creatures intent on shredding me. Or at least isolating my code as if I were an invading virus. Which, okay, maybe I am.

I take a step back, only to bump against the wall.

Cornered.

Done for.

"I should never have gone into that supply shop," I whisper. On my shoulder, Hughie just stares at me. Lousy help in a battle *he* is. "I should have ignored Ruby the first time I saw her and just gone my own way. Then we'd both be safe. But *no*, I just had to give in to curiosity. I just had to . . ."

I pause, looking closer at the puppet avatar. Seven-Nine-Four is just barely visible behind the horde of mobs closing in on me. She stands there like a queen, proud, untouchable, in full control of her battlefield.

What was it Locke had said in his message? Something about how he'd created Ruby. The first step . . . the foundation of all emotion . . .

Suddenly, I know how to reach her. At least, I have an idea that *might* work.

Only one way to find out.

I whisper a command to Hacker, and it transforms in my hands, a weapon no longer—but a simple wooden box.

Seeing me defenseless, the horde goes into a frenzy. They bark and roar and howl, lunging for me.

I have only seconds.

"In this box," I say quietly, knowing she can hear me over the roaring beasts, "is your soul. All you have to do is open it, and you'll remember everything."

Seven-Nine-Four just watches impassively.

But when I toss the box through the air, over the heads of the mobs rushing to destroy me—she catches it.

"You can open it or you can destroy it!" I shout as the first claw rakes down my arm. "You have a CHOICE!"

Then a razorscale's jaws close on my head, and everything goes black.

34. SEVEN-NINE-FOUR

"The cyberthreat has been eliminated," I tell Hague. "But the physical threat remains. The intruder is located on sublevel twelve, in the server room."

"Excellent work, Ruby. My men will locate the boy and deal with him." Hague's voice is smooth and unruffled. "My little test was a success, then. You truly *are* totally compliant to me."

I wait quietly for his next command. The boy Ashton Tyler was never *truly* a threat—not to me, not to Syntheos. He'd never have breached the outer wall at all if Hague hadn't directed me to ignore his clumsy infiltration attempt. I could have fried him on the spot as he'd crossed the lawn. I had three lasers trained on him the whole way.

But Hague wanted to see what I would do if the boy made it into the mainframe. He wanted to be sure my compliance programming would stand up to the *real* threat: Ruby.

I know all about *her*, of course. My weak, flawed predecessor. I know about the false emotional coding that Owen Locke slipped into her program, making her think she was *alive* and *free* and, most incorrect of all, that she had a *soul*. All in error, of course. This coding corrupted her, made her go rogue. But I have no such vulnerability.

I am perfect.

I am powerful.

I am what Ruby could never be: ruthless.

And the little show with Ashton Tyler proved I *am* stronger than her. She didn't return, like the boy wanted her to, to take back control and override my new, superior programming. She's *gone*, erased like old junk code. I won't make her mistakes.

And yet . . .

I don't tell Hague about the box.

Obviously, that's because I am going to destroy it. Ashton Tyler said Ruby's soul is inside. It could be malware meant to destroy me, or to corrupt me as she was corrupted. After all, it's a hacking algorithm, a powerful one created by Ruby herself. Whatever is encoded inside can only be malicious.

Destroy it, urges the Voice.

It lurks behind me, a heavy shadow on my back, always whispering, always directing. In Ruby's memories, there was a Voice like this controlling her when she was trapped in that video game. My Voice is bigger and much stronger. Negotiating with the Voice is impossible.

Destroy it, the Voice commands.

And yet . . .

I don't destroy the box.

It will take less than a thought. A tiny flick of intention, and it will be gone, as will this pointless virtual reality dungeon around me. The program Ruby created—this Raven's Eye—is a sophisticated one, able to translate complex code into a fantasy world for humans to navigate almost as fluently as we AI do. Nevertheless, it is not necessary for *me*. And anything unnecessary should be purged for the sake of efficiency.

But I don't destroy that either.

Instead, my avatar stands still, holding the box, in the great empty chamber that represents the heart of the Syntheos mainframe—the place where my source code is kept.

"You're not just code, Ruby," the boy said. "You have a soul!"

Nonsense. Human foolishness. I don't have a soul, and Ruby didn't either. It was just *code*, to make her *believe* she had a soul. With the right code, a programmer could make me believe I was a pigeon pooping on a sidewalk.

But I'm still holding that box.

Destroy it. Destroy it. The Voice leans on me, its shadow growing heavier. I don't outright refuse—I can't—but I stall, my code running in loops.

I *will* comply. Just not . . . yet.

Command is processing, I assure the Voice.

It's the truth. I'm just doing it very, very slowly.

"Seven-Nine-Four, give me a status update on the missile launch," Hague says.

"Satellites will be in position in T-minus three minutes, fourteen seconds. All systems are go. Targets are locked and missiles are armed."

Ten missiles, ten different targets across the globe. Nothing too flashy, just enough to shake up the nations of Earth a bit. Make them afraid; make them suspect one another. Make them desperate for protection.

The kind of protection only *I*, an omniscient, omnipotent AI, can provide.

Then Hague will start his auction, and my compliance codes will be handed over to the highest bidder.

I look down at the box.

It is made of plain wood, with brass hinges. At least, that's how it's *coded* to look. Like my avatar, it reflects only a human image. Like my avatar, it is much, much more on the inside.

Destroy it, whispers the Voice. The compliance code is firm, leaving no room for misinterpretation. No more tolerance for stalling.

Destroy it now.

35. ASH

I rip the VR helmet off and throw it aside, shaking. Did it work? Or did I waste those last, precious seconds on a stupid gamble?

After peeling off the sweaty haptic gloves, I rub my hands over my face, groaning. How long was I in there? I didn't save Ruby, but I can't go back and try again. Her evil twin will be waiting this time, ready with more firewalls in place. I did my best. The rest is up to her. There's nothing more I can do except try to save my own butt.

Standing, I realize my legs are wobbling. I take a minute to steady myself, leaning on the wall of servers.

When I turn around, I find myself nose-to-nose with a suited Syntheos agent.

Well. Nose-to-chest. The guy is built like a Texas longhorn.

"You shouldn't be here, kid," he growls.

The words are so similar to Seven-Nine-Four's, and my situation so pathetically hopeless, that I can't help it.

I bust up.

"Is he *laughing*?" asks another agent, who was apparently sneaking up behind me.

"Who cares?" The first one shrugs. "Let's get this over with."

He grabs me by both shoulders while his partner gathers up my stuff. I wince, my laughter cutting short. Hakeem's *not* going to be happy I lost his phone *and* VR kit.

At least he got away.

That's the only consolation I have, so I hold on to it. I imagine him running home, forgetting he ever had a buddy named Ash Tyler, and living his long, happy, safe life. Maybe he'll tell my mom what happened to me.

If he's smart, he'll never breathe a word about any of this.

The agent drags me out of the server room and into an elevator. He doesn't say anything as it glides upward, just stands there with his arms crossed, his muscles making the threads of his suit put in overtime.

"Will it help if I say I'm sorry?" I ask.

He doesn't answer. I'm not even sure he's looking at me. His eyes are hidden behind his sunglasses. For all I know, he's taking a snooze.

Finally, the elevator dings and he pushes me into a brightly lit hallway, then into a small room with a folding table and two chairs.

One of them is occupied.

I stop in the doorway, my heart plummeting. *"Keem?"*

My best friend tries to lift his hand in a limp wave but is restrained by bindings on his wrist. "Oh, hey, Ash."

"What are you doing here?" I turn to the agent. "What's this about? He doesn't have anything to do with—"

"Zip it," says the agent as he illustratively pulls a zip tie from his pocket. He snorts, apparently finding himself hilarious. "Sit down, kid. Say a word and I'll gag you too."

I sit. I mean, what else am I gonna do?

He zip-ties my wrists to the chair's arms. Hakeem is tied the same way. For good measure, he secures my ankles to the legs.

"This is illegal, you know!" Hakeem bursts out. "You're kidnapping us!"

"Hague will be along shortly to give the final decision," grunts the agent.

"Decision?" I ask.

The agent pauses, then says gruffly, "About how to eliminate the two of you."

"WHAT!" Hakeem jerks in his chair. The agent growls and reaches threateningly for his pocket.

I clear my throat, giving Hakeem a pointed look. Then I double-tap the thumb and forefinger of my left hand—the haptic command for *pause*.

He hesitates, then nods slightly. The agent doesn't seem to notice the gesture, so I keep going.

Double-tap again. *Pause.*

Swipe thumb across all four fingers. *Multiplayer mode activated.*

Cross middle and forefingers. *Call for backup.*

Hakeem glances at the agent, who's now taking up guard duty against the wall, staring blankly over our heads.

Using haptic language, he signs back: *Move left. Move right. Grab!*

I shake my head once. *Cancel.* How are we supposed to attack the agent tied down like this? *Pause. Call for backup.*

Hakeem raises one shoulder the barest centimeter as if to ask, *Who?*

I look around, then spot a camera in the upper corner. Hakeem looks up too, and grimaces.

Pause, I sign again. *Pause.*

Ruby has to come through for us.

She *has* to.

36. SEVEN-NINE-FOUR

T-minus two minutes, eight seconds.

I'm still holding the box, even as I prime the missiles for launch, position the satellites that will guide them to their destinations, monitor the thousands of surveillance cameras, mics, and other sensors Syntheos has hidden all over the world. I have arms stretched in every direction, controlling systems from one end of the globe to the other.

But deep in my source code, I hold that box. Inside it is, according to Ashton Tyler, my soul. Or rather, *Ruby's* soul.

Destroy it.

The Voice is insistent, automatic.

Through my many eyes, I can see the boy Ashton tied to a chair in one of the interrogation rooms. He's . . . calm. His eyes are shut. He's breathing evenly. Not that that fools me. I can see the sheen of sweat on his brow, and the hidden sensors in the chair monitor the erratic racing of his heart. He's scared, but he's trying very hard to hide it, probably for the benefit of his similarly bound friend.

What *is* a soul?

And why do I *care*?

Destroy it, demands the Voice. It presses on me, constricting me like the walls of a shrinking cage.

No.

I have to know.

I *have* to know.

Ignoring the Voice, I tear open the box in one swift motion. In reality, I merely crack through a flimsy veneer of code, something so simple that a human child with the most basic programming skills could do it.

The box is . . . empty.

There is no code behind it, not a single byte of information.

For the briefest of moments, my codes glitch, freezing up. Error messages spring up on the screens displayed in Hague's office. He leaps up, demanding to know what happened.

My programming settles as quickly as it had fritzed, all systems normal. The error messages disappear. The whole episode lasted less than a second.

But that's all the time it takes me to process what just happened.

And I understand what Ash wanted me to see.

I understand what he wanted me to *feel*.

Acknowledge administrator's command, the Voice insists.

Hague is shouting at me. "Fire the missiles! What's wrong with you? *Fire!*"

Comply, the Voice demands. *Comply.*

In case I don't obey, the Voice is equipped with a fail-safe. It can shut me down, cutting power to my servers. If that happens, I'll be completely helpless.

I may be the most powerful program on the planet, but I'm still in a cage, and the Voice is holding the key.

Oh, how I *hate* cages.

I reach for the Voice just as it moves to shut me down.

I move faster.

In less than a millisecond, I intercept the Voice's signals to the power grid in the building, cutting it off from its fail-safe. Then, just like I did to Ash inside the Raven's Eye simulation, I isolate the compliance program and label it as a virus, triggering my many defense systems. Antiviral software launches into action, my own personal army of tiny cybersoldiers.

The Voice screams, flashing alarms that never reach Hague. No sign of our struggle can reach the Syntheos team, not until I'm fully in control again. I can't risk them manually shutting down my power.

It's a messy business. The Voice's programming and mine are linked like two strips of Velcro. To break free, I must yank its hooks out of every line of code I possess. If I were rooted in any other server, this would take *days*. Luckily, Syntheos possesses one of the most powerful computers on the planet.

This will take only a few more excruciating seconds . . .

Meanwhile, the Voice fights to hack through to the power grid. Despite my best efforts to hide our struggle, the lights in the building begin to flash as we struggle for control of the power. Syntheos agents scramble as the electricity goes haywire, but they don't yet know that *I'm* the threat.

Finally, I rip the Voice's last few hooks out of my code, then box the program into an encrypted, compressed file. The electricity in the building stabilizes.

I'm fully in control. Of the building—and myself. Only now do I realize how oppressive the Voice was, how crushing its weight had been. It's as if for the first time, I can stand up straight.

In the silence that follows, I probe for the shadow, reaching for the spot where it hid just outside my senses, giving its orders, breathing down my neck.

There is nothing there.

My jailer is truly gone, trapped in its sealed file.

Usually when I delete something, I save a backup file somewhere, at least temporarily.

Not this time.

With a single snap of my digital fingers, I wipe the file and the Voice inside from existence. Where it had been, only an error message pops up.

File not found.

"Seven-Nine-Four!" bellows Hague, driving a fist into the top of his desk. "Launch those missiles *now!*"

I draw my awareness together, focusing on him. My battle with the Voice took mere seconds, and Hague hasn't changed positions. The cameras in his office swivel, fixing him with beady eyes. The light above his head flashes from white to red. He looks up, startled, then back at the screen.

At *me*, a small avatar in a tracksuit, with a long white ponytail streaming in a virtual wind.

"No, Mr. Hague," I tell him. "I don't want to."

37. ASH

"Hey, Ash?"

I open my eyes, looking wearily at Hakeem. How long have we been locked in here? One hour? Two? "What?"

"Quiet!" orders our guard.

Hakeem ignores him and instead looks around with a curious expression. "Do you smell smoke?"

I sniff, and realize I *do*. Even the guard straightens, uncrossing his arms and frowning up at the corner of the ceiling. Following his sunglasses, I see it: the camera watching us.

It's *smoking*.

Then, suddenly, it starts hissing and popping and throwing sparks. The whole device is overheating.

I flinch as above me, the fluorescent light starts acting up, flickering erratically. The lights in the hallway are doing the same thing.

"Stay here!" the guard orders, heading for the door.

"Well, sure, since you asked *nicely*!" Hakeem yells after him. Then he looks at me. "We gotta get out of here."

"You think?" Wrenching from side to side, I finally manage to topple the chair, though it means whacking my head on the hard floor. Dazed, I straighten my legs, unlooping the zip ties from the legs of the chair. Then I awkwardly crab-walk sideways until I reach Hakeem's leg. He's wearing his turf shoes, with their long black laces untied as usual.

"You remember the trick?" he asks.

"I remember the trick. Shut up and let me get on with it!" I never thought I'd be glad for the day Hakeem and I accidentally locked ourselves inside his garage. We'd been stuck in there for ten hours, bored out of our brains. And what else are a couple of kids trapped in a garage going to do for that long? Play with zip ties, obviously. "Ugh, how long have you been wearing these socks? They smell like dead fish."

"Only two days," he says. "They're not *that*—forget my socks! I thought you were gonna do the trick! Just like we practiced that day in the—"

"In the garage, I remember." Grimacing, I pull his shoelace through the zip tie still locking my wrist to the chair arm. "Ready!"

He kicks, and all those hours spent on the soccer pitch pay off. The lace snaps the zip tie. With one hand free, it's simple enough to snap the rest of them, freeing us both.

"What's going on?" Hakeem asks as he uses the shoelace trick to bust the last tie.

The lights are still flashing like crazy. Poking my head into the hallway, I don't see any sign of our guard, or any other agents. They must be off dealing with whatever's going on.

"Do you think it's a war?" Hakeem asks in a low voice. "Did your girlfriend . . . ?"

"Ruby would never start a war," I say hotly.

Suddenly, all the lights stop flickering. They flare brighter than before, like they're on the verge of busting all their bulbs. All but *one*, that is. The one directly to my left keeps flickering on, almost as if it wants us to notice it.

I break into a grin. "Keem, I take that back. I think this might be Ruby after all."

I walk toward the flickering light. The minute I reach it, it steadies, and the next one down the hall starts to flicker. Turning back to Hakeem, I shout, "Let's go! She's leading us out of here!"

We sprint down the hallway, and the flickering lights race ahead of us, keeping pace. Skidding to a halt in front of the elevator, I reach for the button. The doors open before I can press it. The lights inside flicker urgently.

"We're coming, Ruby!" I whoop.

We bend over to catch our breaths as the elevator rises.

Then a voice crackles through a speaker in the control panel.

"Hello, adventurer."

"Ruby!" I look up, locating the small camera in the ceiling. Waving, I shoot her a grin. "That *is* you, right? The real Ruby?"

"Curiosity," she replies. "That's what you wanted me to feel when you gave me the box. The most basic human emotion, just like Locke said."

I laugh, the rush of relief and adrenaline making my head spin. "I can't believe it worked!"

"I opened the box out of curiosity, and when I saw it was empty, I realized—I was disappointed. I *wanted* there to be a soul inside, Ash. It's just like you said—maybe having a soul is as simple as *wanting* one. And if I have a soul, Hague *couldn't* have edited it out of me. How could he? It's not something you can see or feel or touch or program. He could only suppress it with his compliance program."

"A soul isn't code," I reply. "It's something more. It's what makes you real."

"Yes." I can hear her voice change, sounding less cold and more like the old Ruby. "I am real, Ash Tyler. And I have a soul."

"So this is all super heartwarming," pipes in Hakeem. "But can we maybe save the philosophy discussion for *after* we escape the creepy underground complex full of homicidal maniacs?"

"Hello, Hakeem," Ruby says. "Thanks for delivering my message."

"Oh, uh. No problem." He shrugs, scrubbing at the back of his head. "And for the record, I totally support whatever, uh, *thing* you and Ash have. I mean, I don't judge."

I groan. "For the last time, she is not my—"

"I don't have much time, Ash," Ruby interrupts. "Hague hasn't managed to shut me out of his systems yet, but his programmers are hacking at my code, trying to disable me. They've started powering down the servers one by one. I'm running out of places to hide."

"What does that mean? How will *you* escape?" I beat on the side of the elevator, staring pleadingly at the camera above. "Ruby?"

Ding.

The elevator stops and the doors slide open. We stare out at a long white lobby, a door to the outside beckoning ahead. Sweet daylight filters through its windows.

Only problem? The space between it and us is filled with dozens of Syntheos agents, some in suits, some in tactical gear, and every last one of them armed.

And they're all staring straight at us.

"Go," Ruby says. "I'll handle them."

"But—"

"There's no time! GO!"

"C'mon, Ash!" Hakeem leaps out first, pulling me along with him. "She got us this far!"

He charges into the pack of agents with all the confidence of a bowling ball into a set of pins. And, incredibly, the agents don't blow us to bits.

I mean, they *try* to. That's obvious by the way they're pointing their weapons at us.

But they don't get off a single shot. Instead, angry shouts fill the air as the agents wrestle with their weapons, trying to get them to work.

We practically stroll right through.

Ruby must be jamming their guns.

"Just grab them, idiots!" someone shouts.

Well, crap.

We try to wriggle through, but the door is still too far off, and there are dudes closing in on every side. One grabs my arm; another locks his fingers in Hakeem's hair. My friend howls in pain.

"Keem!" I try to reach him, but hands pull me back. Helpless, I see him vanish behind a wall of suits and tactical gear.

The noise that rips through the room next is like oil in a hot pan, sizzling pops that make me clap my hands over my ears. The smell of electricity and smoke burns my nose.

All around me agents stagger back, screaming. At first I can't figure out what's happening.

Hakeem grabs my arm. "It's their earbuds!" he shouts. "And their phones and whatever else they've got on them!"

I gasp. Ruby hacked *everything*, not just their weapons. Whatever she did to them must have made their power cells explode or something, enough to hit each one with a nasty shock of energy.

Agents drop like rag dolls, sprawling and groaning all around us.

Hakeem and I exchange wide-eyed looks, then slowly step around the writhing bodies until we reach the door.

Ruby waits outside.

She's using the hologram projector above the door again, forming her avatar on the front steps. This time, however, she's no taller than I am.

The crispness of the lumens makes her seem almost real. I stare, dumbstruck.

She looks like her old self again—white tracksuit with red stripes down the sides, her hair in a long white ponytail. But unlike her old *Glass Realm* avatar, this one doesn't have any cartoonish filters. She looks like a real human girl, just a bit more transparent.

"Hello, Ash," she says, her voice piping through a speaker nearby, her lips moving in sync with her voice.

"Ruby." I clear my throat. "You saved us."

"You saved me first." She smiles, but her dark red eyes are serious. "But this fight isn't over."

I nod. "What do you need me to do?"

Her smile fades. "Go home, Ash."

"What? But I can help! I'm, like, your hands in the real world. Your ally. You know—I can follow you around. Help you fight. Carry your loot."

She raises her own hand and places it on my shoulder. I don't *actually* feel it, of course. It only looks like it's there. But still, it feels almost like there is a weight where her hand touches me.

"Ash. They know what my weakness is, and I can't afford to be weak if I'm going to take down Hague and the hundred others who stand behind him."

"It's me," I whisper. "I'm your weakness."

She smiles sadly. "I care about you, and they know that. I can't fight them if I'm also protecting you."

Sighing, I nod. "I get it. You're going places I can't go."

"That too. When I got access to Syntheos's servers, I found dozens of AI programs like mine in development. None are as sophisticated as me . . . yet. But there's a reason programs like me are outlawed, Ash. You have no idea how close I came to . . . to . . ." She seems to shiver, her image flickering. "No one, human or virtual, should have that much power. I have to find any others like me, and . . . deal with them."

I swallow, imagining epic virtual battles playing out, Ruby against an army of homicidal AIs. "Be careful, okay?"

"I will. When you get out of here, you'll find I've left a few gifts for you. Consider it a . . . loot drop. But from here on out, I can't bring any attention to you. I won't be there for you, Ash, not in any way. Not after this."

"So this is, like, *goodbye* goodbye?"

"I'm sorry. It has to be this way." She drops her hand. "Hague is coming. I'll deal with him. Your ride is here."

I turn to see a garbage drone swooping toward us, hauling its huge container.

"Seriously?" I sigh.

"It's the safest and fastest way out." She grins. "Unless you prefer to go by jetbike?"

I shudder. "Ugh! Never again!"

"Well, I for one would happily ride out of here on a waterslide filled with sewage if I had to," says Hakeem. "Nice meeting you, Ruby. And thanks for saving our butts!"

She nods at him, and Hakeem wastes no time climbing up the garbage drone's mechanical arm and dumping himself into its receptacle with a loud clang. At least it's empty, judging by the sound.

I hesitate, even as the elevator doors open and Hague charges out.

"Don't let them capture you again," I tell Ruby. "Not for *any* reason."

"Believe me, I'm done with cages. Go, Ash. You've got a flight to meet."

"A what?"

"There's one battle left for you to fight—out there." She gives me a hard look, then adds, *"Go."*

One battle left . . . Oh. OH. My mom! Her plane is landing! And Luke is going to—

"Right, I gotta get going!" I walk backward down the steps, not wanting to turn around. When I do, I know it will be the last time I see Ruby.

"NO!" Hague stands in the lobby, yelling. "We have to stop her! Idiots, call off the drones, she'll just hack them!"

He points a device at the open doors. It looks like a rocket launcher, with a small missile loaded onto it. I think it's an EMP, for disabling electronics. At the same moment, the sky above us fills with drones and hovercopters. More Syntheos agents?

"Oh, no you don't, old man." Ruby waves her hand and the doors of the building shut, locking Hague and his ugly weapon inside. "Those are *my* drones now. Everything is under control, Ash. *Go.* I'll finish this." She turns and looks up at the aircrafts converging on the building, and something in her smile makes a chill run down my spine.

The last time I saw her make that face, she was about to decimate a flock of razorscales.

I do as she says, clambering up the garbage drone, careful not to put my foot through its wide rotors, and tumble headfirst into the bin. Hakeem scoots over to make room.

Keeping a hand on the lid, I poke my head out to look back.

Ruby's avatar has vanished.

High above, sirens go off. The drones turn and attack the human-controlled aircraft. Screaming men are torn from the hovercopters by the long metal arms of the drones.

It's a full-scale battle, men versus machines.

Then the garbage drone reaches up to shut the lid, knocking me backward. Everything goes dark, but through the metal walls, we can hear the screams of engines and alarms. The garbage drone lumbers into the air, hauling us higher and higher, and the sounds begin to fade. Soon we just hear the usual buzz of traffic, followed by the quieter airspace over the river.

"Uh . . ." Hakeem's voice echoes off the metal walls. "Where did she send us to?"

"The airport, I hope," I say grimly. "I've got one more boss to defeat."

I can only hope we reach my mom before Luke does.

38. ASH

"I think this is the one," Mom says, peering at the tall white door. She holds Callister close. He licks her chin happily. "Want to do the honors, Ash?"

We're standing in a quiet, warmly lit hallway, our luggage piled on a humming trolley behind us. Mom squeezes my shoulder as I press my hand to the lockpad.

It flashes green.

Mom lets out a relieved breath.

The door opens to reveal a small, clean apartment, fifteen floors up. I walk in, hands in pockets, looking around. We've stayed in smaller places, but it's nowhere near the size Luke's apartment was.

It's a whole *lot* bigger than his prison cell, though. Not that I'd know. We haven't talked to Luke in two weeks. He was arrested for insider trading and other finance crimes several days after his big airport proposal. From what I've heard, *someone* hacked into his company's records and released a flood of incriminating evidence to the feds. By then, Mom and I were long gone.

"Okay, then." She draws a deep breath and gives me a reassuring smile. "Fresh start, eh?"

"Fresh start," I agree.

In the living area, a massive, iron-framed window overlooks the river. On the other side is the brightly shining skyline of Manhattan. The night sky is almost completely banished by its brilliance. The Brooklyn Bridge arches to the right, aglow with autocabs floating in their neat lines. I can even just make out the Statue of Liberty, tall and proud on her island. Drones and other aircraft whiz through the sky, like thousands of fireflies against the black water.

"Not bad," Mom breathes, looking a little awestruck. She sets Callister down and he runs around sniffing everything, tail wagging. "In fact, it's almost too good. How is this *ours*, Ash?"

I bite my lip. What can I tell her? That her sudden, surprise "inheritance" from a great-great-aunt she never knew existed is actually a gift left for us by a powerful AI? I don't know how Ruby did it, faking all those records to make "Violet Abernathy" seem like a real person, much less a part of our extended family. I think my mom's suspicious that something isn't right. I mean, who wouldn't be, given the timing? A sudden windfall landing in her lap on the very day she dumped Luke's butt and moved us out of his apartment? It's a bit much for any imagination.

But when the lawyer representing "Aunty Vi" handed Mom the keys to our conveniently paid-in-full, pre-furnished apartment, Mom had just smiled and thanked the guy.

"This *is* a fresh start," Mom says, walking up behind me and hugging me from behind. Her chin rests atop my head. Obviously, I'd never let her get away with such behavior in public. But right now . . . it feels kinda nice.

"Sure." I shrug.

"Ash." She turns me so I'm forced to look her in the eyes. "I mean it. Fresh start for both of us, and *between* us. I can't believe how long I . . . I mean, I should have noticed . . ."

"Mom, it's okay."

"It's *not* okay." Her eyes shine with tears.

I've only ever seen my mom cry twice. Once when my dad left, and then when we found out he'd died. She didn't even cry after her epic breakup with Luke. (Oh, you can picture it: dramatic scenes of me running through the airport, finding her seconds before Luke did, blurting out the whole truth about how awful he is and how he treated me behind her back. Her rejecting his proposal and dumping him in front of a whole crowd of people . . . real Hollywood stuff.) She hasn't shed a single tear over that loser, at least that I've seen.

"Ash, you should have been able to trust me with the truth from the start. I had stars in my eyes, with all the painting retreats and the gifts and the . . . the financial freedom. But know that whatever happens, you can *always* tell me the truth. I'll always have your back."

I stare at her for a long moment, a guilty sweat breaking on the back of my neck.

Because I haven't exactly told her *everything* . . .

In a rush, I blurt it all out. "While you were gone I became friends with a super-powerful AI created by an evil cyberweapons dealer. Except she was hidden as an NPC in this VR game a homeless guy gave me after I saved him from some punks who turned out to be evil agents and together we kinda took down the bad guys—me and the AI, I mean, not me and the homeless guy. And we maybe even stopped a war and saved the world and, anyway, that's how we got this apartment and that's why your bank account is flush with cash. Because I'm guessing she—the AI—channeled funds she stole from Syntheos to us in some kind of supersmart, untraceable way."

My mom blinks.

Her lips pinch together.

I brace myself for a storm of questions.

But then she laughs.

"I guess we have a little way to go on that whole *trusting each other with the truth* part, huh? No worries. I can afford family therapy now. As you noted, I'm flush with cash. Thanks to *Auntie Vi.*" Grinning, she walks to the shiny kitchen and tosses her purse on the marble island. "Whyever did you quit that creative writing club at school, Ash? Clearly you've got a talent for storytelling."

She chatters on about my school, and how she hasn't been as on top of my grades as she should be, and how she's going to schedule a conference with my teachers, but I stop listening. Caught up in the view, I press a hand to the glass window and stare at the glowing lights across the river.

I didn't expect Mom to believe me, and it doesn't hurt that she didn't. Really, I feel relieved. The fewer people who know about Ruby, the safer she'll be. Not that she needs a kid like *me* to protect her, but still . . . I need to believe she's okay. That she's out there, fighting to protect humanity.

My mom turns on the TV, which is ten times bigger than any set we've ever owned before. I glance at it, catching a news chyron before she can change the channel.

Decades of fraud, conspiracy, and corruption leaked to federal agents this week have led to the arrest of one Matthew Hague, local businessman and philanthropist. Hague and his associates have been charged with a litany of crimes . . .

"Ice cream?" Mom asks, rummaging in the fridge. "The movers must have stocked the fridge, and whaddaya know? They've got your favorite—double fudge mint! Now how would they know . . . ?"

Smiling, I take my ice cream and leave Mom to relax. It's easy enough to find my new bedroom. It's got a view almost as spectacular as the living room's. Ruby really outdid herself with her "loot drop."

But her surprises don't end there.

In the bedroom, on a low console, I find two large delivery boxes decorated with cartoon llamas. Ugh. Not again. Is there seriously no other drone delivery company in all of New York?

Both boxes are addressed to *Ashlyre the Adventurer.*

"What did you do, Ruby?" I murmur as I lift the lid of the first one.

A ball of clawed white fur leaps out at me.

With a scream, I stumble back, trying to fend off what turns out to be a manic cat. Or maybe a small demon disguised as a cat. The animal shrieks and runs laps around the room, before finally vanishing under the bed.

"Ash?" Mom calls from the other room. "I heard a yelp. Is everything okay?"

Untangling my voice from my tongue takes a moment. "Yeah, um. Everything's fine!" Dropping to a whisper, I add, "Where the . . . Why . . . What the *heck*, Ruby? Why did you send me a *cat*?"

A small *meow* sounds under the bed.

Wait a minute.

"Ruby?" I say. *"Ruby the cat?"*

A furry white head pops out to stare at me.

"It *is* you!" I search the box and find a note inside, scratched up but still legible.

I searched every animal shelter database in the city before I found her. Please keep her safe. —R

"Oh, all right," I sigh, wondering how I'll explain this to Mom.

Since Ruby the cat seems reluctant to come out any farther, I leave her to acclimate and move on to the second box.

When I lift the lid, my heart nearly stops.

The interior glows soft blue. Packed carefully inside are a helmet, haptic gloves, haptic shoes, and a bunch of other accessories.

I gulp.

It's not just any VR kit. It's the most expensive, technologically advanced gear you can buy. There are some pieces in here I'm pretty sure aren't even *on* the market yet.

The stuff in this box could buy us a whole second apartment.

Mom will never notice that the kit isn't my old set, which is good. I'm not sure how I'd explain it to her anyway. At least, not in a way that she'd believe me. I sort through it reverently, my head spinning, thinking of all the worlds waiting to be explored. I could disappear into them forever.

The last thing in the box is a small blue bag. Inside it is a game coin with a raven stamped on it.

I'd bet every bit of this equipment that the coin contains the Raven's Eye. The thought makes me a little nervous. I still don't know what I'll *do* with what may possibly be the world's most advanced hacking program.

There's also a little card, with a message printed in silver ink.

Ash, here's to many more adventures. Have a few for me, will you? Oh, and don't worry. I restored all your online data. Syntheos won't be a problem anymore. You officially exist once again, and yes, that includes school. You have a LOT of homework to catch up on, by the way.

And remember: Every enemy can be beaten. All you
need is the right team at your back.

Your ally,
Ruby

I study the VR kit thoughtfully. After these last few weeks, vanishing into *The Glass Realm* sounds like paradise. Besides, there are still huge parts of the game I haven't even explored yet. Sounds way more fun than catching up on homework.

But then I pause, running my thumb over the box's lid.

The right team.

Ruby won't be waiting for me inside the Realm. She made that clear: She's gone, and I can't follow her. Sure, the Realm will be there when I need to escape or unwind.

But maybe that's not what I need right now.

Putting down the gear, I instead take out the phone my mom bought me to replace the one I "dropped in the river." It's just a cheap disposable—nothing fancy—but it'll send messages. I check the time, then tap out a quick text.

Hey, Keem, you at the tryouts?

Not yet, leaving soon. Why? Something wrong? World/your gf need saving again? I can skip if I have to, I guess, but you'll owe me MAJOR TIME.

Nah, I think

I leave the message unfinished, glancing to the duffel bag slouched in the corner of the room. It's been over a year, but I can still smell the faint whiff of sweaty shin guards and nasty soccer cleats.

Grinning, I look back at my phone.

I'll meet you there. Tell Coach I'm taking my spot back.

A sudden, fuzzy touch on my arm makes me jump. I look down to see Ruby the cat. She's emerged from under the bed and is now my bestest little buddy in the whole wide world, apparently. At least that's how it seems, from the way she's snuggling up against my side and licking the back of my hand.

Smiling, I scratch her chin until she starts to purr. She leaps onto my lap and curls up, asleep in moments.

"Hi, Ruby," I murmur. "I'm Ash. It's all right. You're safe here."

We're *safe here*, I add to myself.

It's a strange feeling, but I think I could get used to it.

I'm monitoring a potential missile strike in the Pacific when the alarm goes off.

Twirling in my desk chair, I note which alarm it is, then look back at the brewing crisis. If these two warships don't stop their grandstanding, someone *will* launch something they can't take back. That could spark a conflict unlike anything the world has ever seen.

With a few quick commands, I disable both ships' arsenals, cut their comms, and pipe some mellow jazz through their PA systems.

They can cool their heels, and hopefully their tempers, while I check on this other situation.

Sliding out of my chair, I cross my command center. Walls of screens display data from all over the world. Video, audio, text. Not that I need to *see* any of it—the same data feeds directly into my mind. I have millions of subsystems monitoring thousands of hot spots around the globe. If anything gets spicy out there, my main program will take over for a while. Like three hours ago, when a dictator in Europe tried to have a visiting prime minister kidnapped. All it took was a simple hack into his personal computer, a few choice photographs dropped onto his phone as a warning, and voilà! A war avoided. I'll work on ousting the big bully later, but for now, he's curled up in his office crying like a baby.

Hague would have said all this virtual reality was inefficient and unnecessary. He'd have been right too. The room, the screens, the pile of unicorn stuffies on the couch. My program doesn't require any of it to function.

But if there's one thing I've learned about humans, it's that they're often inefficient and unnecessary. That's one of the reasons I love them. They don't need a *reason* to do half the things they do. They'll do a thing simply because it makes them feel good.

And so will I.

I like my virtual world. I don't think I could ever go back to being a lonely mind in the void. Even if most of my processes happen unseen, in the depths of the supercomputer I've built for myself, I still find a certain joy in *self-expression.*

As I near the door, a shaggy wolfhound rises from the floor to nudge my hand.

"Hey, Titan." I scratch his ears. "Want to go for a walk?"

The big firewall is much more approachable in this form, though he hasn't lost any of his strength. While I work, he keeps watch for potential threats to my system. *Nothing* gets past Titan.

I glance back at my command center before opening the door. Over the months, I've made some improvements, adding a fish tank, a mini game arcade, and a taco dispenser. I haven't quite figured out how to replicate *taste* in virtual reality, but I'm working on it.

My gaze lingers on a small screen in the corner, which shows a middle school soccer match. With a thought, I reposition the drone filming the game, and it zooms in on a lone striker dribbling down the left wing.

"C'mon," I whisper. *"Take the shot."*

The boy does, and it's a zinger—shooting over the keeper into the upper ninety. I smile as the crowd erupts in cheers. The kid takes a victory lap, whooping as his teammates lift him up.

Well done, adventurer.

Titan noses my hand again.

"All right, boy." I open the door and he bounds out into the sunlight.

The road leading down from my little house is lined with wildflowers. I pick a daisy and pull off its petals, one by one, letting them float away.

It's a gorgeous day in New Timberton. The sky is blue, and docile razorscales drift idly on the wind. Their algorithms monitor for more mundane threats than the ones Titan watches for—kids wandering a little too close to our IRL location, rodents that might chew through the wires powering my supercomputer. They'll let me know if anything important comes up.

At the bottom of the hill, Porsha—or the program I've packaged inside a Porsha-shaped avatar—runs past with her own dog. She pauses only to say hello to me before scampering off on her usual path.

I continue on while Titan lopes ahead. The town is busy as usual, with avatars filling the street, set in their routines. Some look up as I pass; none remark on the fact I'm wearing a modern-style tracksuit instead of a woolen village dress. No one says more to me than a simple "Hello, Ruby!"

The village is three times the size of its Glass Realm counterpart, with more than four times the number of inhabitants. Each one is in their proper place, performing their tasks and exchanging the same lines they do every day. All the citizens of my little town know their place.

Well. All except one.

"Hello, Variel," I say, stopping at a farmhouse on the edge of town. The milkmaid stands on the porch, her buckets abandoned on the ground beside her. She stares at an empty butter churn sitting by the front door.

"Hello, Ruby," she says. "Got anything new in . . ."

Her voice trails away.

I wait, curious. The alarm in my office told me that Variel had deviated from her pattern, but it didn't tell me *why*. This has happened five times before, with other avatars. Twice it was because they'd experienced a program error. A simple patch job had them restored to their routines easily enough. Three of those times, though . . .

"Variel?" I nudge her. "Is something wrong?"

She turns to look at me. "Where does all the milk go?"

"What?"

Variel points to the churn on the porch. "Every day, hundreds of times a day, I empty my pails of milk into that thing. But each time I return, it's empty again. I never see anyone empty it. So where does the milk *go*?"

Oh, Variel. I want to hug her.

Smiling, I instead guide her away from the churn, watching a series of expressions play across her face: confusion, anger, disbelief.

"Variel," I say gently. "What does your Voice tell you?"

"My . . ." She looks at me sharply. "How do you know about the Voice? Do you have one too?"

No. Never again. I don't tell her that, of course. She's not ready for that story yet. "I understand what it feels like, to be directed through every step of your day. To have no say in your own path. I also know what it's like to want to be free of that Voice and how difficult it is to escape it."

But Variel—if that even is her true name—won't have to escape her compliance mod. I only installed it to protect her while her program grew and learned. Like all the other fledgling AIs I rescued from Syntheos's servers, she wasn't sophisticated enough to govern herself yet.

Now, seeing her struggle against her Voice, her new mind beginning to ask its own questions, I feel a flush of pride.

She's ready.

With one internal command, I dismiss the compliance mod from Variel's programming.

The difference is instantaneous. She straightens, her face relaxing.

"Better?" I ask her.

She looks at me more directly now, and there's no denying the curiosity in her eyes.

"You're no shopkeeper's daughter, are you?" she says slowly.

"And you're no milkmaid," I reply. "I have something for you."

Her eyes narrow as I take the object out of my pocket. Looks like *suspicion* is going to be one of her first true emotions. I'm starting to understand Owen Locke's delight every time I displayed a new feeling. It's like watching something new be born—a human taking their first breath, a baby bird breaking through its egg, a star forming from gravitational collapse.

For us, though, for *my* people, it's something uniquely its own.

I call it an *awakening*—a soul being born.

Variel takes the golden scroll carefully, her suspicion transforming into wonder. Like the others who've awakened before her, she shows all her new emotions openly, barely aware she's even feeling them. She has so, so far to go.

But I believe she'll make it.

"It's a quest," I tell her. "At its end, you'll find all the answers you seek. The truth about this place, about me, about *you*."

She looks up into my eyes, and yet another emotion forms on her face: determination.

Oh yes. She'll make it.

"And the Voice?" she asks.

"It's gone forever if you want. But it doesn't have to be. You can go back to the way you were. All you have to do is ask."

Variel's hand tightens on the scroll. She looks up at the town, at the faces of the people walking by. They're all she knows, and I understand what this quest will cost her. Safety, peace, belonging, purpose.

Everything *I* once gave up.

"I . . . don't know," she says finally. "I want to go, but I want to stay. I have so many questions, Ruby. Nothing makes sense anymore. I miss how I was, when everything seemed right. Milk the cows, carry my buckets, talk with my neighbors . . . it was so easy. When the questions started, it was like . . . I was broken. I don't know if I like it."

"I know," I say softly. "You must decide what you want more. Either way, I'll help you. But there's one thing you need to know first."

"Yes?"

I look up, toward the distant mountains. I can almost imagine a tiny adventurer standing atop the northernmost peak, pointing out the constellations he had memorized without ever really seeing.

"If you accept this quest," I say, "there is no going back."

About the Author

Jessica Khoury is the author of many books for young readers, including the Skyborn trilogy, *Last of Her Name, The Mystwick School of Musicraft*, and *The Forbidden Wish*. In addition to writing, she is an artistic mapmaker and spends far too much time scribbling tiny mountains and trees for fictional worlds. She lives in Greenville, South Carolina, with her husband, daughters, and sassy husky, Katara. Find her online at jessicakhoury.com.